Praise for *Vanishing Girls*

'This is a tight, tense psychological thriller; a fascinating look at the complicated mixture of love, loathing and rivalry that can exist between sisters.'   *The Times*

'This brilliant thriller has a killer twist.'   *Sun*

'A tense, clever psychological thriller, with a devastating denouement that will make you want to start the book all over again. A perfect showcase for Oliver's exceptional talents.'   *Daily Mail*

'Perfect for readers who devoured *We Were Liars*, it's the sort of novel that readers will race to finish, then return to the beginning to marvel at how it was constructed – and at everything they missed.'   *Publishers Weekly*

'Bestselling Oliver weaves a taut mystery interspersed with blog posts about Madeline's disappearance, and the story is made all the more compelling by Nick and Dara's close but troubling relationship, marked by both love and intense jealousy.'   *Booklist*

'The twists and turns this novel take the reader on are both shocking and gripping . . . The carefully layered prose and intense emotions threaded through the pages kept me absorbed and intrigued from beginning to end. The writing style very much reminded me of Gillian Flynn . . . Thrilling, dark, and full of susp̲e̲n̲s̲e̲ ̲t̲' ̲ ̲ ̲ ̲ ̲ ̲ ̲ ̲ ̲ ̲ ̲ ̲ ̲ ̲ ̲ ̲ ̲ ̲ ̲ psychological journey tha̲ kbag

Lauren Oliver is the author of *Before I Fall*, *Panic*, *Rooms* and the Delirium trilogy: *Delirium*, *Pandemonium* and *Requiem*, which have been translated into more than thirty languages and are *New York Times* and international bestselling novels. She is also the author of three novels for younger readers, *The Spindlers*, *Liesl & Po*, and *Curiosity House: The Shrunken Head*. Lauren's novel *Panic* has been optioned for film by Universal Studios. A graduate of the University of Chicago and NYU's MFA program, Lauren now lives in Brooklyn. You can visit her online at www.laurenoliverbooks.com

Also by Lauren Oliver

Standalone:

BEFORE I FALL
PANIC

For older readers:

ROOMS

The Delirium trilogy:

DELIRIUM
PANDEMONIUM
REQUIEM

HANA: A DELIRIUM SHORT STORY (an original eBook)
RAVEN: A DELIRIUM SHORT STORY (an original eBook)
ANNABEL: A DELIRIUM SHORT STORY (an original eBook)
ALEX: A DELIRIUM SHORT STORY (an original eBook)

For younger readers:

LIESL & PO
THE SPINDLERS

With H. C. Chester:

CURIOSITY HOUSE: THE SHRUNKEN HEAD

VANISHING GIRLS

LAUREN OLIVER

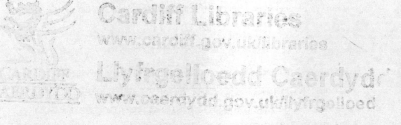

HODDER

First published in the United States of America in 2015 by
HarperCollins Publishers

First published in Great Britain in 2015 by Hodder & Stoughton
An Hachette UK company

First published in paperback in 2016

2

A CIP catalogue record for this title is available from the British Library

B-format ISBN 978 1 444 78681 1
A-format ISBN 978 1 444 78682 8

Typeset in ITC Berkeley OldStyle Std by Palimpsest Book Production Limited,
Falkirk, Stirlingshire

Printed and bound by Clays Ltd, St Ives plc

Hodder & Stoughton policy is to use papers that are natural, renewable and
recyclable products and made from wood grown in sustainable forests. The
logging and manufacturing processes are expected to conform to the environ-
mental regulations of the country of origin.

Hodder & Stoughton Ltd
Carmelite House
50 Victoria Embankment
London EC4Y 0DZ

www.hodder.co.uk

To the real John Parker, for the support and inspiration –
and to sisters everywhere, including my own

THE FUNNY THING ABOUT ALMOST-DYING IS THAT AFTERWARD everyone expects you to jump on the happy train and take time to chase butterflies through grassy fields or see rainbows in puddles of oil on the highway. *It's a miracle,* they'll say with an expectant look, as if you've been given a big old gift and you better not disappoint Grandma by pulling a face when you unwrap the box and find a lumpy, misshapen sweater.

That's what life is, pretty much: full of holes and tangles and ways to get stuck. Uncomfortable and itchy. A present you never asked for, never wanted, never *chose*. A present you're supposed to be excited to wear, day after day, even when you'd rather stay in bed and do nothing.

The truth is this: it doesn't take any skill to almost-die, or to almost-live, either.

BEFORE

nick

'WANT TO PLAY?'

These are the three words I've heard most often in my life. *Want to play?* As four-year-old Dara bursts through the screen door, arms extended, flying into the green of our front yard without waiting for me to answer. *Want to play?* As six-year-old Dara slips into my bed in the middle of the night, her eyes wide and touched with moonlight, her damp hair smelling like strawberry shampoo. *Want to play?* Eight-year-old Dara chiming the bell on her bike; ten-year-old Dara fanning cards across the damp pool deck; twelve-year-old Dara spinning an empty soda bottle by the neck.

Sixteen-year-old Dara doesn't wait for me to answer, either. 'Scoot over,' she says, bumping her best friend Ariana's thigh with her knee. 'My sister wants to play.'

'There's no room,' Ariana says, squealing when Dara leans into her. 'Sorry, Nick.' They're crammed with a half-dozen other people into an unused stall in Ariana's parents' barn, which smells like sawdust and, faintly, manure. There's a bottle of vodka, half-empty, on the hard-packed ground, as well as a few six-packs of beer and a small pile of miscellaneous items of clothing: a scarf, two mismatched mittens, a puffy jacket, and Dara's tight pink sweatshirt with *Queen B*tch* emblazoned across the back in rhinestones. It all looks like some bizarre ritual sacrifice laid out to the gods of strip poker.

'Don't worry,' I say quickly. 'I don't need to play. I just came to say hi, anyway.'

Dara makes a face. 'You just got here.'

Ariana smacks her cards faceup on the ground. 'Three of a kind, kings.' She cracks a beer open, and foam bubbles up around her knuckles. 'Matt, take off your shirt.'

Matt is a skinny kid with a slightly-too-big-nose look and the filmy expression of someone who is already on his way to being very drunk. Since he's already in his T-shirt – black, with a mysterious graphic of a one-eyed beaver on the front – I can only assume the puffy jacket belongs to him. 'I'm cold,' he whines.

'It's either your shirt or your pants. You choose.'

Matt sighs and begins wriggling out of his T-shirt, showing off a thin back, constellated with acne.

'Where's Parker?' I ask, trying to sound casual, then hating myself for having to try. But ever since Dara started . . . *whatever* she's doing with him, it has become impossible to talk about my former best friend without feeling like a Christmas tree ornament has landed in the back of my throat.

Dara freezes in the act of redistributing the cards. But only for a second. She tosses a final card in Ariana's direction and sweeps up a hand. 'No idea.'

'I texted him,' I say. 'He told me he was coming.'

'Yeah, well, maybe he *left*.' Dara's dark eyes flick to mine, and the message is clear. *Let it go.* I guess they must be fighting again. Or maybe they're not fighting, and that's the problem. Maybe he refuses to play along.

'Dara's got a *new* boyfriend,' Ariana says in a singsong, and Dara elbows her. 'Well, you do, don't you? A *secret* boyfriend.'

'Shut up,' Dara says sharply. I can't tell whether she's really mad or only pretending to be.

Ari fake-pouts. 'Do I know him? Just tell me if I *know* him.'

'No way,' Dara says. 'No hints.' She tosses down her cards and stands up, dusting off the back of her jeans. She's wearing fur-trimmed wedge boots and a metallic shirt I've never seen before, which looks like it has been poured over her body and then left to harden. Her hair – recently dyed black, and blown out perfectly straight – looks like oil poured over her shoulders. As usual, I feel like the Scarecrow next to Dorothy. I'm wearing a bulky jacket Mom bought me four years ago for a ski trip to Vermont, and my hair, the unremarkable brown of mouse poop, is pulled back in its trademark ponytail.

'I'm getting a drink,' Dara says, even though she's been having beer. 'Anyone want?'

'Bring back some mixers,' Ariana says.

Dara gives no indication that she's heard. She grabs me by the wrist and pulls me out of the horse stall and into the barn, where Ariana – or her mom? – has set up a few folding tables covered with bowls of chips and pretzels, guacamole, packaged cookies. There's a cigarette butt stubbed out in a container of guacamole, and cans of beer floating around in an enormous punch bowl full of half-melted ice, like ships trying to navigate the Arctic.

It seems as if most of Dara's grade has come out tonight, and about half of mine – even if seniors don't usually deign to crash a junior party, *second semester* seniors never miss any opportunity to celebrate. Christmas lights are strung between the horse stalls, only three of which contain actual horses: Misty, Luciana, and Mr Ed. I wonder if any of the horses are bothered by the thudding bass from the music, or by the fact that every five seconds a drunk junior is shoving his hand across the gate, trying to get the horse to nibble Cheetos from his hand.

The other stalls, the ones that aren't piled with old saddles and muck rakes and rusted farm equipment that has somehow landed and then expired here – even though the only thing Ariana's mom farms is money from her three ex-husbands – are filled with kids playing drinking games or grinding on each other, or, in the case of Jake Harris and Aubrey O'Brien, full-on making out. The tack room, I've been informed, has been unofficially claimed by the stoners.

The big sliding barn doors are open to the night, and frigid air blows in from outside. Down the hill, someone is trying to get a bonfire started in the riding rink, but there's a light rain tonight, and the wood won't catch.

At least Aaron isn't here. I'm not sure I could have handled seeing him tonight – not after what happened last weekend. It would have been better if he'd been mad – if he'd freaked out and yelled, or started rumors around school that I have chlamydia or something. Then I could hate him. Then it would make *sense*.

But since the break-up he's been unfailingly, epically polite, like he's the greeter at a Gap. Like he's *really* hoping I'll buy something but doesn't want to seem pushy.

'I still think we're good together,' he'd said out of the blue, even as he was giving me back my sweatshirt (cleaned, of course, and folded) and a variety of miscellaneous crap I'd left in his car: pens and a phone charger and a weird snow globe I'd seen for sale at CVS. School had served pasta marinara for lunch, and there was a tiny bit of Day-Glo sauce at the corner of his mouth. 'Maybe you'll change your mind.'

'Maybe,' I'd said. And I really hoped, more than anything in the world, that I would.

Dara grabs a bottle of Southern Comfort and splashes three inches into a plastic cup, topping it off with Coca-Cola. I bite the inside of my lip, as if I can chew back the words I really want to say: This must be at *least* her third drink; she's already in the doghouse with Mom and Dad; she's supposed to be staying out of trouble. She landed us both in *therapy*, for God's sake.

Instead I say, 'So. A new boyfriend, huh?' I try to keep my voice light.

One corner of Dara's mouth crooks into a smile. 'You know Ariana. She exaggerates.' She mixes another drink and presses it into my hand, jamming our plastic cups together. 'Cheers,' she says, and takes a big swig, emptying half her drink.

The drink smells suspiciously like cough syrup. I set it down next to a platter of cold pigs in blankets, which look like shriveled thumbs wrapped up in gauze. 'So there's no mystery man?'

Dara lifts a shoulder. 'What can I say?' She's wearing gold eyeshadow tonight, and a dusting of it coats her cheeks; she looks like someone who has accidentally trespassed through fairyland. 'I'm irresistible.'

'What about Parker?' I say. 'More trouble in paradise?'

Instantly I regret the question. Dara's smile vanishes. 'Why?' she says, her eyes dull now, hard. 'Want to say "I told you so" again?'

'Forget it.' I turn away, feeling suddenly exhausted. 'Goodnight, Dara.'

'Wait.' She grabs my wrist. Just like that, the moment of tension is gone, and she smiles again. 'Stay, okay? *Stay*, Ninpin,' she repeats, when I hesitate.

When Dara gets like this, turns sweet and pleading, like her old self, like the sister who used to climb onto my chest and beg me, wide-eyed, to wake up, wake up, she's almost impossible to resist. Almost. 'I have to get up at seven,' I say, even as she's leading me outside, into the fizz and pop of the rain. 'I promised Mom I'd help straighten up before Aunt Jackie gets here.'

For the first month or so after Dad announced he was leaving, Mom acted like absolutely nothing was different. But recently she's been *forgetting*: to turn on the dishwasher, to set her alarm, to iron her work blouses, to vacuum. It's like every time he removes another item from the house – his favorite chair, the chess set he inherited from his father, the golf clubs he never uses – it takes a portion of her brain with it.

'Why?' Dara rolls her eyes. 'She'll just bring cleansing crystals with her to do the work. Please,' she adds. She has to raise her voice to be heard over the music; someone has just turned up the volume. 'You *never* come out.'

'That's not true,' I say. 'It's just that you're *always* out.' The words sound harsher than I'd intended. But Dara only laughs.

'Let's not fight tonight, okay?' she says, and leans in to give me a kiss on the cheek. Her lips are candy-sticky. 'Let's be happy.'

A group of guys – juniors, I'm guessing – huddled together in the half-dark of the barn start hooting and clapping. 'All right!' one of them shouts, raising a beer. 'Lesbian action!'

'Shut up, dick!' Dara says. But she's laughing. 'She's my *sister*.'

'That's definitely my cue,' I say.

But Dara isn't listening. Her face is flushed, her eyes bright with alcohol. 'She's my sister,' she announces again, to no one and also to everyone, since Dara is the kind of person other people watch, want, follow. '*And* my best friend.'

More hooting; a scattering of applause. Another guy yells, 'Get it on!'

Dara throws an arm around my shoulder, leans up to whisper in my ear, her breath sweet-smelling, sharp with booze. 'Best friends for life,' she says, and I'm no longer sure whether she's hugging me or hanging on me. 'Right, Nick? Nothing – *nothing* – can change that.'

AFTER

At 11:55 p.m., Norwalk police responded to a crash on Route 101, just south of the Shady Palms Motel. The driver, Nicole Warren, 17, was taken to Eastern Memorial with minor injuries. The passenger, Dara Warren, 16, who was not wearing her seat belt, was rushed by ambulance to the ICU and is, at the time of this posting, still in critical condition. We're all praying for you, Dara.

Sooo sad. Hope she pulls through!
posted by: mamabear27 at 6:04 a.m.

i live right down the road heard the crash from a half mile away!!!
posted by: qTpie27 at 8:04 a.m.

These kids think they're indestructible. Who doesn't wear a seat belt??
She has no one to blame but herself.
posted by: markhhammond at 8:05 a.m.

Have some compassion, dude! We all do stupid things.
posted by: trickmatrix at 8:07 a.m.

Some people stupider than others.
posted by: markhhammond at 8:08 a.m.

Dara,
I'm so sorry. Please wake up.
I want to make it up to you
                    Parker

http://www.theShorelineBlotter.com/july15_arrests

It was a busy night for the Main Heights PD. Between midnight
and 1:00 a.m. on Wednesday, three local teens perpetrated a rash
of minor thefts in the area south of Route 23. Police first responded
to a call from the 7-Eleven on Richmond Place, where Mark Haas,
17, Daniel Ripp, 16, and Jacob Ripp, 19, had threatened and
harassed a local clerk before making off with two six-packs of beer,
four cartons of eggs, three packages of Twinkies, and three Slim
Jims. Police pursued the three teens to Sutter Street, where they
had destroyed a half-dozen mailboxes and egged the home of Mr
Walter Middleton, a math teacher at the teens' high school (who
had, this reporter learned, earlier in the year threatened to fail Haas
for suspected cheating). The police at last caught and arrested the
teens in Carren Park, but not before the three boys had stolen a
backpack, two pairs of jeans, and a pair of sneakers from next to
the public pool. The clothes, police reported, belonged to two
teenage skinny-dippers, both of whom were brought into the Main
Heights police station . . . hopefully, after recovering their clothing.

Dannnnnnny . . . ur a legend.
posted by: grandtheftotto at 12:01 p.m.

Get a life.
posted by: momofthree at 12:35 p.m.

The irony is that these boys will probably be working in the
7-Eleven before too long. Somehow I don't see these three
boys as brain surgeons.
posted by: hal.m.woodward at 2:56 p.m.

Skinny-dipping? Weren't they freezing?? :P
posted by: prettymaddie at 7:22 p.m.

How come the article doesn't give us the names of the 'two
teenage skinny-dippers'? Trespassing is a criminal offense, isn't
it?
posted by: vigilantescience01 at 9:01 p.m.

Thanks for posting. It is, but neither teen was charged.
posted by: admin at 9:15 p.m.

Mr Middleton sux.
posted by: hellicat15 at 11:01 p.m.

nick

'SKINNY-DIPPING, NICOLE?'

There are many words in the English language that you never want to hear your father say. *Enema. Orgasm. Disappointed.*

Skinny-dipping ranks high on the list, especially when you've just been dragged out of the police station at three in the morning wearing police-issue pants and a sweatshirt that likely belonged to some homeless person or suspected serial killer, because your clothing, bag, ID, and cash were stolen from the side of a public pool.

'It was a joke,' I say, which is stupid; there's nothing funny about getting arrested, almost ass-naked, in the middle of the night when you're supposed to be asleep.

The headlights divide the highway into patches of light and dark. I'm glad, at least, that I can't see my dad's face.

'What were you *thinking*? I would never have expected this. Not from you. And that boy, Mike—'

'Mark.'

'Whatever his name was. How old is he?'

I stay quiet on that. *Twenty* is the answer, but I know better than to say it. Dad's just looking for someone to blame. Let him think that I was forced into it, that some bad-influence guy made me hop the fence at Carren Park and strip down to my underwear, made me take a big bellyflop into a deep end so cold it shocked the breath right out of my body so I came up laughing, gulping air, thinking of Dara, thinking she should have been with me, that she would understand.

I imagine a huge boulder rising up out of the dark, an accordion-wall of solid stone, and have to shut my eyes and reopen them. Nothing but highway, long and smooth, and the twin funnels of the headlights.

'Listen, Nick,' Dad says. 'Your mom and I are worried about you.'

'I didn't think you and Mom were talking,' I say, rolling down the window a few inches, both because the air conditioning is barely sputtering out cold air and because the rush of the wind helps drown out Dad's voice.

He ignores that. 'I'm serious. Ever since the accident—'

'Please,' I say quickly, before he can finish. 'Don't.'

Dad sighs and rubs his eyes under his glasses. He smells a little bit like the menthol strips he puts on his nose at night to keep him from snoring, and he's still wearing the baggy pajama pants he's had for ever, the ones with reindeers on them. And just for a second, I feel really, truly terrible.

Then I remember Dad's new girlfriend and Mom's silent, taut look, like a dummy with her strings pulled way too tight.

'You're going to have to talk about it, Nick,' Dad says. This time his voice is quiet, concerned. 'If not with me, then with Dr Lichme. Or Aunt Jackie. Or *someone*.'

'No,' I say, unrolling the window all the way, so the wind is thunderous and whips away the sound of my voice. 'I don't.'

dara's diary entry

Dr Lick Me — I'm sorry, Lichme — says I should spend five minutes a day writing about my feelings.

So here I go:

I hate Parker.

I hate Parker.

I hate Parker.

I hate Parker.

I hate Parker.

I feel better already!

It's been five days since THE KISS and today in school he didn't even breathe in my direction. Like he was worried I would contaminate his oxygen circle or something.

Mom and Dad are on the shitlist this week, too. Dad because he's acting all serious and somber about the divorce, when inside you know he's just turning backflips and cartwheels. I mean, if he doesn't want to leave, he doesn't have to, right? And Mom because she doesn't even stand up for herself, and didn't cry once about Paw-Paw, either, not even at the funeral. She just keeps going through the motions and heading to

SoulCycle and researching goddamn quinoa recipes as if she can keep the whole world together just by getting enough fiber. Like she's some weird animatronic robot wearing yoga pants and a Vassar sweatshirt.

Nick is like that too. It drives me crazy. She didn't used to be, I don't think. Maybe I just don't remember. But ever since she started high school, she's always doling out advice like she's forty-five and not exactly eleven months and three days older than I am.

I remember last month, when Mom and Dad sat down to tell us about the divorce, she didn't even blink. 'Okay,' she said.

Oh-fucking-kay. Really?

Paw-Paw's dead and Mom and Dad hate each other and Nick looks at me like I'm an alien half the time.

Listen, Dr Lick Me, here's all I have to say: It's not okay.

Nothing is.

nick

SOMERVILLE AND MAIN HEIGHTS ARE ONLY TWELVE MILES APART, but they might as well be in different countries. Main Heights is all new: new construction, new storefronts, new clutter, newly divorced dads and their newly bought condos, a small cluster of Sheetrock and plywood and fresh paint, like a stage set built too quickly to be realistic. Dad's condo looks out over a parking lot and a line of skinny elm trees that divides the housing complex from the highway. The floors are carpeted and the air conditioner never makes a sound, just silently churns out frigid, recycled air, so it feels like living inside a refrigerator.

I like Main Heights, though. I like my all-white room, and the smell of new asphalt, and all the flimsy buildings clinging to the sky. Main Heights is a place where people go when they want to forget.

But two days after the skinny-dipping incident, I'm heading home to Somerville.

'It'll be good for you to get a change of scenery,' Dad says, for the twelfth time, which is stupid because it's the exact thing he said when I moved out to Main Heights. 'And it'll be good for your mother to have you home. She'll be happy.'

At least he doesn't lie and say that Dara will be happy, too.

Too fast, we're entering Somerville. Just like that, from one side of the underpass to the other, everything looks old. Enormous trees line the road, weeping willows fingering the earth, tall oaks casting the whole car in flickering shadow; through the curtain of swaying green, enormous houses ranging from turn-of-the-century to colonial to who-the-hell-knows-how-long-ago are visible. Somerville used to be the seat of a booming mill and cotton factory, the largest town in the whole state. Now half the town has been granted landmark status. We have a Founders' Day and a Mill Festival and a Pilgrims' Parade. There's something backward about living in a place so obsessed with the past; it's like everyone's given up on the idea of a future.

As soon as we turn onto West Haven Court, my chest goes tight. This, too, is the problem with Somerville: too many memories and associations. Everything that happens has happened a thousand times before. For a second, an impression surfaces of a thousand other car rides, a thousand other trips home in Dad's big Suburban with the rust-colored coffee stain on the passenger seat – a composite memory of family trips and special dinners and group errands.

Funny how things can stay the same for ever and then change so quickly.

Dad's Suburban is now for sale. He's looking to trade it in for a smaller model, like he traded his big house and four-person family for a downsized condo and a perky, pint-size blonde named Cheryl. And we'll never drive up to number 37 as a family again.

Dara's car is in the driveway, boxed in between the garage and Mom's: the pair of fuzzy dice I bought her at a Walmart still hanging from the rearview, so dirty I can make out hand-prints near the gas tank. It makes me feel a little better that she hasn't thrown them away. I wonder if she's started driving again yet.

I wonder if she'll be home, sitting in the kitchen alcove, wearing a too-big T-shirt and barely-there shorts, picking her toenails like she always does when she wants to drive me crazy. Whether she'll look up when I come in, blow the bangs out of her eyes, and say, 'Hey, Ninpin,' as if nothing has happened, as if she hasn't spent the past three months avoiding me completely.

Only once we're parked does Dad seem sorry for off-loading me.

'You gonna be okay?' he asks.

'What do you think?' I say.

He stops me from getting out of the car. 'This will be good for you,' he repeats. 'For both of you. Even Dr Lichme said—'

'Dr Lichme's a hack,' I say, and climb out of the car before he can argue. After the accident, Mom and Dad insisted I ramp up my sessions with Dr Lichme to once a week, like they were worried I'd crashed the car deliberately or maybe that the concussion had permanently screwed up my brain. But they finally stopped insisting I go after I spent a full four sessions at $250 an hour sitting in complete and total silence. I have no idea whether Dara's still going.

I rap once on the trunk before Dad pops it. He doesn't even bother getting out of the car to give me a hug, not that I want one – just rolls down his window and lifts his arm to wave, like I'm a passenger on a ship about to set sail.

'I love you,' he says. 'I'll call you tonight.'

'Sure. Me too.' I sling my duffel over one shoulder and start traipsing toward the front door. The grass is overgrown and clings wetly to my ankles. The front door needs painting and the whole house looks deflated, like something integral inside has collapsed.

A few years ago my mom became convinced that the kitchen was slanted. She would line up frozen peas and show Dara and me how they rolled from one end of the counter to the other. Dad thought she was crazy. They got in a big fight about it, especially since he kept stepping on peas whenever he went barefoot to the kitchen for water at night.

It turned out Mom was right. Finally she had someone take a look at the foundation. Because of the way the ground had settled, it turned out our house leaned a half-inch to the left – not enough to see, but enough to feel.

But today the house looks more lopsided than ever.

Mom hasn't yet bothered to switch out the storm door for the screen. I have to lean on the handle before it will open. The hallway is dark and smells faintly sour. Several FedEx boxes are stacked underneath the hall table, and there's a pair of rubber gardening boots I don't recognize, soles caked with mud, abandoned in the middle of the floor. Perkins, our sixteen-year-old tabby, lets out a plaintive meow and trots down the hall, twining himself around my ankles. At least *someone* is happy to see me.

'Hello?' I call out, embarrassed that I suddenly feel so awkward and disoriented, as if I'm a stranger.

'In here, Nick!' Mom's voice sounds faint through the walls, as if it's trapped there.

I dump my bags in the hall, careful to avoid the mud splatter, and make my way toward the kitchen, the whole time imagining Dara: Dara on the phone, Dara with knees up in the windowsill, Dara with new streaks of color in her hair. Dara's eyes, clear as pool water, and the small upturned knob of her nose, the kind of nose people pay for. Dara waiting for me, ready to forgive.

But in the kitchen, I find Mom alone. So. Either Dara's not home, or she has decided not to grace me with her presence.

'Nick.' Mom seems startled when she sees me, though of course she heard me come in and has been expecting me all morning. 'You're too thin,' she says when she hugs me. Then: 'I'm very disappointed in you.'

'Yeah.' I take a seat at the table, which is piled high with old newspapers. There are two mugs, both half-filled with coffee now showing a milk-white sheen, and a plate with a piece of half-eaten toast on it. 'Dad said.'

'Really, Nick. Skinny-dipping?' She's trying to pull the disapproving-parent act, but she isn't as convincing as Dad was, as if she's an actress and already the lines are boring her. 'We're all dealing with enough as it is. I don't want to have to worry about you, too.'

There she is, shimmering between us like a mirage: Dara in short-shorts and high heels, lashes thick with mascara, leaving dust on her cheeks; Dara laughing, always laughing, telling us not to worry, she'll be safe, she never drinks, even as her breath smells like vanilla vodka; Dara the beautiful one, the popular one, the problem child everyone loves – my baby sister.

'So don't,' I say bluntly.

Mom sighs and takes a seat across from me. She looks like she's aged a hundred years since the accident. Her skin is chalky and dry, and the bags under her eyes are a bruise-y yellow color. The roots are showing at her scalp. For a second I have the worst, most vicious thought: *No wonder Dad left.*

But I know that isn't fair. He left even before things got shitty. I've tried to understand it a million times, but still, I can't. Afterward, sure. When Dara got metal pins in her knee-caps and swore she would never speak to me again, and when Mom went silent for weeks and started taking sleeping pills every night and waking up too groggy to go to work and the hospital bills kept coming, kept coming, like autumn leaves after a storm.

But why weren't we good enough before?

'Sorry about the mess.' Mom gestures to encompass the table and the window seat, cluttered with mail, and the countertop, also heaped with mail and groceries half unpacked from a bag and then abandoned. 'There's always so much to do. Ever since I started work again . . .'

'That's okay.' I hate hearing my mom apologize. After the accident, all she did was say *I'm sorry.* I woke up in the hospital and she was holding me, rocking me like a baby, repeating it over and over. Like she had anything to do with it. Hearing her apologize for something that wasn't her fault made me feel even worse.

I was the one driving the car.

Mom clears her throat. 'Have you thought about what you'll do this summer, now that you're home?'

'What do you mean?' I reach over and take a bite of the toast. Stale. I spit it out into a balled-up napkin, and Mom doesn't even lecture me. 'I still have shifts at the Palladium. I'll just have to borrow Dara's car and—'

'Absolutely not. No way you're going back to the Palladium.'

Mom turns, suddenly, into her old self: the principal-for-one-of-the-worst-public-high-schools in Shoreline County, the mom who broke up physical fights between the senior boys and made absentee parents get it together, or at least do a better job of pretending. 'And you're not driving, either.'

Anger itches its way up through my skin. 'You're not serious.' At the start of the summer, I landed a job behind the concessions kiosk at the Palladium, the movie theater at Bethel Mall just outside of Main Heights: the world's easiest, stupidest job. Most days the whole mall is empty except for moms in spandex pushing baby strollers, and even when they come to the Palladium they never order anything but Diet Coke. All I have to do is show up and I get $10.50 an hour.

'I'm dead serious.' Mom folds her hands on the table, her knuckles gripped so tightly I can see every bone. 'Your father and I think you need a little more structure this summer,' she says. Amazing that my parents can only find time to stop hating each other to team up against me. 'Something to keep you busy.'

Busy. Like *stimulated*, that word is parent-speak for: supervised at all times and bored out of your mind.

'I'm busy at the Palladium,' I say, which is a complete lie.

'You mix butter into popcorn, Nicki,' Mom says. A crease appears between her eyebrows, as if someone has just pressed a thumb to her skin.

Not always, I nearly say.

She stands up, cinching her bathrobe a little tighter. Mom runs summer-school sessions Monday through Thursday. I guess since it's Friday she didn't bother getting dressed, even though it's after 2:00 p.m. 'I've spoken to Mr Wilcox,' she says.

'No.' The itch has become a full-blown panic. Greg Wilcox

is a creepy old guy who used to teach math at Mom's school, until he chucked academia for a job managing the world's oldest, most pathetic amusement park, Fantasy Land. Since the name makes it sound like a strip club, everyone calls it FanLand. 'Don't even say it.'

Apparently she isn't listening. 'Greg said he's short-staffed this summer, especially after—' She breaks off, making a face as if she's sucking on a lemon, meaning she almost said something she shouldn't have. 'Well, he could use an extra pair of hands. It'll be physical, it'll get you outside, and it will be good for you.'

I'm getting pretty sick of my parents forcing me to do things while pretending it's for my benefit.

'This isn't fair,' I say. I almost add, *You never make Dara do anything*, but I refuse to mention her, just like I refuse to ask where she is. If she's going to pretend I don't exist, I can do the same for her.

'I don't have to be fair,' she says. 'I'm your mom. Besides, Dr Lichme thinks—'

'I don't care what Dr Lichme thinks.' I shove away from the table so hard the chair screeches on the linoleum. The air in the house is thick with heat and moisture: no central air. This is what my summer will be like: instead of lying in Dad's spare bedroom with the AC cranked up and all the lights off, I'll be sharing a house with a sister who hates me and slaving away at an ancient amusement park solely attended by freaks and old people.

'Now you're starting to sound like her, too.' Mom looks totally exhausted. 'One is enough, don't you think?'

It's typical of Dara that she can become not only the topic of but also a force in the conversation even when she isn't in the room. For as long as I can remember, people have been comparing me to Dara instead of the other way around. *She's not as pretty as her younger sister . . . shyer than her younger sister . . . not as popular as her younger sister . . .*

The only thing I was ever better at than Dara was being ordinary. And field hockey – like running a ball down a field is a great basis for a personality.

'I'm nothing like her,' I say. I leave the kitchen before Mom can respond, almost tripping on the stupid gardening boots in the hall before taking the stairs two at a time. Everywhere are signs of the unfamiliar, little details missing and others added, like several plastic gnome-shaped night-lights outside Mom's room and nothing but a bare patch of carpet in the office where Dad's favorite, ugly-ass leather chair used to sit, plus more and more cardboard boxes full of junk, as if another family is slowly moving in or we're slowly moving out.

My room, at least, is untouched: all the books organized spine-out and the powder-blue coverlet nicely folded and my stuffed animals from when I was a baby, Benny and Stuart, propped up on my pillows. On my bedside table, I spot the framed picture of Dara and me from Halloween when I was a freshman; in it, we're both dressed like scary clowns, and in our face paint, grinning, we look nearly identical. I cross the room quickly and turn the picture facedown. Then, thinking better of it, I slide the photograph into a drawer.

I don't know which is worse: that I'm home and so much is different, or that I'm home and so much feels the same.

Overhead, I hear a pattern of creaks. Dara, moving around her attic bedroom. So she *is* home. Suddenly I'm so angry I could hit something. This is all Dara's fault. Dara's the one who decided to stop speaking to me. It's Dara's fault I've been walking around feeling like I've got a bowling ball in my chest, like at any second it might drop straight through my stomach and spill my guts on the floor. It's her fault I can't sleep, I can't eat, and when I do I just feel nauseous.

Once upon a time, we would have laughed together about Dad's girlfriend, and Dara would have made up a mean code name so we could refer to her without her knowing. Once upon a time, she might have come to work with me at FanLand just to keep me company, just so I wouldn't have to deal with scrubbing out old-person smell and little-kid vomit from the ancient rides all by myself, and we would have competed over who could spot the most fanny packs in an hour or drink the most Coke without barfing.

Once upon a time, she would have made it fun.

Before I've fully decided what I'm going to say to her, I head back into the hall and up the attic stairs. The air is even hotter up here. Mom and Dad moved Dara from the ground-floor bedroom to the attic in the middle of freshman year, thinking it would be harder for her to sneak out at night. Instead she started climbing out the window and using the old rose trellis as her own personal ladder.

Dara's bedroom door is closed. One time after we had a fight she painted KEEP OUT in big red letters right on the door. Mom and Dad made her cover it over, but in certain lights you can still make out the words shimmering under the layering of Eggshell #12.

I decide against knocking. Instead I fling open the door like cops do on TV shows, as if I'm expecting her to jump out at me.

Her room is a wreck, as always. The sheets are pulled halfway off the bed. The floor is piled with jeans, shoes, sequined shirts, and halter tops, as well as a covering, fine as leaves, of the kind of thing that accumulates at the bottom of a purse: gum wrappers, Tic Tacs, spare change, pen caps, broken cigarettes.

The air still smells, faintly, like cinnamon: Dara's favorite scent.

But she's gone. The window is open and a breeze distorts the curtains, making ripple patterns, faces that appear and disappear. I cross the room, doing my best to avoid stepping on anything breakable, and lean out the window. As always, instinctively, my eyes go first to the oak tree, where Parker used to hang a red flag when he wanted us to come play and we were supposed to be doing homework or sleeping instead. Then Dara and I would sneak down the rose trellis together, trying desperately not to giggle, and run, holding hands, to meet him at our secret spot.

There is no red flag now, of course. But the trellis is swaying slightly, and several petals, recently detached, twirl on the wind toward the ground. I can make out the faint imprints of footsteps in the mud. Looking up, I think I see a flash of skin, a bright spot of color, a flicker of dark hair moving through the woods that crowd up against the back of our house.

'Dara!' I call out. Then: 'Dara!'

But she doesn't turn around.

dara

I HAVEN'T CLIMBED DOWN THE ROSE TRELLIS SINCE THE ACCIDENT, and I'm worried my wrist won't hold. It got pulverized in the crash; for a month, I couldn't even hold a fork. I have to drop the last few feet, and my ankles let me know it. Still, I've made it down in one piece. I guess all that PT is good for something.

No way do I want to see Nick. Not after what she said.

I'm nothing like her.

Perfect Nicki. The Good Child.

I'm nothing like her.

As if we didn't spend practically our whole lives sneaking into each other's rooms to sleep in the same bed, whisper about our crushes, watch moon patterns on the ceiling and try to pick out different shapes. As if we didn't once cut our fingers and let them bleed together so we'd be bonded for ever, so we'd be made not just of the same genes but of each other. As if we didn't always swear that we'd live together even after college, the Two Musketeers, the Dynamic Duo, Light and Dark, two sides of the same cookie.

But now Perfect Nick has started to show some cracks.

The woods run up against another yard, neatly mowed, and a house staring at me through the trees. Turning left will bring me past the Duponts' house to Parker's, and the hidden break in the fence that Nick, Parker, and I engineered when we were kids so we'd be able to sneak back and forth more easily. I turn right instead and get spat out at the end of Old Hickory Lane, across the street from the bandstand in Upper Reaches Park. There's a four-person band onstage, of a combined age of about one thousand, dressed in old-fashioned straw hats and candy-striped jackets, playing an unfamiliar song. For a moment, standing in the middle of the road, watching them, I feel completely lost – as if I've stumbled into someone else's body, into someone else's life.

There was one good thing about the accident – and in case you're wondering, it wasn't the broken kneecaps or shattered pelvis, the shattered wrist and fractured tibia and dislocated jaw and scars where my head went through the passenger window, or getting to lie around in a hospital bed for four weeks and sip milkshakes through a straw.

The good thing was: I got to cut school for two and a half months.

It's not that I mind going to school. At least, I didn't *used* to mind it. The classes suck, sure, but the rest of it – seeing friends, skipping out between classes to sneak cigarettes behind the science lab, flirting with the seniors so they'll buy you lunch off campus – is just fine.

School is only hard when you care about doing well. And when you're the stupid one in the family, no one *expects* you to do well.

But I didn't want to see anyone. I didn't want to watch everyone feel bad for me while I limped across the cafeteria, when I couldn't sit down without wincing, like an old man. I didn't want to give anyone an excuse to pity me, or pretend to pity me while feeling secretly satisfied that I'm not pretty anymore.

A car blares its horn, and I move quickly out of the road, stumbling a little on the grass, but grateful for the sense of strength returning: this is practically the first time I've left the house in months.

Instead of passing, the car slows, and time slows, and I feel a hard fist of dread squeeze in my chest. A beat-up white Volvo, its bumper attached to the undercarriage with thick ropes of duct tape.

Parker.

'Holy shit.'

That's what he says when he sees me. Not *Oh my God, Dara. It's so good to see you.* Not *I'm so sorry. I've been thinking of you every day.*

Not *I was afraid to call, so that's why I didn't.*

Just: *Holy shit.*

'Pretty much,' I say, since it's the only response I can think of. At that moment, the band decides to stop playing. Funny how silence can be the loudest sound of all.

'I'm . . . wow.' He shifts in the car but makes no move to get out and hug me. His dark hair has grown long and hangs practically to his jaw now. He's tan – he must be working outside, maybe mowing lawns again, like he did last summer. His eyes are still the same in-between color, not quite blue or green but something closer to gray, like the fifteen minutes just before the sun rises. And looking at him still makes me want to puke and cry and kiss him all at once. 'I really didn't expect to see you.'

'I live around the corner, in case you forgot,' I say. My voice sounds harder, angrier, than I'd meant it to, and I'm grateful when the band strikes up again.

'I thought you were gone,' he says. He keeps both hands on the steering wheel, squeezing tightly, like he does when he's trying not to fidget. Parker always used to joke he was like a shark – if he ever stopped moving, he would die.

'Not gone,' I say. 'Just not seeing anyone.'

'Yeah.' He's watching me so intensely I have to turn away, squinting into the sun. This way, he can't see the scars, still angry and raw-red, flattened across my cheek and temple. 'I figured – I figured you didn't want to see me. After what happened . . .'

'You figured right,' I say quickly, because otherwise I might say what I really feel, which is: *not true.*

He flinches and looks away, returning his attention to the road. Another car passes, and has to pull out into the oncoming traffic to avoid Parker's car. He doesn't seem to notice, even when the passenger, an old man, rolls down his window and yells something rude. The sun is warm and sweat moves down my neck. I remember, then, lying between Parker and Nick last summer in Upper Reaches Park on the day after school ended, while Parker read out loud all the weirdest news he could find from around the country – interspecies relationships; bizarre deaths; unexplained agricultural patterns that could only, Parker insisted, be caused by aliens – inhaling the smell of charcoal and new grass and thinking, *I could stay here for ever.* What the hell changed?

Nick. My parents. The accident.

Everything.

I suddenly feel like crying. Instead I wrap my arms around my waist and squeeze.

'Listen.' He rakes a hand through his hair, which immediately swings back into place. 'You need a ride somewhere or something?'

'No.' I don't want to tell him that I have nowhere to go. I'm not heading anywhere except *away*. I can't even go back for my car keys or I risk seeing Nick, who no doubt is finding reasons to complain about the fact that I wasn't there to cheerlead her arrival.

He makes a face like he's accidentally swallowed his gum. 'It's good to see you,' he says. But he doesn't look at me. 'Really good. I've been thinking about you . . . all the time, basically.'

'I'm doing just fine,' I say.

Good thing lying comes naturally to me.

East Norwalk PD are reporting the possible abduction of nine-year-old Madeline Snow from a car outside Big Scoop Ice Cream & Candy off Route 101 in East Norwalk on the evening of Sunday, July 19, sometime between 10:00 p.m. and 10:45 p.m. Her family has released the accompanying picture of Madeline and asked that anyone with any knowledge of her whereabouts get in contact immediately with Chief Lieutenant Frank Hernandez at 1-200-555-2160, ext. 3.

Please join me in praying that Madeline makes it home safe – and soon – to her family.

> This article is surprisingly undetailed. Was she with her parents when she was 'abducted'? Statistically, it's usually the parents' fault when a child disappears.
> posted by: alikelystory at 9:45 a.m.

> Thanks for your comment, @alikelystory. The police haven't released any further details, but I'll be sure to update as soon as they do.
> posted by: admin at 10:04 a.m.

> @alikelystory 'It's usually the parents' fault when a child disappears.' Where do you get this so-called 'statistic'?
> posted by: booradleyforprez at 11:42 a.m.

> Poor Madeline. The whole congregation at St Jude is praying for you.
> posted by: mamabear27 at 1:37 p.m.

Hey all, for up-to-the-minute info, go to www.FindMadeline.
tumblr.com. It looks like they just got the site up and running.
posted by: weinberger33 at 2:25 p.m.

see additional 161 comments.

JULY 20

nick

MY NEW JOB STARTS ON MONDAY, BRIGHT AND EARLY.

Mom's still sleeping when I leave the house at seven. Dara, too. In the two days since I've been home, Dara's done a near-perfect job of avoiding me. I have no idea what she does up in her room all day – sleeps, most likely, and of course Mom never bugs her about it; Dara's off-limits since the accident, as if she's a glass figurine that might break if we handle it – and every morning I see broken rosebuds in the garden, evidence that she's been shimmying up and down the trellis again.

I know her only by the trace evidence: iPod left blaring through the speakers in her room, footsteps overhead, the things she leaves behind. Toothpaste crusted on our shared bathroom sink, because she always uses too much and never bothers to put the cap on. A bag of chips, half-eaten, discarded on the kitchen table. Thick wedge heels lying on the stairs; the faint smell of pot that filters down from the attic at night. This way I form an impression of her, of her life, of what she's doing, the way we used to rush downstairs on Christmas morning and know Santa Claus had come because the cookies we'd left had been eaten and the milk consumed. Or the way an anthropologist does, constructing whole civilizations out of the scraps of pottery they left behind.

It's already hot, even though the sun has just edged over the horizon and the sky is still stained a deep blue. The crickets are going crazy, threshing the air into layers of sound. I peel the banana I pulled from the kitchen before realizing it's rotten. I chuck it into the woods.

On the bus, which is mostly empty, I take the last seat. Someone has carved the initials *DRW* into the window, big. Dara's initials. I briefly imagine her sitting where I'm sitting, bored, taking a penknife to the glass while on her way to God knows where.

The number 22 goes from Somerville all the way down the coast, and curves along Heron Bay and its clutter of cheap motels and faux-timber resorts, past a long blur of diners and T-shirt shops and ice cream parlors, into East Norwalk, a place thick with bars and shitty lingerie stores and XXX-video stores and strip clubs. FanLand is right off Route 101, only a mile or so away from the crash site: a no-name place of low-lying marshland and twisted shrubbery and studded outcroppings of rock, carried down to the beach by some long-ago glacier, still getting sawed slowly into sand by the motion of the waves.

I don't know what we were doing there. I don't remember why we crashed, or how. My memory is looped over a single moment, like a thread snagged on something sharp: the moment my hands were off the wheel and the headlights lit up a wall of rock. Dad suggested not too long ago that I visit the site of the crash, said that I might find it 'healing.'

I wonder if my license plate is still there, lying mangled in the sun-bleached grass, if there's glass still glittering between the rocks.

By the time we reach FanLand – which shares a parking lot with Boom-a-Rang, the state's Largest Firecracker Emporium, according to the sign – the only other person on the bus is an ancient man with a face the color of a tobacco stain. He disembarks with me but doesn't even glance up, just heads slowly across the lot toward Boom-a-Rang, head down, as if he's moving against a hard wind.

Already I'm sweating through my T-shirt. Across the street, the gas station parking lot is full of cop cars. One of the sirens is turning soundlessly, sweeping the walls and pumps with intermittent red light. I wonder whether there was a robbery; this area has gotten worse over the years.

FanLand has a mascot, a pirate named Pete who's featured on billboards and placards all over the park, warning people not to litter and about the height minimum for various rides. The first thing I see when I enter the park through the gate, which is unlocked, is Mr Wilcox, scraping gum off a twelve-foot-tall Pirate Pete grinning a welcome down to park visitors. A big, glossy sign is tacked to Pirate Pete's shoulder, concealing the parrot I know should be there. It reads CELEBRATING 75 YEARS!!

'Nick!' When he sees me, he puts an arm above his head to wave, as if I'm four hundred feet away from him instead of fourteen. '*Great* to see you. Great to see you. Welcome to FanLand!' He pulls me into a crushing hug before I can resist. He smells like Dove soap and, weirdly, car oil.

Two things about Mr Wilcox: he always says things twice, and he obviously missed a few educational seminars on sexual harassment. Not that he's a creep. He's just big into hugs.

'Hi, Mr Wilcox,' I say, my voice muffled by his shoulder blade, which is roughly the size of a ham hock. Finally I manage to extract myself, though he keeps a hand on my back.

'Please,' he says, beaming. 'Here at FanLand, I'm just Greg. You'll call me Greg, won't you? Come on, come on. Let's get you suited up. I was thrilled when your mom told me you were back in town and looking for work, just absolutely thrilled.'

He pilots me toward a small yellow building half-concealed behind a wall of fake potted palms, and in through a door he unlocks with one of the keys he has strung to a massive key ring on his belt. The whole time, he never stops talking, or smiling.

'Here we are, the keys to the castle. This is the front office – nothing too fancy, you'll see, but it does the job quite nicely. If I'm not out and about, I'll usually be in here, and we've got some first aid kits, too, if anybody loses a finger. Kidding, kidding. But we do have first aid kits.' He gestures to the saggy shelves above a desk cluttered with receipts, rolls of ride tickets, and various scrawled drawings that look to be from children thanking 'Pirate Pete' for such a great day. 'Don't touch the Coke in the fridge, or Donna – she's my secretary, you'll meet her soon enough – will have your head, but you're welcome to any of the waters, and if you want to BYO lunch and keep it cold, go right ahead.' He slaps the refrigerator to emphasize the point. 'Same thing with valuables – phone, wallet, love letters – kidding, kidding! – we can lock 'em up right here at the start of your shift and they'll be safe as anything. *Here* you are. Throw this on' – this, as he tosses me a scratchy red T-shirt emblazoned with an image of Pirate Pete's grinning face, which I can tell is going to sit right over my left boob – 'and we'll get you started. Welcome to the team! Bathrooms are just past the photo booth on the left.'

I leave my bag in the office with Mr Wilcox and head to the bathrooms, which are indicated by means of a wooden parrot sign. I haven't been to FanLand since I was maybe eight or nine and much of it feels unfamiliar, though I'm sure it hasn't changed, and I have a brief flash of memory as soon as I enter the bathroom stall of standing with Dara in our wet bathing suits, water pooling on the concrete, shivering and giggling after a long day in the sun, our fingers sticky with cotton candy, running ahead of our parents, holding hands, while our flip-flops slapped on the puddled pavement.

Just for a second, I feel a moment of grief so intense it hollows me out: I want my family back. I want my Dara back.

I quickly swap out my T-shirt for the official uniform, which is about three sizes too big, and return to the office, where Mr Wilcox is waiting for me.

'Nick!' he booms, as if he's seeing me for the first time. 'Looking good, looking good.'

He wraps an arm around my shoulder and pilots me down one of the paths that wind through the park, past fake ship-wrecks and more plastic palm trees, plus rides with names like Splish 'n' Splash or the Plank. I see a few other employees, quickly visible in their vivid red, sweeping leaves from the boardwalk or changing filter traps or calling out instructions to one another, and I have the weird sense of walking backstage just before a play and seeing all the actors in half make-up.

Then Mr Wilcox is pumping an arm high in the sky and calling out to another girl, roughly my height, wearing all red. 'Tenneson! Over here! Tenneson! New meat for ya!' He lets out a booming laugh. The girl begins jogging toward us, and

Wilcox fires out another explanation: 'Tenneson's my right-hand man. But a girl, of course! This is her fourth summer with us at FanLand. Anything you need, you ask her. Anything she can't answer, you don't need to know!' With another laugh he releases me and retreats, waving again.

The girl looks maybe half-Asian and has long black hair, worn in multiple braids, and a tattoo of a snail just below her left ear. She looks like someone Dara would know, except that she's smiling and she has the bright eyes of someone who *really* likes mornings. Her front teeth overlap a little, which makes me like her.

'Hey,' she says. 'Welcome to FanLand.'

'I've heard that a few hundred times already,' I say.

She laughs. 'Yeah, Greg's a little . . . enthusiastic about the new recruits. About everything, actually. I'm Alice.'

'Nicole,' I say. We shake hands, even though she can't be much older than I am. Twenty, tops. She gestures for me to follow her, and we turn right toward the Cove, the 'dry' half of the park, where all the big rides, plus the game booths and food vendors, are. 'Most people call me Nick.'

Her face changes, an almost imperceptible switch, as if a curtain has come down behind her eyes. 'You're – you're Dara's sister.'

I nod. She turns away, making a face as if she's sucking on something sour. 'I'm sorry about the accident,' she blurts out at last.

My whole body goes hot, like it always does when someone brings up the accident, as if I've just walked into a room where people have been whispering about me. 'You heard, huh?'

To Alice's credit, she looks sorry to have mentioned it. 'My cousin goes to Somerville. Plus, since John Parker . . .'

Hearing Parker's name – his *full* name – makes something

glitch in my chest. I haven't thought of Parker in months. Or maybe I've been trying not to think about him for months. And nobody calls him by his full name. He and his older brother have been Big Parker and Little Parker for as long as I can remember. Even his mom calls her sons the Parkers.

John Parker makes him sound like a stranger.

'Since John Parker what?' I prompt.

She doesn't answer, and doesn't have to, because at that moment I see him: shirtless, straddling an open toolbox and fiddling with something beneath the undercarriage of the Banana Boat, a ride that, true to its name, looks like a giant airborne banana with multicolored sides.

Maybe he hears his name or senses it or maybe it's just coincidence, but at that moment he looks up and sees me. I lift a hand to wave but freeze when I see his expression – horrified, practically, as if I'm a ghost or a monster.

Then I realize: he probably blames me too.

Alice is still talking. '. . . put you on crew with Parker this morning. I have a shit ton of work to do for the anniversary party. He can show you the ropes, no problem, and I'm around if you need anything.'

Now Parker and I are separated by no more than ten feet. Finally he ducks under the steel support beams, sweeping up his T-shirt at the same time and using it to quickly wipe his face. He seems to have grown another two inches since I last saw him in March, so he towers over me.

'What are you doing here?' he says. With his shirt off I can see the half-moon shape on his shoulder blade, a smooth white scar, where he and Dara burned themselves with lighters freshman year while they were drunk on Southern Comfort. I was supposed to do it, too, but chickened out at the last second.

Stupidly I tug at my T-shirt. 'Working,' I say. 'My mom forced me into it.'

'Wilcox got to your mom, too, huh?' he says. He's still not smiling. 'And I'm supposed to play tour guide?'

'I guess so.' My whole body feels itchy. Sweat moves between my breasts, down to my waistband. For years, Parker was my best friend. We spent hours watching bad B horror movies on his couch, experimenting with ways to mix chocolate and popcorn together, or rented foreign films and disabled the subtitles so we could make up the plots ourselves. We texted in pre-calc when we were bored, until Parker got busted and had his phone taken away for a week. We hopped his older brother's scooter and piled on: me, Parker, and Dara; and had to abandon it and run for the woods when a cop spotted us.

Then, last December, something changed. Dara had just broken up with her latest boyfriend, Josh or Jake or Mark or Mike – I could never keep them straight, they cycled in and out of her life so fast. And suddenly she would crash movie night with Parker, wearing short-shorts and a tissue-thin shirt that showed the black lacy cups of her bra. Or I would see them riding the scooter together in the freezing cold, her arms wrapped around his chest, her head tilted back, laughing. Or I would walk into the room and he would jerk quickly backward, flashing me a guilty look, while she kept a long, tan leg draped across his lap.

Suddenly I was the third wheel.

'Look.' My throat feels like it's coated in sand. 'I know you might be mad at me—'

'Mad at you?' he interjects, before I can say more. 'I figured you were mad at me.'

I feel very exposed in the high glare, as if the sun is a big telescope and I'm the bug on the slide. 'Why would I be?'

His eyes shift away from mine. 'After what happened with Dara . . .' Her name sounds different in his mouth, special and strange, like something made of glass. I'm half tempted to ask whether he and Dara are still hooking up, but then he would know we aren't speaking. Besides, it's none of my business.

'Let's just start over,' I say. 'How about that?'

Finally he smiles: a slow process, beginning in his eyes, lightening them. Parker's eyes are gray, but the warmest gray in the world. Like the gray of a flannel blanket washed a hundred times. 'Sure,' he says. 'Yeah, I'd like that.'

'So are you going to play tour guide or what?' I reach out to punch his arm, and he laughs, pretending I've hurt him.

'After you,' he says, with a flourish.

Parker takes me on a tour of the park, pointing out all the places, both official and unofficial, I'll need to know: Wading Lake, informally known as the Piss Pool, where all the toddlers splash around in their diapers; the DeathTrap, a roller coaster that might, Parker tells me, someday live up to its name, since he's pretty sure it hasn't been inspected since the early nineties; the small, fenced-in area behind one of the snack bars (which for some reason at FanLand have been renamed 'pavilions'), which contains the maintenance hut, where the employees go to smoke or hook up in between shifts. He shows me how to measure the chlorine in the Piss Pool – '*always* add a little extra; if it starts burning off your eyelashes, you'll know you've gone too far' – and how to operate the hand crank on the bumper boats.

By eleven o'clock, the park is crowded with families and camp groups, and the 'regulars': usually old people, wearing sun visors and fanny packs, who totter between the rides announcing to no one in particular every way in which the park has changed. Parker knows a bunch of them by name and greets everyone with a smile.

At lunchtime, he introduces me to Princess – actual name
Shirley, though Parker cautions me never to call her that – an
ancient blond woman who runs one of the four snack bars
– excuse me, *pavilions* – and clearly has a major crush on
Parker. She gives him a free bag of chips and me a long scowl.

'Is she that nice to everyone?' I say, when Parker and I take
our hot dogs and sodas outside, to eat under the shadow of
the Ferris wheel.

'You don't get a name like Princess without working for it,'
he says, and then smiles. Every time Parker smiles, his nose
wrinkles. He used to say it didn't like to be left out of the fun.
'She'll warm up eventually. She's been here almost since the
beginning, you know.'

'The very beginning?'

He turns his attention to a miniature relish pack, trying to
work the green goop out of the plastic with a thumbnail. 'July
29, 1940. Opening day. Shirley joined up in the fifties.'

July 29. Dara's birthday. This year, FanLand will turn seventy-
five on the day she turns seventeen. If Parker makes the connection, he doesn't say so. And I'm not about to point it out.

'Still eating alien slime, I see?' I say instead, jerking my chin
toward the relish.

He pretends to be offended. '*Le* slime. It's not alien. It's
French.'

The afternoon is a blur of rounds: scooping up litter,
changing trash bags, dealing with a five-year-old kid who has
somehow gotten separated from his camp group and stands,
bawling, underneath a crooked sign pointing the way to the
Haunted Ship. Someone throws up on the Tornado, and Parker
informs me it's my job, as the new girl, to clean it – but then
does all the work himself.

There's fun stuff, too: riding the Albatross to see whether the gears feel sticky; washing down the carousel with an industrial hose so powerful I can barely keep it in my hands; downtime between jobs when I talk with Parker about the other kids who work at FanLand and who hates who and who's hooking up or breaking up or getting back together.

I finally find out why FanLand is so short-staffed this summer.

'So there's this guy Donovan.' Parker starts into the story while we're taking a break between shifts, sitting in the shade of an enormous potted palm. He keeps swatting at the flies. Parker's hands are constantly in motion. He's like a catcher telegraphing mysterious signs to an invisible teammate: hand to nose, tug on ear, tuck the hair. Except the signs aren't mysterious to me. I know what all of them mean, whether he's happy or sad or stressed or anxious. Whether he's hungry, or had too much sugar, or too little sleep.

'First name or last?' I interrupt.

'Interesting question. Not sure. Everyone just calls him Donovan. Anyway, he'd been working at FanLand for ever. Way longer than Mr Wilcox. Knows the whole place inside and out, everyone loves him, really great with the kids—'

'Wait – was he here longer than Princess?'

'Nobody's been here longer than Princess. Now stop interrupting. So he was a good guy, okay? At least, that's what everyone thought.' Parker pauses dramatically, deliberately making me wait.

'So what happened?' I say.

'The cops busted down his door a few weeks ago.' He raises one eyebrow. His eyebrows are very thick and practically black, like he has vampire blood somewhere far back in his ancestry. 'Turns out he's some kind of pedo. He had, like, a hundred pictures of high school girls on his computer. It was some crazy sting operation. They'd been tracking him for months.'

'No way. And no one had any idea?'

Parker shook his head. 'Not a clue. I only met him once or twice, but he seemed normal. Like someone who should be busy coaching soccer and complaining about mortgage rates.'

'Creepy,' I say. Years ago, I remember learning about the mark of Cain in Sunday school and thinking that it wasn't such a bad idea. How convenient if you could see what was wrong with people right away, if they wore their sicknesses and crimes on their skin like tattoos.

'Very creepy,' he agrees.

We don't talk about the accident, or Dara, or about the past at all. And suddenly it's three o'clock and the first shift of my new job is over, and it didn't totally suck.

Parker walks me back to the office, where Mr Wilcox and a pretty, dark-skinned woman I assume is Donna, the woman who hoards all the Cokes, are arguing about additional security for the anniversary party, in the good-natured, easy tones of people who have spent years arguing without ever essentially disagreeing. Mr Wilcox breaks off long enough to give me another hearty slap on the back.

'Nick? You enjoy your first day? Of course you did! Best place in the world. See you tomorrow, bright and early!'

I retrieve my backpack. When I re-emerge into the sunshine, Parker is waiting for me. He has changed shirts, and his red uniform is balled up under one arm. He smells like soap and new leather.

'I'm glad we get to work together,' I blurt as we walk into the parking lot, still crowded with cars and coach buses. FanLand is open until 10:00 p.m., and Parker has told me that the night crowd is totally different: younger, rowdier, more unpredictable. Once, he told me, he caught two people having sex on the Ferris wheel; another time he found a girl snorting coke off a sink in one of the men's toilets. 'I'm not sure I could handle Wilcox all by myself,' I add quickly, because Parker is looking at me strangely.

'Yeah,' he says. 'I'm glad, too.' He tosses his keys a few inches and catches them in his palm. 'So you want a ride home? I think the Chariot's missed you.'

Seeing his car, so familiar, so *him*, I have a quick flash of memory, like an explosion in my brain: the windshield fogged up, patterned with rain and body heat; Parker's guilty face; and Dara's eyes, cold and hard, gloating, like the eyes of a stranger.

'That's all right,' I say quickly.

'You sure?' He pops open the driver's-side door.

'I have Dara's car,' I say quickly. The words come out before I can think about them.

'You do?' Parker seems surprised. I'm grateful the lot is crowded, so my lie isn't immediately obvious. 'All right, then. Well . . . I guess I'll see you tomorrow.'

'Yeah,' I say, willing away another image of that night, of the way it felt to know, deep down, that everything had changed; that nothing would ever be the same between the three of us again. 'See you.'

I've already started to turn away – lingering, now, so that Parker won't see that I'm headed toward the bus stop – when he calls me back.

'Look,' he says, all in a rush. 'There's a party at the Drink tonight. You should come. It'll be super low-key,' he goes on. 'Like twenty people, max. But bring whoever you want.' He says the last part in a funny voice, half-strangled. I wonder whether it's a hint, and he's asking me to bring Dara along. Then I hate myself for having to wonder it. Before they hooked up, there was never any weirdness between us.

One more thing that Dara ruined because she felt like it, because she had an itch, an urge, a whim. *He's so fuckable*, I remember her saying one morning, out of the blue, when we'd all gone across the street to Upper Reaches Park to watch his Ultimate Frisbee game. *Did you ever notice that he's undeniably fuckable?* As we were watching him run across the ball field, chasing the bright red disk of the Frisbee, arm outstretched – the same *boy-body-arm* I'd known my whole life was transformed, in an instant, by Dara's words.

And I remember looking at her and thinking that she, too, looked like a stranger, with her hair (blond and purple, then) and the thick dusting of charcoal eyeshadow on her lids, lips red and exaggerated with pencil, legs stretched out for miles underneath her short-shorts. How could my Dara, Little Egg, Nosebutton, who used to wrap her arms around my shoulders and stand on my toes so we could pretend to be one person as we staggered around the living room, have turned into someone who used the word *fuckable*, someone I barely knew, someone I feared, even?

'It'll be just like old times,' Parker says, and I feel a hard ache in my chest, a desperate desire for something lost long ago.

Everyone knows you can't go back.

'Yeah, maybe. I'll let you know,' I say, which I won't.

I watch him get into his car and drive off, waving, smiling big behind the glare, and pretend to be fumbling for keys in my bag. Then I walk across the parking lot to wait for the bus.

BEFORE

nick

'OW.' I OPEN MY EYES, BLINKING FURIOUSLY. DARA'S FACE, FROM this angle, is as big as the moon, if the moon were painted in crazy colors: coal-black eyeshadow, silver liner, a big red mouth like a smear of hot lava. 'You keep poking me.'

'You keep moving. Close your eyes.' She grabs my chin and blows, gently, on my eyelids. Her breath smells like vanilla Stoli. 'There. You're done. See?' I stand up from the toilet, where she's installed me, and join her at the mirror. 'Now we look like twins,' she says happily, putting her head on my shoulder.

'Hardly,' I say. 'I look like a drag queen.' Already I'm sorry I agreed to let Dara do my make-up. Normally I use ChapStick and mascara – and that's only for special occasions. Now I feel like a kid who went crazy at a carnival face-painting booth.

The funny thing is that Dara and I *do* look alike, mostly – and yet, everywhere she's delicate and well-made and pretty, I'm lumpy and plain. Our hair is the same indeterminate brown, although hers is currently dyed black (*Cleopatra* black, she calls it) and has previously been platinum, auburn, and even, briefly, purple. We have the same hazel eyes spaced a little too far apart. We have the same nose, although mine is a teensy bit crooked, from where Parker accidentally clobbered me with a softball in third grade. I'm actually taller than Dara is, though you'd never know it – currently, she has on a pair of crazy wedge platform boots with a translucent dress that barely clears her underwear, plus black-and-white-striped tights that on anyone else would look idiotic. Meanwhile, I'm wearing what I always wear to the Founders' Day Ball: a tank top and skinny jeans, plus comfortable ankle boots.

That's the thing about Dara and me: we're both similar and worlds apart. Like the sun and the moon, or a starfish and a star: related, sure, but at the same time totally and completely different. And Dara's always the one doing the shining.

'You look beautiful,' Dara says, straightening up. On the sink, her phone starts vibrating and does a half turn next to the toothbrush cup before falling silent again. 'Doesn't she, Ari?'

'Beautiful,' says Ariana, without looking up. Ariana has long, wavy blond hair and a facial-cleanser-and-Swiss-Alps kind of complexion, which makes her tongue ring, nose ring, and the tiny stud above her left eyebrow always seem out of place. She's perched on the edge of the bathtub, stirring her warm vodka orange juice with a pinkie. She takes a sip and gags expressively.

'Too strong?' Dara asks, faking innocence. Her phone starts going again. She quickly silences it.

'No, it's great,' Ariana says sarcastically. But she takes another sip. 'I was looking for an excuse to burn away my tonsils. Who needs 'em?'

'You're welcome,' Dara says, reaching for the cup. She takes a big swig and passes it to me.

'No, thanks,' I say. 'I'll keep my tonsils.'

'Come on.' Dara hooks an arm around my shoulder. In her heels, she's even taller than my five-seven. 'It's Founders' Day.'

Ariana stands up to take the cup back. She has to pick her way across a bathroom floor littered with bras and underwear, dresses and tank tops – all discarded outfit selections. 'Founders' Day,' she repeats, in her best impression of our principal's voice. Mr O'Henry not only chaperones the dance, which takes place every year in the gym, he participates in the lame historical re-enactment of the Battle of Monument Hill, after which the original British settlers determined all the area west of the Saskawatchee a part of the British Empire. I think it's a little politically insensitive to basically mime the massacre of a bunch of Cherokee Indians every year, but whatever. 'The most important day of the year, and a seminal moment in our proud history,' Ariana finishes, hefting her cup in the air.

'Hear, hear,' Dara says, and mimes drinking from a glass, keeping her pinkie high.

'They really should have called it Royal Fuck-Up Day,' Ari says in her normal voice.

'Doesn't have the same ring to it,' I say, and Dara giggles.

Three hundred years ago, colonial explorers looking for the Hudson River believed they'd found it and settled instead on the banks of the Saskawatchee, chartering the town for England and inadvertently forming what would later become Somerville, about five hundred miles south-west of their initial destination. At some point, they must have realized their mistake, but I guess by then they were too settled to do anything about it.

There's a metaphor in that somewhere – like all of life is

about ending up somewhere you didn't expect, and learning to just be happy with it.

'Aaron's going to freak when he sees you,' Dara says. She has the uncanny ability to do that: to pluck a thought out of my head and finish it, like she's unspooling some tangled invisible sweater. 'One look, and he's going to forget all about the promise club.'

Ariana snorts.

'For the last time,' I say, 'Aaron's not *in* the promise club.' Ever since Aaron was cast as Jesus in our Christmas pageant – in *first grade* – Dara has been convinced that he's a religious freak and a sworn virgin until marriage, an idea confirmed, in her mind, by the fact that we've been together for two months and haven't gotten much past second base.

I guess it hasn't occurred to her that the problem might be with me.

Thinking of him now – his long dark hair, the way he always smells, mysteriously, a bit like toasted almonds, even after his basketball games – makes something squeeze up in my stomach, half pleasure, half pain. I love Aaron. I do.

I just don't love him enough.

Dara's phone starts vibrating again. This time she snatches it up, sighs, and drops it into a small sequined bag, patterned all over with tiny skulls.

'Is that the guy who—?' Ariana starts to ask, and Dara shushes her quickly.

'What?' I turn to Dara, suddenly suspicious. 'What's the big secret?'

'Nothing,' she says, giving Ariana a stern look, as if daring her to argue. Then she turns back to me, all smiles, so beautiful, the kind of girl you want to believe, the kind of girl you want to follow. The kind of girl you want to fall in love with. 'Come on,' she says, taking my hand and squeezing it so hard my fingers ache. 'Parker's waiting.'

Downstairs, Dara bullies me into finishing the last few sips of Ariana's lukewarm drink, which is full of pulp, but at least it lights up my chest, helps me get into the mood.

Then Dara pops open a metal pill case and fishes out something small and round and white. Instantly my good feeling fades.

'Want?' she says, turning to me.

'What is that?' I say, even as Ariana holds out a palm for one.

Dara rolls her eyes. 'Breath mint, dummy,' she says, and sticks her tongue out at me, showing off the mint, slowly dissolving. 'And trust me, you need one.'

'Yeah, right,' I say, but hold out my hand, the good feeling returning. Dara, Parker, and I have always gone to Founders' Day together, even in middle school, when instead of a dance the school put on a weird variety show, and for the past few years Ariana has been tagging along. So what if Parker and Dara *are* something now? So what if I won't get shotgun? So what if I haven't talked to Parker, really talked, since he and Dara started hooking up? So what if my best friend seems to have completely and totally forgotten that I exist?

Details.

We have to take the long way, because neither Ariana nor Dara can make it through the woods in their heels and Ariana wants to smoke a cigarette anyway. It's freakishly warm, and all the ice is running off the trees into the gutters, soft snow *whoomphing* down from roofs, the air layered with that rich smell, the pulpy promise of spring, even though it's a false promise: we're supposed to get more snow next week. But for now, I'm wearing only a light jacket, and Dara's walking beside me, mostly sober, laughing, and we're heading to Parker's house: just like old times.

Every block brings back memories. That old maple where Parker and I once competed to see who could climb higher, until he crashed through the high, flimsy branches and broke his arm – for a whole summer he couldn't swim, and I wore a cast of paper towels and masking tape out of solidarity; Old Hickory Lane, Parker's street, our favorite spot to trick-or-treat, because Mrs Hanrahan could never distinguish between the kids on the block and kept forking over Snickers bars even when we rang three, four, five times in a row; the stretch of woods where we convinced Dara that fairies lived who would steal her away to a horrible underworld if she didn't do what we said; concentric circles of growth, spreading outward, like the rings of a tree marking off time.

Or maybe we're passing from the outer rings *in*, back to the start, the root and the heart, because as we get closer to Parker's house the memories get thicker and come faster, of summer nights and snowball fights and our whole lives layered together, until we're standing on his porch and Parker opens the door with warm light spilling out behind him and we're here; we've arrived at the center.

Parker's actually bothered to put on a button-down, although I can see a T-shirt peeking out from the open collar, and he's still wearing jeans and his blue Surf Siders, covered over with faded ink marks and doodles. *Nick is the* ~~greatest SMELLIEST~~ *greatest!!* is written beneath the left sole in Sharpie.

'My best girls,' Parker says, opening his arms wide, and just for a second, when our eyes meet, I forget and start to move toward him.

'Hotness,' Dara says, moving past me, and then I remember.

So I take a quick step backward, turning away, letting her get to him first.

AFTER

dara

ARE YOU GOING TO PARTY @ THE DRINK? PARKER TOLD ME about it.

The note is wedged under my door when I get out of the shower, written on Nick's cream-white stationery. (Nick is the only person under the age of a hundred who actually *uses* stationery, and her handwriting is so neat it looks like each letter is a minuscule piece of architecture. My handwriting looks like Perkins ingested some letters and then puked them onto a page.)

I stoop down, wincing as pain snakes up my spine, and scoop up the note before crumpling it and overhanding it toward the trash can in the corner. The note hits the rim and rebounds into a pile of dirty T-shirts.

I pull on a pair of cotton shorts and a tank top and take my computer onto the bed, clicking quickly away from Facebook as soon as it pops up, catching a brief glimpse of all the messages, unliked, unanswered, posted on my wall.

We miss you!
Thinking of you!!
We love you so much!!!

I haven't posted since the accident. Why would I? What could I possibly say?

I'm bored to tears alone on a Saturday night.
I'm hopelessly scarred for life.
I'm finally able to bend my knees like a normal person!

I click over to YouTube but keep imagining Parker's face, the way he squints against the light reflected in the windshield, his nails, trim and neat, the way a guy's should be. His eyebrows, thick and dark, drawn together. Everyone else in Parker's family is totally Norwegian-looking, blond and fair and smiley, like they should be out hauling catches of herring on the open ocean, which somehow makes Parker's dark hair and olive skin even cuter, like it was a mistake.

Suddenly I can't stand the idea of another night at home, watching stupid videos or queuing up TV shows. I get the old itch, a heat between my shoulder blades, like my skin might suddenly sprout wings to carry me away.

I need out. I need to prove that I'm not afraid of seeing him, or my old friends, or anyone. I'm not afraid of Nick, either, and the way she makes me feel now: as if I'm broken. Every time I hear her blasting music downstairs – indie pop, shiny happy music, since Nick doesn't get depressed – or shouting for Mom to help her find her favorite jeans; every time I come into the bathroom and find it still humid from her shower, still smelling like Neutrogena; every time I see her running shoes on the stairs or find her field hockey T-shirt tangled up with my laundry, she may as well be hammering a stake into the ground. TOWN: NORMAL. POPULATION: 1.

Maybe she always made me feel that way, but it's only since the accident that I've been able to admit it.

I pull on my best skinny jeans, surprised by their fit. Weirdly, even though I've barely left the house, I must have lost weight. But with a studded tank top and my favorite slouchy boots, I look all right, especially from a distance.

When I head downstairs to the bathroom, I see Nick's door is still closed. I press my ear to the door but hear nothing. Maybe she's already left for the party. I briefly imagine her standing next to Parker, laughing, maybe competing to see who can throw their beer cans farther.

Then my brain spits out a whole series of memories, flip-book-style, from our lives together: struggling on my tricycle to keep up with Parker and Nick, both on shiny new two-wheelers; watching from the pool deck while they took turns cannonballing into the deep end when I was too small to join them; hearing them burst into laughter because of an inside joke I didn't understand.

Sometimes I think I didn't even fall in love with Parker. Sometimes I think it was really all about Nick, and proving I could finally be her equal.

Downstairs, Mom is standing in the kitchen, talking on the phone, probably to Aunt Jackie, the only person she ever calls. The TV is on behind her, barely audible, and I get a jolt when the camera pans to a familiar stretch of highway not far from the place Nick drove us into a solid face of rock. The place is crawling with cops, as it must have been after the accident; the whole scene is lit up with floodlights and sirens, like a nighttime movie set. Words scroll across the bottom of the screen: *Cops Launch Massive Search for Missing Nine-Year-Old . . .*

'Yeah, of course. We expected a period of adjustment, but—' Mom breaks off when she sees me, points to the Stouffer's lasagna box on the kitchen table and then to the microwave, mouthing *Dinner?* In the quiet, I can make out the newscaster's voice: 'Police are searching for witnesses or clues in the disappearance of Madeline Snow, who vanished Sunday night . . .' I shake my head and my mom turns away, her voice muffled as she passes out of view. 'But I'm hanging in there. It's starting to feel a little more like a house again.'

I punch the TV off and grab Nick's favorite field hockey hoodie from the peg near the front door. Though it's likely still in the mid-eighties, with the hood up my scars will be mostly concealed. Besides, it gives me a thrill to wear Nick's clothes unasked, as if I can shrug on a new identity. The sweatshirt still smells like Nick – not like perfume, since Nick never wears any, but like coconut shampoo and the general, indefinable odor of cleanliness, outdoors, and competency at sports.

I pull the hood up and cinch it under my chin, stepping onto the grass and enjoying the slick feel of the moisture around my ankles, seeping through my jeans. I feel like a burglar, or someone on a secret mission. My car is blocked in, and I don't want to ask Mom to move the Subaru, which would then involve a lot of questions and concerned, quizzical looks. I'm not even sure she would say yes – she put a moratorium on driving after the accident.

I drag my ancient bike out from the garage – I haven't ridden in forever, except once two summers ago, as a joke, after Ariana and I dropped mushrooms and Nick found us flopping on the grass like fish, gasping with laughter. I'm a little unsteady at first, but soon enough, I get the rhythm back. My knees are bugging me, but no worse than usual. Besides, the Drink is only a few miles away.

The Drink is actually a nickname for the Saskawatchee River. Sometime in the previous decade, back when a rush of Realtors and speculators descended on Shoreline County like an army of money-crazed locusts, chewing their way through our land, a development group decided to raze the woods and build a clutter of sleek waterfront stores on its banks: coffee houses, art galleries, and high-rent restaurants, smack-dab in the middle of Somerville.

Construction was approved and materials shipped before the residents freaked. Apparently, for a town built on history, the threat of new buildings and new parking lots and new cars bearing in tides of new people was too much. Somerville managed to have the entire area west of the river declared a piece of national park land. I'm surprised the town board hasn't mandated we start wearing hoop skirts yet.

Someone was supposed to have cleaned up the mounds of gravel and the piles of concrete. But no one bothered. There's even an abandoned hard hat, meticulously and mysteriously preserved by the people who hang out there.

I can hear the party almost as soon as I turn off Lower Forge and bump off the road and into the woods, keeping to the path that has been carved through the undergrowth because of a constant Friday-night procession of kids, coolers, bikes, and, occasionally, Chris Handler's ATV. In the woods, the air is cooler, and leaves slap wetly against my thighs and calves as I jerk along the uneven ground, holding tight to the handlebars to avoid being bucked off. As soon as I see lights through the woods – people moving around, using their phones as flashlights – I dismount, wheeling my bike out into the open and leaning it next to several others on the grass.

The party's pretty big: forty or fifty people, most of them in shadow, milling around on the slope leading down to the river or perched on broken pieces of concrete. No one notices me yet, and for a second I get this moment of panic, a feeling like being a little kid again on the first day of school and watching the stream of kids through the double doors. I haven't felt like an outsider in a long time.

I don't know why you always have to be the center of attention, Nick said to me once, not long before the accident. I'd been wriggling into a pair of leather pants I'd bought and then concealed from our parents by hiding them underneath the sweaters folded at the back of my closet.

Well, I don't know why you're so scared of being noticed, I responded. It's like Nick gets power from being totally, inoffensively correct: nice jeans, tight but not too tight, white T-shirt, translucent but not transparent, just enough make-up so it looks like she isn't wearing any. I bet if Somerville *did* start mandating hoop skirts, she'd be the first to sign up and grab one. She'd probably add in a pair of ruffled pantaloons for good measure.

I don't see Nick, or Parker, either. But when the crowd shifts, I spot a keg and a bunch of red Solo cups stacked in the ice.

I feel better, much more myself, once I've poured myself a beer, even though it's mostly foam. The first few sips dull some of my anxiety, and it's dark enough that I even take off my hood, shaking out my hair. I see Davis Christensen and Ben Morton standing, pinkie fingers linked, on the other side of a small knot of people. Both of them notice me at the same time, and Mark's mouth forms an O of surprise. Davis whispers something to him before lifting her cup and extending two fingers in a kind of wave.

I slug back the beer, turn to the keg, and refill. When I look up again, Ariana has materialized, just appeared out of the crowd like something spit up on a tide. She's cut her hair short. In her black shorts, wedge sneakers, and heavy eyeliner, she looks like a deranged pixie. I feel a sudden squeeze of pain. My best friend.

My *former* best friend.

'Wow.' Ariana stares at me as if I'm a new species of animal that hasn't yet been categorized. 'Wow. I didn't expect to see you here. I didn't expect to see you *out*.'

'Sharon's had me on lockdown,' is all I say, because I don't feel like getting into it. It's an old joke of ours that my mom is a jailer, and I'm expecting Ariana to laugh. But instead she just nods really fast, as if I've said something interesting.

'How is your mom?' she asks.

I shrug. 'The same,' I say. 'She started working again.'

'Good.' Ariana is still nodding. She looks a little like a puppet whose strings are being tugged. 'That's really good.'

I take another sip of my beer. I'm past the foam now, into the flat bitter burn. Now I see that my presence has caused a disturbance, a ripple effect as the news travels from one group to the next. Various people swivel in my direction. Once, I might have welcomed the attention, even enjoyed it. But now I feel itchy, evaluated, the way I do during standardized tests. Maybe this is the effect of wearing Nick's sweatshirt – maybe some of her self-consciousness is seeping into my skin.

'Look.' Ariana takes a step closer and talks low and really fast. She's breathing hard, too, as if the words are a physical effort. 'I wanted to tell you I'm sorry. I should have been there for you. After the accident, I should have reached out or done something, but I couldn't – I mean, I didn't know what to do—'

'Don't worry about it,' I say, taking a step backward and nearly stumbling on a bit of cement half-embedded in the grass. Ariana's eyes are wide and pleading, like a little kid's, and I feel suddenly disgusted. 'There's nothing you could have done.'

Ariana exhales, visibly relieved. 'If you need anything—'

'I'm fine,' I say quickly. 'We're fine.' Already, I regret coming. Even though I can't make out individual faces, I can feel the weight of people staring. I tug on my hood, making sure my scars are concealed.

Then the crowd shifts again, and I see Parker, hopping over concrete rubble, coming toward me with a big smile. I'm seized by the sudden desire to run; at the same time, I forget how to move. He's wearing a faded T-shirt, but I still recognize the logo of the old campgrounds where our families vacationed together for a few summers. At least Ariana has vanished.

'Hey,' Parker says. He hops off an old ledge into the grass in front of me. 'I didn't expect to see you.'

It would have helped if you'd invited me, I almost say. But that would mean admitting I care. It might even make it seem as if I'm jealous he invited Nick. For the same reason, I won't, I *refuse* to, ask whether she's here.

'I wanted to get out of the house,' I say instead. I shove my free hand into the front pocket of Nick's sweatshirt, gripping my beer with the other. Being around Parker makes me hyper-aware of my body, as if I've been taken apart and put together just a little bit wrong – which I guess I have. 'So. FanLand, huh?'

He grins, which annoys me. He's too easy, too smiling, too different from the Parker who pulled over to talk to me yesterday, awkward and stiff-backed, the Parker who didn't even climb out to give me a hug. I don't want him to think we'll be buddy-buddy again, just because I showed up at the Drink.

'Yeah, FanLand's all right,' he says. His teeth flash white. He's standing so close I can smell him, could lean forward six inches and place my cheek against the soft fabric of his T-shirt. 'Even if they're a little heavy on pep.'

'Pep?' I say.

'You know. Smells like teen spirit. Drinking-the-Kool-Aid kind of stuff.' Parker raises a fist. 'Go, FanLand!'

It's a good thing Parker was always such a nerd. Otherwise he would have been stupid popular. I look away.

'One time my sister nearly drowned trying to surf a kick-board in the wave pool.' I don't say I was the one who dared Nick to surf the kickboard, after she dared me to go down the Slip 'N Slide backward.

'That sounds like her,' Parker says, laughing.

I look away, taking another sip of beer. Standing this close to him, and looking at the familiar shape of his face – his nose, slightly crooked and still lined faintly with a scar, from where he ran smack into another guy's elbow during a game of Ultimate; the planes of his cheeks, and his eyelashes, which are almost as long as a girl's – makes my stomach hurt.

'Look.' Parker touches my elbow and I shift away, because if I don't shift away I'll only lean into him. 'I'm really glad you came. We've never really talked, you know, about what happened.'

You broke my heart. I fell for you, and you broke my heart. Period, done, end of story.

I can feel my heart opening and closing in my chest, like a fist trying to get a grip around something. It was the bike ride. I'm still weak. 'Not tonight, okay?' I force a smile. I don't want to hear Parker apologize for not loving me back. That will be worse, even, than the fact that he doesn't. 'I'm just here to have a good time.'

Parker's smile falters. 'Yeah, okay,' he says. 'I get it.' He touches his cup briefly to mine. 'Then how about a refill?'

Across the circle, I see Aaron Lee, a guy Nick was with for a while before the accident: nice guy, decent body, hopeless nerd. His eyes light up and he waves, arm up, as if hailing a taxi. He must think I brought Nick with me.

'I'm good,' I say. The beer isn't having its usual effect. Instead of feeling warm and loose and careless, I just feel queasy. I dump the rest of my beer onto the ground. Parker takes a quick step backward to avoid getting splashed. 'I'm actually not feeling so hot. I might head home.'

Now his smile is all-the-way gone. He tugs on his left ear. Parker-speak for *not happy*. 'You just got here.'

'Yeah, and I'm just leaving.' More and more people are swiveling in my direction, sneaking quick, curious looks before turning away again. My scars are burning, as if a flashlight has been shone on them. I imagine them glowing, too, so that everyone can see. 'Is that okay with you, or do I need a hall pass?'

I know I'm being mean, but I can't help it. Parker ditched me. He's been avoiding me ever since the accident. He can't parade back into my life and expect me to throw confetti at his feet.

'Wait.' For a moment, Parker's fingers, ice-cold from touching the beer, graze the inside of my wrist.

Then I pull away, turning clumsily in the uneven grass, dodging areas lumpy with deteriorating stone, pushing through a crowd that parts for me easily, too easily. As if *I'm* contagious.

Colin Dacey's trying to get a fire going in the pit, a blackened depression lined with gravel and nubs of stone. So far, he's succeeded mostly in sending huge, stinking geysers of smoke toward the sky. Stupid. It's already too hot, and cops are always patrolling in summertime. Girls back away from the fire, shrieking with laughter, fanning away the smoke. One of them, a sophomore whose name I can't remember, comes down hard on my toe.

'I'm sooo sorry,' she says. Her breath smells like amaretto. And then Ariana, barely sidestepping me, smiling huge and fake and overly nice, like she's a salesperson trying to douse me with perfume, says, 'You're leaving *already*?'

I don't stop. And when I feel a hand close down on my arm, I spin around, shaking off the grip, and say, 'What? What the hell do you want?'

Aaron Lee takes a quick step backward. 'Sorry. I didn't mean to – sorry.'

My anger immediately sizzles down to nothing. I've always felt vaguely sympathetic toward Aaron, even though we've barely spoken. I know what it's like to trot after Nick, to worship her from three steps behind. I've been doing it since I was born.

'That's all right,' I say. 'I was just leaving.'

'How've you been?' Aaron says, as if he hasn't heard me. He's nervous; that's obvious. He's holding his arms rigidly by his sides, like he's waiting for me to order him on a march. Aaron is six-four, the tallest Chinese guy in school – the tallest Chinese guy I've ever met, actually – and in that moment he really *looks* it. Gangly and awkward, too, like he's forgotten what his arms are for. Even before I can answer, he says, 'You look good. I mean, you always looked good, but considering—'

Just then, someone screams.

'Cops!'

All at once, people are running, yelling, laughing, scattering down the hill and into the trees even as beams of light come cutting across the grass. The chant rises up on the night, swelling the way the crickets did when evening fell.

'Cops! Cops! Cops!'

Someone rockets into me, knocking me off my feet; Hailey Brooks, barefoot and laughing, disappears into the woods, her blond hair streaming behind her like a banner. I try to protect my wrist when I fall and wind up crashing down on my elbow instead. A cop has Colin Dacey bent over double, arms behind his back, crime show–style. Everyone is screaming and the cops are shouting and there's a blur of bodies everywhere, silhouetted against the smoke and the sweep of flashlights. Suddenly there's a moon-big glow directly in my eyes, dazzling.

'All right,' the cop – a woman – says. 'Up you go.'

I roll away to my feet just as she gets a hand around the back of my sweatshirt, dropping her flashlight in the process.

'Gotcha.' But she's breathing hard, and I know that even on damaged legs I'll be able to outrun her.

'Sorry,' I say, half to her, half to Nick, because this sweatshirt is her favorite. Then I unzip and wriggle my arms free, one after the other, as the cop stumbles backward with a short cry of surprise and I run, limping, bare-armed, into the heavy wet darkness of the trees.

dara's diary entry

Today in Remedial Science — wait, sorry, Science Exploration, since we can't use the word remedial anymore — Ms. Barnes was droning on and on about the forces that keep all the planets circling around the sun and the moons circling around Saturn and all the different orbits carved out like railroad tracks in the middle of a great big piece of nothing, keeping everything from smashing together and imploding. And she said it was one of the greatest miracles: that everything, every bit of matter in the universe, could stay in its little circle, imprisoned in its own individual orbit.

But I don't think it's a miracle. I think it's sad

My family's like that. Everyone's just locked up in a spiraling circle, spinning past everyone else. It makes me want to scream. It makes me hope for a collision.

Lick Me told me last week that he thinks my family has trouble dealing with conflict. He said it with this really serious look on his face, like he was in the process of farting out some really important wisdom. Did he have to get a degree in psychology just to say really obvious shit?

My name is Dr Lichme, PhDuh.

For example: I caught Nick in my room today. She acted like she was just looking for her blue cashmere sweater, the one that used to belong to Mamu. As if I would believe that. She knows I'd rather wear chain link than pastels, and she knows I know she knows it and was just trying for an excuse. I bet Mom sent her to spy on me and root around to make sure I'm not getting into any trouble.

Just in case it happens again: HI, NICK!!! GET THE HELL OUT OF MY ROOM AND STOP READING MY DIARY!!

And to save you time — the weed's stashed in the flowerpot and my cigarettes are in the underwear drawer. Oh, and Ariana has a friend who works at Baton Rouge, and he says he knows someone who can get us Molly this weekend.

Don't tell Mom and Dad, or I'll tell them that their little angel isn't such an angel after all. I heard what you and Aaron did in the boiler room during the Founders' Day Ball. Naughty, naughty. Is that why you've been carrying around condoms in your bag?

That's right, N. Two can play at this game.

Love,
Lil Sis

JULY 21
nick

IT'S DAY TWO OF MY FANLAND CAREER AND I'M ALREADY RUNNING late. I'm in the kitchen, slugging Mom's coffee, which tastes alarmingly like something you'd use to clean drainpipes, when the knocking starts.

'I'll get it!' I shout, partly because I'm on my way out and partly because Mom's still in the bathroom, doing whatever she does in the morning, creams and lotions and layers of make-up and a slow transformation from pouchy and puckered to put-together.

I grab my bag from the window seat and jog down the hall, noticing that the unfamiliar gardening boots are still lying in the middle of the hall, as they have been for the whole five days I've been home. Suddenly annoyed – Mom always used to bug us about picking up after ourselves, and now she can't be bothered? – I pick them up and chuck them in the coat closet. A fine layer of dirt flakes from the thick rubber soles.

I'm unprepared for the cop standing on the front porch,

and for a moment my whole chest seizes and time stills or leaps backward and I think, *Dara. Something happened to Dara.*

Then I remember that Dara came home last night. I heard her, clomping around upstairs and playing snippets of weird Scandinavian dance tech, as though deliberately trying to annoy me.

The cop, a woman, is holding my favorite field hockey sweatshirt.

'Are you Nicole Warren?' She pronounces my name as if it's a dirty word, reading off the old camp label still stitched to the inside of the collar.

'Nick,' I say automatically.

'What's going on?'

Mom has come halfway down the stairs, her face only half made up. Foundation lightens her face, makes her pale lashes and eyebrows nearly disappear, giving her whole face the look of a blank mask. She's wearing her bathrobe over work pants.

'I don't know,' I say.

At the same time, the cop says, 'There was a party by the construction site at the Saskawatchee River last night.' The cop holds the sweatshirt a little higher. 'We took this off your daughter.'

'Nick?' Mom now comes all the way downstairs, cinching her belt tighter. 'Is that true?'

'No. I mean, I don't know. I mean—' I take a deep breath. 'I wasn't there.'

The cop ticks her eyes from me to the sweatshirt and then back to me. 'This belong to you?'

'Obviously,' I say, starting to get annoyed. Dara. Always goddamn Dara. Despite the accident, despite what happened, she just can't help but get into trouble. It's like it feeds her somehow, like she draws energy from chaos. 'My name's in it. But I wasn't there. I stayed in last night.'

'I doubt the sweatshirt walked over to the Drink on its own,' the cop says, smirking like she made a joke. It bothers me that she calls it the Drink. That's our name for it, a nonsense nickname that stuck, and it feels wrong that she knows – like a doctor probing your mouth with his fingers.

'Well, then, it's a mystery,' I say, grabbing the sweatshirt back from her. 'You're a cop. You figure it out.'

'Nick.' Mom's voice turns hard. 'Enough.'

Both of them are staring at me, wearing twin expressions of disappointment. I don't know when every grown-up masters that look. Maybe it's part of the college curriculum. I almost blurt it out: how Dara uses the rose trellis as a ladder; how she probably stole my sweatshirt and then got drunk and forgot it.

But years ago, back when we were kids, Dara and I swore that we would never rat each other out. There was never a formal declaration like a pact or a pinkie-swear. It was an implicit understanding, deeper than anything that could be stated.

Even when she started to get in trouble, even when I found cigarettes stubbed out on her windowsill or little plastic bags filled with unidentifiable pills stashed beneath the pencil cup on her desk, I didn't tell. Sometimes it killed me, lying awake and listening to the creak of the trellis, a muffled burst of laughter outside and the low roar of an engine peeling away into the night. But I couldn't bring myself to tell on her; I felt I'd be breaking something that could never be replaced.

Like as long as I kept her secrets, she would stay safe. She would stay mine.

So I say, 'Okay. Yeah, okay. I was there.'

'I don't believe this.' Mom turns a little half circle. 'First Dara. Now you. I just don't fucking believe it. Sorry.' This directed at the cop, who doesn't even blink.

'It's no big deal, Mom.' Ridiculous that I'm defending myself for something I didn't even do. 'People party at the Drink all the time.'

'It's trespassing,' the cop says. She's obviously enjoying herself.

'It *is* a big deal.' Mom's voice is creeping higher and higher. When she's really angry, it sounds like she's whistling instead of speaking. 'After what happened in March, *everything* is a big deal.'

'If you were drinking,' the cop goes on, she and Mom like a tag team of shitty, 'you could have been in a lot of trouble.'

'Well, I wasn't.' I shoot her a glare, hoping she'll shove off now that she's gotten to play bad cop this morning.

But she remains resolutely, squarely where she is, solid and unmoving, like a human boulder. 'You ever do any community service, Nicole?'

I stare at her. 'You can't be serious,' I say. 'This isn't *Judge Judy*. You can't make me—'

'I can't make you,' the cop interrupts me. 'But I can ask you, and I can *tell* you that if you don't help out, I'm going to write you up for partying at the Drink last night. Sweatshirt proves it, as far as I'm concerned.' For a moment, her expression softens. 'Look, we're just trying to keep you kids safe.'

'She's right, Nick,' Mom says, in a strangled voice. 'She's just doing her job.'

She turns back to the cop. 'It won't happen again. Will it, Nick?'

I'm not going to swear off doing something I didn't do in the first place. 'I'm going to be late for work,' I say, shouldering my bag. For a second, the cop looks like she might stop me from going. Then she sidesteps me and I feel a rush of triumph, as if I really have gotten away with doing something wrong.

But she grabs my elbow before I can pass her.

'Wait a minute.' She presses a flyer into my hand – from the way it's folded, it looks as if she's been carting it around in her back pocket. 'Don't forget,' she says. 'You do good, I do good for you. See you tomorrow.'

I wait until I'm halfway across the lawn before unfolding the flyer.

Join the Search for Madeline Snow.

'We're going to talk about this later, Nick!' Mom calls.

I don't answer her.

Instead I fish my phone out of my bag and key in a text to Dara – who's still asleep, I'm sure, her hair tangled on a cigarette-scented pillowcase, her breath still smelling like beer or vodka or whatever else she managed to flirt off of someone last night.

You owe me, I write. *Big-time.*

HELP US FIND MADELINE! JOIN THE SEARCH.

Hi all,

Thank you for all of the outpouring of support you've shown to the site, the Snows, and to Madeline in the past few days. It means the world to us.

Many of you have been asking how you can help. We are not currently accepting donations. But please join our search party July 22 at 4 p.m.! We will assemble in the parking lot at Big Scoop Ice Cream & Candy, 66598 Route 101, East Norwalk.

Please help spread the word to friends, families, and neighbors, and remember to follow @FindMadelineSnow on Twitter for the latest updates.

Let's bring Madeline home safely.

I'll be there!!!!!
posted by: allegoryrules at 11:05 a.m.

Me too. ☺
posted by: katywinnfever at 11:33 a.m.

>>>>comment deleted by admin<<<<

nick

THERE'S A FUNDAMENTAL RULE OF THE UNIVERSE THAT GOES LIKE this: if you're running late, you will miss your bus. You'll also miss your bus if it's raining or if you have somewhere really important to go, like the SATs or a driver's test. Dara and I have a word for that kind of luck: *crapdiment*. Just crap smeared on top of more crap.

My morning is already full of crapdiment.

By the time I get to FanLand, I'm nearly twenty-five minutes late. The traffic was bad along the shore. It was announced that Madeline Snow vanished from her sister's car two days ago outside Big Scoop Ice Cream & Candy, and the news has blown up across the entire state. Even more tourists are flooding the beach than usual. Sick how people like tragedies – maybe it makes them feel better about the crapdiment of their own lives.

The front gate is hanging open, even though the park won't officially open for another half hour, but there's no one in the front office, no sound except for the gentle whir of the refrigerator that contains all of Donna's precious Diet Cokes. I grab my red shirt from my assigned cubby – yes, I get a cubby, like in kindergarten – and do a quick armpit sniff. Not bad, but I'll definitely have to wash it after today. Already the parrot-shaped thermometer registers ninety-three degrees.

I re-emerge, blinking, into the sun. Still no one. I take the path that winds down past the big public bathrooms, toward the Lagoon – also known informally as the Martini, the Cesspool, and the Piss 'N' Play – where all the water rides are. The wind rustles the leaves, both plastic and real, lining the path, and I have a memory of watching Dara, knock-kneed and skinny as a stick, running ahead of me, laughing. Then I turn the corner and see the park employees, all of them, sitting in a semicircle in the sunken outdoor amphitheater the park uses for birthday parties and special performances. Mr Wilcox is standing on an overturned wooden crate, like a crazy man spouting off about religion. Fifty pairs of eyes turn to me simultaneously.

Funny that even in a crowd, it's Parker I see first.

'Warren, so nice of you to join us!' Mr Wilcox booms. But he doesn't sound too angry. I can't actually picture him angry; it's like trying to imagine a skinny Santa Claus. 'Come on, cop a squat, pull up a chair.'

There are no chairs, of course. I sit cross-legged at the edge of the crowd, my face hot, wishing everyone would stop staring. I catch Parker's eye and try to smile, but he turns away.

'We were just discussing plans for the big day,' Mr Wilcox says, addressing me. 'FanLand's seventy-fifth-anniversary party! We'll need all hands on deck, and we'll be coordinating a special volunteer force, too, with some local middle school recruits. The concession stands and pavilions will be working double time, and we're expecting more than *three thousand people* over the course of the day.'

Mr Wilcox rattles on about delegating special task forces and the importance of teamwork and organization, like we're heading out to do major battle instead of throwing a party for a bunch of pukey children and their exhausted parents. I half listen, while thinking of Dara's birthday two years ago and how she insisted we go out to this sleazy under-eighteen club near Chippewa Beach with a Halloween theme all year long. She knew the DJ – Goose or Hawk or something – and I remember how she stood on the table to dance, her mask looped around her neck, fake blood oozing down into the hollow of her clavicle.

Dara's always liked that kind of thing: dressing up, green on Saint Patrick's Day, bunny ears for Easter. Any excuse to do something out of the ordinary.

If there's one thing she's bad at, it's ordinary.

After the staff meeting, Mr Wilcox instructs me to help Maude 'prep' the park. Maude has a pinched face, almost as if it went through a vise; short hair, white-blond with blue streaks; and spacers in her ears. She's dressed like a hippie from the sixties, wearing a long flowing skirt and leather sandals that make her standard red T-shirt look even more ridiculous. She looks like a Maude; it's easy to imagine that in forty years she'll be hand-knitting a cover for her toilet seat and cursing at all the neighborhood kids pegging her porch with baseballs. Her face is twisted into a permanent scowl.

'What's the point of a dry run?' I ask, trying to make conversation. We're standing in front of the Cobra, the park's largest, and oldest, roller coaster. I shield my eyes against the sun and watch the empty cars rattle along the toothy track, eating it. From a distance, it does look like a snake.

'Gotta warm 'em up,' she says. Her voice is surprisingly deep and husky, like a smoker's. Definitely a Maude. 'Get 'em on their feet, wake 'em up, make sure there's no glitches.'

'You're talking about them like they're alive,' I say, only half joking. This makes her scowl even harder.

We make the rounds, testing the Plank and the Whirling Dervish, Pirate's Cove and Treasure Island, the Black Star and the Marauder. The sun is creeping higher in the sky and the park has officially opened; the concession stands and gamers have unshuttered their booths, and already the air is scented with fried dough. Families are streaming in, little kids trailing the paper flags we give out at the entryway, moms shouting for them to *Slow down, slow down.*

Mr Wilcox is parked by the front gate, talking with two cops wearing identical mirrored sunglasses and scowls. With them is a girl who looks familiar. Her blond hair is pulled into a high ponytail, her eyes swollen like she's been crying.

In the distance, I spot Alice and Parker painting a long canvas banner stretched between them on the pavement. I can't make out what the banner says:. just blocky red and black lettering and blue splashes that might be flowers. Parker is shirtless again, his hair hanging long over his eyes, the muscles in his back contracting every time he moves the brush. Alice catches me watching and gives me a big wave, smiling broadly. Parker looks up, too, but when I wave to him he looks down, frowning. It's the second time today he's avoided eye contact. Maybe he's mad that I skipped the party.

'All done,' Maude says, after we send the line of interconnected boats through the Haunted Ship and watch them emerge, passenger-less, on the other side. Faint screams and roars emanate from inside: a scream track, Alice told me yesterday, to get everyone into the right mood.

'What about that one?' I point to a ride that looks like a single metal finger, pointed to the sky. GATEWAY TO HEAVEN is painted on the side of a grounded sixteen-seater cart, which, given the name, presumably shoots up into the sky before dropping.

'That one's closed,' she says, already turning away from me.

As soon as she says it, I can see that she's right; the Gateway looks as if it hasn't been used in ages. The paint is flaking from the metal, and the whole thing has the sad, disused look of an abandoned toy. 'How come?'

Maude whirls around, barely suppressing a sigh. 'It's been closed *for ever.*'

For some reason, I don't want to let it drop. 'But why?'

'Some girl fell out of the chair, like, ten years ago,' Maude says flatly, as if she's reading off the world's most boring grocery list.

Even though we're standing in the sun and it must be one hundred degrees, a tiny shiver snakes up my spine. 'Did she die?'

Maude squints at me. 'No, she lived happily ever after,' she says, and then shakes her head, snorting. 'Of *course* she died. That thing is, like, one hundred and fifty feet high. She fell from the very top. Straight to the pavement. Splat.'

'Why don't they tear it down?' I ask. Suddenly the Gateway looks not sad, but ominous: a finger raised not to get attention but as a warning.

'Wilcox won't. He still wants to get it running again. It was the girl's fault, anyway. They proved it. She wasn't wearing her harness correctly. She unlocked it as a joke.' Maude shrugs. 'Now they're all automated. The harnesses, I mean.'

I have a sudden image of Dara, unbelted, falling through

space, her arms pinwheeling through empty air, her screams swallowed by wind and the sound of children laughing. And the accident: a brief photo explosion in my head, the sound of screaming, a jagged face of rock lit up by the headlights and the wheel jerking out of my hands.

I close my eyes, swallow, will away the image. Breathe in through my nose and out through my mouth, ticking off long seconds, like Dr Lichme taught me to do – the *only* useful thing he taught me. Where were we coming from? Why was I driving so fast? How did I lose control?

The accident has been clipped from my memory, just clean lifted away, as though surgically excised. Even the days before the accident are lost in murk, submerged in deep, sticky strangeness: every so often a new image or picture gets spit out, like something surfacing from the mud. The doctors told my mom it may have had something to do with the concussion, that memory would return to me slowly. Dr Lichme said, *Trauma takes time.*

'Sometimes her dad still comes to the park and just, like, stands there, staring up at the sky. Like he's still waiting for her to fall down. If you see him, just get Alice. She's the only one he'll talk to.' Maude curls her upper lip, revealing teeth that are surprisingly small, like a child's. 'He once told her she reminded him of his daughter. Creepy, right?'

'It's sad,' I say. But Maude doesn't hear. She's already walking away, skirt swishing.

Alice directs me to spend the rest of the morning helping out at the booths that line Green Row (so named, she explains, because of all the money that passes hands there), distributing stuffed parrots and keeping the kids from bawling when they don't manage to peg the wooden sharks with their water pistols.

By twelve thirty I'm sweating and starving and exhausted. More and more visitors keep arriving, flooding the gates, a tidal wave of grandparents and kids and birthday parties and campers dressed identically in bright orange T-shirts: a dizzying, kaleidoscope vision of people, more people.

'What's the matter, Warren?' Mr Wilcox, weirdly, isn't sweating. If anything, he looks even better and cleaner than he did this morning, as if his whole body had recently been vacuum-cleaned and ironed. 'Not hot enough for you? Go on. Why don't you grab some lunch and take a break in the shade? And don't forget to drink water!'

I head for the opposite side of the park, toward the pavilion Parker showed me yesterday. I'm not particularly looking forward to braving another conversation with Shirley, or *Princess*, but the other pavilions are absolutely packed, and the idea of trying to fight my way through a crowd of sweaty pre-teens is even less appealing. I have to pass under the shadow of the Gateway again. Impossible not to look at it: it's so high, the sun looks like it might impale itself on the metal. This time, it's Madeline Snow I picture, the girl from the news, the one who disappeared: free-falling through the air, hair blowing behind her.

It's quieter on the eastern side of the park, probably because the rides are sedate and farther apart, separated by long tracks of manicured parkland and benches nestled beneath tall spruces. Alice told me that this section of FanLand is known as the Nursing Home, and I see mostly older people here, a few couples tottering along together with their grandkids; a man with a face full of liver marks napping, upright, on a bench; a woman making painstaking progress toward the canteen with her walker, while a younger woman next to her does a bad job of pretending to be patient.

There are only a few people eating at the pavilion, sitting beneath the metal awning at metal picnic tables. I'm surprised to see Parker behind the counter.

'Hey.' I step to the window, and Parker straightens up, his face moving through an array of expressions too quick for me to decipher. 'I didn't know you were manning the grill.'

'I'm not,' he says shortly, not smiling. 'Shirley had to pee.'

Next to the window are dozens of multicolored flyers, layered like feathers over the glass, advertising different special events and discounted specials and, of course, the anniversary party. A new one has been recently added to the mix, this one glaringly out of place: a grainy photograph of the missing girl, Madeline Snow, face tilted to the camera, gap-toothed and grinning. In big block letters above her image it says simply: MISSING. Now it strikes me that the girl with the blond ponytail, the one who was standing with the cops and seemed somehow familiar, must be related to Madeline Snow. They have the same wide-spaced eyes, the same subtly rounded chin.

I touch my finger to the word *Missing*, as if I could erase it. I briefly think about the story Parker told me, about Donovan, an everyday guy just walking around wearing a big smile and collecting kiddie porn on his computer.

'You going to order, or what?' Parker says.

'Is everything okay?' I'm careful not to look at him. My throat is still as dry as chalk. I want to buy a water but don't want to ask Parker to get it. 'You seem a little . . .'

'A little what?' He leans forward on his elbows, eyes dark, unsmiling.

'I don't know. Mad at me or something.' I take a deep breath. 'Is it because of the party?'

Now it's Parker's turn to look away – over my head, squinting, as if something fascinating is happening mid-air. 'I was hoping we could, you know, actually hang out.'

'Sorry.' I don't bother pointing out that technically, I never said I would come, only that I would think about it. 'I wasn't feeling well.'

'Really? Didn't seem like it.' He makes a face. Then I remember I spent the whole day with him at work, laughing, talking, threatening to splash each other with the industrial cleaning hose. He knows I was feeling just fine.

'I wasn't in the mood to party.' There's no way I can tell him what I really feel: that I was hoping my note would bring Dara to my door, that she would knock a half second before letting herself in, wearing one of her backless, strapless, gravity-defying tank tops and a thick covering of eyeshadow; that she would insist that I change into something *sexier,* that she would grip my chin and force make-up on me, as if I were the younger sister. 'Did you have fun?'

He just shakes his head and mutters something I can't hear.

'What?' I'm starting to get angry.

'Forget it,' he says. I spot Shirley waddling toward us, scowling as usual. Parker must see her at the same time, because he backs up, toward the door sandwiched between the deep fryer and the microwave. When he opens the door, a wedge of light expands across the narrow space, touching boxes of hamburger buns and towering stacks of plastic soda lids.

'Parker—'

'I said forget it. Seriously. It's no big deal. I'm not mad.' Then he disappears, silhouetted momentarily before vanishing, and Shirley takes his place, shuffling up to the counter, huffing, moisture clinging to the bleached-blond hair on her upper lip.

'You gonna order something, or just sit there staring?' she says to me. Big dark rings have expanded under her breasts, like the shadows of two groping hands.

'Not hungry,' I say. Which, thanks to Parker, is true.

MISSING

Madeline Snow, 9 yrs. old

LAST SEEN: Sunday, July 19th at 10:05 p.m. wearing Disney princess pajama bottoms and a Greenville Soccer sweatshirt.

Please contact (212) 555-4770 with any information, or visit findmadeline.tumblr.com

(212) 555-4770 (212) 555-4770 (212) 555-4770 (212) 555-4770 (212) 555-4770 (212) 555-4770 (212) 555-4770 (212) 555-4770

JULY 22

dara

SARAH SNOW AND HER BEST FRIEND, KENNEDY, WERE BABYSITTING
Madeline Snow on Sunday, July 19. Madeline was running a
low fever. Still, she demanded ice cream from her favorite place
on the shore, Big Scoop, and eventually Sarah and Kennedy
gave in.

By the time they arrived, it was after 10:00 p.m. and Madeline
had fallen asleep. Sarah and Kennedy went inside together,
leaving Madeline in the backseat. Sarah may have locked the
doors, but she may not have.

There was a long line. Big Scoop has been in business since
the late seventies, and has become, for the residents of Shoreline
County and the tens of thousands of vacationers who descend
on the shore every summer, a landmark. It took twenty-five
minutes for Sarah and Kennedy to get their order: Rum Pecan
Punch for Kennedy; Double Trouble Chocolate for Sarah;
Strawberries and Cream for Madeline.

But when they returned to the car, the back door was hanging
open and Madeline was gone.

The cop who tells us all this, Lieutenant Frank Hernandez, doesn't look like a cop, more like a weary dad trying to coach his son's soccer team back from a really bad loss. He's not even wearing a uniform, but scuffed-up sneakers and a dark-blue polo shirt. There's mud on the cuffs of his jeans, and I wonder whether he was one of the guys at the Drink two nights ago, maybe even the cop who arrested Colin Dacey and made him spend the night sleeping it off at the boxy little station downtown. Rumor has it that the bust was related to Madeline's disappearance. The cops start getting shit in the media – no leads, no suspects – so they decide to prove their worth by raiding a keg party.

Colin is here, looking miserable and pale, like a tortured saint; I spot Zoe Heddle and Hunter Dawes and assume both of them were forced to volunteer, too.

Even though Nick covered for me when the cop showed up on our front porch this morning, she made it clear she has no intention of taking the rap for a party she didn't even attend.

This time, the note was on the toilet seat.

Cop busted 'me' at the Drink. Thanks for asking whether you could borrow my sweatshirt. Since 'I' went to a party, 'I'm' volunteering today. Big Scoop parking lot, 4:00 p.m. Have fun.—N

'At this point, we're still hoping for a positive outcome,' the cop says, in a tone of voice that suggests they're fearing the opposite. He's climbed up onto the concrete divider that separates the Big Scoop parking lot from the beach, and he speaks into the air above the crowd, which is larger than I'd expected. There must be two hundred people packed into the lot, along with three news vans and a cluster of journalists hefting heavy equipment and sweating in the sun. Maybe these are the same journalists who've been writing bad things about the Shoreline County cops and budget cuts and incompetence. With their cameras and boom lights and microphones, hovering at the edge of the crowd, they look like members of a futuristic army, waiting for the chance to attack.

Standing a short distance away is a couple I recognize from the news as the Snows. The man looks like he's been standing all day in a raw wind: his face is red, chapped, and bloated-looking. The woman is swaying on her feet and keeps one hand gripped, clawlike, on the shoulder of a blond girl standing in front of her. Madeline's older sister, Sarah. Next to her is Kennedy, the best friend. She has dark hair cut in a severe fringe across her forehead, and she's wearing a bright-red tank top that looks surprisingly cheerful given the occasion.

I arrived early, when the crowd was thinner, and a few dozen people were milling around, keeping a careful distance from the yellow police tape marking off the scene of the disappear-ance. We all had to sign in, like we're guests at someone's really awful wedding. I've watched enough *Law & Order* to know the cops are probably hoping the pervert – if there is a pervert – will show up to get his rocks off and smirk about being smarter than the cops.

Reflexively I fish my cell phone from my bag. No further word from Nick. No texts from Parker, either. I'm not surprised, but I still get a little dip of disappointment in my stomach, like going over a hill too fast.

'This is how it's going to go. We're going to move east in a line. You should be close enough to touch your neighbors' shoulders.' The cop holds out his arms like a drunk trying to steady his balance on the line. 'Keep your eyes on the ground and look for anything and everything that doesn't belong. A barrette, a cigarette stub, a headband, whatever. Maddie had a favorite bracelet – silver, with turquoise charms. She was wearing it when she disappeared. If you see something, give a shout.'

He hops off the concrete divider, and the crowd responds like a uniform pool of water, rippling outward, dispersing, breaking apart into smaller groups. The search party fans out across the beach, while cops shout orders and instructions and the camera crews click and buzz away. From above we might look like we're playing a complicated game, an intricate pattern of Red Rover, all of us spread out in a line and silently calling for Madeline to come over, to come back. The sand is studded with the kind of trash that accumulates at the edge of parking lots: pulpy cigarette packs, plastic wrappers, soda cans. I wonder whether any of it is important. I imagine a featureless man sitting outside on Friday night, sipping a warm Coke, watching the firefly flicker of taillights in and out of the Big Scoop parking lot, watching two girls, Kennedy and Sarah, walking with their arms linked to the warm bright glow of the ice-cream shop, leaving a small girl huddled in the backseat.

I hope she's alive. Even more: I *believe*. It strikes me that that's the point of the search party. Not actually to turn up clues, but as if the power of our collective belief, our joint effort, will keep her alive. As if she's Tinker Bell, and all we have to do is keep clapping.

At least it's a little cooler when we move down toward the water, but the mosquitoes and the horseflies are worse, swarming up from hidden pockets and piles of beach wood. The going is painfully slow, but even so, moving across the sand is exhausting. Every few minutes someone shouts, and the cops rush over and squat, prodding at some garbage with long, white-gloved fingers: a tattered piece of fabric, an empty beer can, the remains of somebody's fast-food lunch, probably chucked out of a passing car. The cops bag a silver bracelet, though I see Madeline Snow's mother shaking her head, lips pressed together. The beach is barely a quarter mile wide; at no point are we out of sight of either the parking lot or the houses and motels perched high on the dunes. It seems impossible to imagine that anything bad could happen here, in this short strip of land, so close to the everyday churn of cars and restaurants and people sneaking outside to smoke cigarettes on the beach.

But something bad *did* happen here. Madeline Snow is gone. Nick and I used to pretend that there were goblins waiting in the woods; she told me that if I listened hard enough, I could hear them singing.

If you don't watch out, they'll grab you, she'd say, tickling me around the middle until I shrieked. *They'll take you to the underworld and turn you into a bride.*

And just for a second, I imagine Madeline vanishing into thin air, lured by a song too soft for the rest of us to hear.

'You're Sharon Warren's daughter, aren't you?' the woman on my left blurts out. She's been blatantly staring at me for the past ten minutes, and I've been doing my best to ignore her. Her face is sugared with too-heavy make-up, and she's been tottering along in wedge heels over the sand, windmilling her arms like she's on a balance beam.

I almost deny it but decide there's no point. 'Uh-huh.'

'I'm Cookie,' she says, blinking at me, as if expecting me to know her. Of course her name is Cookie. No one who wears bright-pink lipstick and heels to search for a missing girl could possibly have any other name. 'Cookie Hendrickson,' she adds, when I say nothing. 'I live in Somerville, too. I did admin at MLK High when your mom was principal there. I knew your grandfather, too. Great man. I was' – she lowers her voice as if she's telling me a secret – 'at the funeral.'

Last December, three days after Christmas, my grandfather died. He'd lived in Somerville all his life and, in fact, worked for two summers for the last mill before it got shuttered in the fifties. Later on he coached Little League and even briefly got elected town chairman, a position he abdicated as soon as he, and the rest of town, realized that he didn't give a shit about politics. Nick and I called him Paw-Paw, and half of Somerville was at his funeral in January. Everybody loved him.

Later that night Nick, Parker, and I got blitzed on SoCo in Parker's basement. Nick went upstairs to get water, and I started crying, and Parker put his arm around me and I kissed him. When Nick came downstairs again she made the funniest face, like she'd just walked into a party where she didn't know anyone.

Still, Nick and I slept together that night, side by side, the way we did when we were kids. It was the last time.

'How's your mama doing?' She's putting on the accent real thick, like we're in Tennessee. Women do that, I've noticed, when they're about to say something you won't like, like dropping all the consonants makes it harder to hear what they're saying. Sugared face, sugared words. 'I know she went through a little . . . depression.' She says it like it's a bad word.

'She's fine,' I say. We've stopped moving again. We're almost at the water now. The ocean shimmers like metal just beyond a short, dark strip of wet sand. A woman – a reporter? – has taken an interest in our conversation. She starts edging toward us, clutching a mini tape recorder. 'We're all fine.'

'That's good to hear. You tell your mama Cookie says hello.'

'I'm sorry to interrupt.' The reporter has reached us and, without acknowledging Cookie, shoves her iPhone in my face, looking not at all sorry. She's overweight, wearing a nylon suit with big sweat marks soaking the underarms. 'I'm Margie. I work for the *Shoreline Blotter*.' She pauses, as if expecting me to applaud her. 'I was just hoping to ask you a few questions,' she adds, when I say nothing. Cookie lets out a little chirp of surprise as the reporter, undeterred, steps in front of her, effectively blocking Cookie's view.

'Aren't you supposed to be doing something *useful*?' I cross my arms. 'Like interviewing the Snows?'

'I'm looking for a variety of human interest stories,' she says smoothly. She has big eyes, weirdly protruding, and she doesn't blink very much, giving her face the impassive look of a particularly stupid frog. But she's not stupid. That I can tell right away. 'I live just outside Somerville. You're from Somerville, is that right? You were in that terrible accident. It wasn't that far from here, was it?'

Cookie makes a disapproving noise. 'I'm sure she doesn't want to talk about all that,' she coos, but with a wink in my direction, as if she's hoping I will anyway.

Sweat is moving freely down my back by now, and the horseflies are fat, droning in thick clusters. Suddenly all I want is to strip down and get clean, scrub off this day, scrub off Cookie and the reporter with her reptilian eyes, watching me lazily as if I'm an insect she's waiting to swallow.

Down the beach, the cop who looks like a dad is waving his arms and shouting something I can't hear. But the gesture's clear enough. *We're done here,* he's saying. *Pack up and go home.* I feel an immense, overwhelming surge of relief.

'Look,' I say. My voice sounds high-pitched, foreign, and I clear my throat. 'I just came to help out, like everybody else. I really think we should, you know, keep the focus on Madeline. Okay?'

Cookie murmurs something that manages to sound both appreciative and disappointed. The reporter, Margie, is still standing there clutching her stupid iPhone like it's a magic wand. I turn around and start moving back toward the parking lot, as the crowd disperses into smaller groups, everyone speaking in low tones, reverent almost, as if church has just finished and we're afraid to use our regular voices too soon.

'What do *you* think happened to Madeline Snow?' Margie calls after me, her voice loud and easy – too easy.

I freeze. It might be imagination, but I imagine that the crowd freezes too, that for a second the whole day stills and becomes a picture, *filter: sepia*, a whitewash of grays and yellows and a flat silver sea.

I turn around. Margie is still watching me, unblinking.

'Maybe she just got tired of everyone bothering her,' I say. My throat is raw from the heat and the salt. 'Maybe she just wanted to be left alone.'

WE NEED YOU!
Sign Our Petition and Join the Fight for Safer Streets!

On Sunday, July 19, nine-year-old Madeline Snow was abducted from her sister's car just outside the Big Scoop Ice Cream & Candy Shop, a Shoreline County institution. This follows a year in which police budgets were slashed by 25 percent county-wide, leaving many police departments understaffed and underfunded.

Police commissioner Gregory Pulaski has spoken up about the need to demand that the state legislature expand the police budget to pre-recession levels: 'When times are hard, people get desperate. When people get desperate, they do desperate things. In order to function efficiently as a unit, we need to expand our presence on the streets, develop our training programs, and recruit and keep the best men and women for the job. That costs money. Period.'

Join the fight to secure safer streets. Sign the petition below, and demand that the General Assembly take action.

Sign the Petition!
Enter full name:
Enter zip code:
SUBMIT

Glad someone is finally taking action. Forwarded to everyone I know. Let's hope the town actually listens.
posted by: soccerdadrules at 6:06 p.m.

25 percent?? No wonder there's graffiti all over my neighborhood.
posted by: richardthefirst at 7:04 p.m.

Graffiti isn't a crime. It's an art form, dickwad.
posted by: iambanksky at 8:55 p.m.

How many more children will have to disappear before Congress takes note? Poor Maddie. And poor Sarah! I can't imagine how devastated she must be.
posted by: mamabear27 at 12:00 a.m.

Sarah Snow is a liar.
posted by: anonymous at 1:03 a.m.

dara

I MAKE IT BACK TO THE PARKING LOT WITHOUT SEEING THE reporter again, thank God. Still no texts from Parker, and no word from Nick, either. Just a creepy text from a number I don't recognize.

Yo. WTF. Tried calling. R u dead?

I delete the text without replying. Probably some asshole I made out with once.

My whole body feels filmy with sweat, and my legs are killing me. I half jog, half wobble across the street to the gas station. I buy a Coke and chug it in basically a single gulp, then lock myself in the bathroom, which is surprisingly clean and as cold as a meat freezer. I splash water on my face, dampening my hair and shirt in the process and not even caring. I towel off with the scratchy brown paper towel unique to public restrooms, the kind that smells like wet earth.

I try not to look too long in the mirror – funny how I used to *like* to look at myself, could stand for hours with

Ariana at my mom's vanity before we went out, comparing lip and eye shades and making funny faces – and sweep my hair over my right shoulder, which helps conceal the scars below my jawline. There's nothing I can do about the scars on my cheek and temple, although I half wish I had Nick's hoodie again.

Already I feel better. Still, I spend some time rifling through the rack of weird miscellaneous crap all gas stations sell: Christian rock CDs, sun visors, plastic razors. When Parker first got his license, six months before Nick, we used to play this game where we'd all pile into the car and hit up the local pawn shops and gas stations, competing over who could find the weirdest items for sale. One time at a Gas 'n Go he found two old beanbag toys, fur clotted with dust, stuffed behind a row of condoms and energy-pill bottles. Nick got the horse because she used to ride, and I got the bear, which I named Brownie.

I wonder whether he remembers that day.

I wonder what he would think if he knew that Brownie still sleeps with me every night.

The parking lot across the street is now mostly empty, and both the cops and the news vans have dispersed. The sun is hovering low over the trees, and I can see stretches of the bay lying puddle-like between the clutter of businesses and condos.

When I step outside, I'm surprised to see Sarah Snow standing a few feet away, angled behind a big SUV, smoking a cigarette with hard, rapid pulls. She starts when she sees me, dropping her cigarette. Then, after a momentary hesitation, she comes toward me.

'Hey.' She brings her hand to her mouth quickly, then drops it, as though still smoking a phantom cigarette. Her fingers are trembling. 'Don't I know you?'

Whatever I thought she might say, it wasn't that. I shake my head. 'I don't think so,' I say.

She keeps watching me. Her eyes are huge, as if she's not *seeing* but actually devouring me through her eyeballs. 'You look familiar.'

Even though it's a long shot, I say, 'Maybe you know my sister?'

'Yeah.' She starts nodding. 'Yeah, maybe.' She looks away, squinting, wiping her hands on the back of her jeans. The seconds tick on. I wonder what it would be like to have to be here, on the beach, surrounded by strangers, holding hands with some sweating neighbor and calling for your sister to come home.

'Listen,' I say, fighting a sudden feeling of suffocation. I was never good at this: words of comfort or hope. 'I'm really sorry. About your sister. I'm sure . . . I'm sure she's okay.'

'You think?' When she turns back to me, her face is so raw, so full of grief and fear and something else – anger – I almost turn away. But then she steps forward and grabs my wrist, squeezing so hard I can feel the impression of each individual finger.

'I was trying so hard to protect her,' she says, speaking in a sudden rush. 'It's all my fault.' She's so close I can smell her breath, sour, stinking of tobacco. 'The lying is the hardest part, isn't it?'

'*Sarah.*' Across the street, Kennedy is standing at the edge of the parking lot, holding a hand to her eyes to shield them from the sun. She's frowning.

Once again, Sarah's face transforms. Before I can respond, she releases me, spinning around, her blond hair fanning behind her shoulder blades, trailing the faint smell of smoke.

nick's gratitude list

Why is it so hard to find five things to be thankful for? It's only been a month and already keeping a gratitude journal might be the hardest New Year's resolution I ever made, especially after our crap show of a Christmas. I can think of a billion things I'm not happy about. Like the fact that Dara's not speaking to me ever since she caught me reading her journal. Or the fact that Mom spends all her time at work. Or the fact that Dad's new girlfriend always has lipstick on her teeth, even first thing in the morning.

Okay, bad start. Here goes. For real this time:

1. I'm grateful that I don't have lipstick on my teeth, ever, because I never wear any.

2. I'm grateful for the Toyota Dad got me! Okay, it's like twenty years old and Parker says the upholstery smells like cat food, but it drives, and this way Dara and I don't always have to fight over the keys.

3. I'm grateful for Perkins, my little walking ball of fluffy.

4. I'm grateful that Margot Lesalle started that stupid rumor about what Aaron and I were doing in the boiler room at the

Founders' Day Ball. Thank God for Margot. She always goes for the most obvious rumors.

And:

5. I'm super, extra, mega grateful that no one knows what really happened. That no one will ever know. They say that you're supposed to tell the truth. Dr Lichme says that, anyway.

But don't they also say that what you don't know can't hurt you?

BEFORE

nick

'DARA!' I PAW THROUGH THE PILE OF CLEAN LAUNDRY ON MY BED, cursing under my breath. The stuffed cat Aaron gave me for Valentine's Day – *You're puuurrfect,* it says in a creepy high voice when you squeeze it – is perched between my pillows, watching me with glittering glass eyes. 'Dara? Have you seen my blue sweater?'

No answer from above: no footsteps, no signs of life. Christ. It's already after seven o'clock. No way can I be late to homeroom again, not after Mr Arendale threatened me with detention.

From my closet, I grab a broom – or what was a broom, anyway, before Perkins clawed out most of the bristles – and thump the ceiling with the handle, a method of communication (I've found) far more effective than screaming or calling or even texting, which Dara has been known to do when she's really hung over. (*Can u bring up some water? Pleeeeeeease?*)

'I know you can hear me!' I shout, punctuating every word with a *thwack.*

Still nothing. Cursing again – out loud, this time – I shove my phone in my pocket, grab my bag, and take the stairs up to the attic, two at a time. Dara pretends everything I own is too boring for her to borrow, but recently my favorite sweaters and T-shirts have been disappearing and reappearing strangely altered, reeking of cigarettes and pot, sporting new stains and holes.

Dara hates that her door has no lock and militantly insists that we knock before entering, which is why I swing the door open with no warning, hoping it will annoy her.

'What the hell?' I say. She's sitting up in bed, facing away from me, still wearing her sleep shirt, her hair ratty with knots. 'I've been calling you for like twenty—'

Then she turns around and I can't finish my sentence.

Her eyes are swollen and her skin is splotchy and bloated in places, like overripe fruit. Her bangs are plastered to her damp forehead. Her cheeks are streaked with mascara, as if she fell asleep without washing her face and has been crying all night long.

'Jesus.' As always, Dara's room looks as if it's been the recent victim of a small and concentrated tsunami. I almost trip three times moving toward the bed. The radiators are going overtime; her room is stifling hot, heavily scented with cinnamon and saline and clove smoke and, just faintly, sweat. 'What happened?'

I sit down next to her and try to put an arm around her shoulder, but she pulls away. Even from a distance, I can feel heat radiating from her skin.

She takes a shuddering breath, but when she speaks her voice is dull, monotone. 'Parker dumped me. Again.' She mashes a fist into her eye as if she's trying to physically press back tears. 'Happy fucking Valentine's Day.'

I count to three in my head so I don't say anything dumb. Since they started hooking up or going out or whatever they're doing, Dara and Parker have broken up three times that I know about. And Dara always cries and freaks and tells me she'll never talk to him again, and a week later I see her in school with her arms wrapped around his waist, stretching onto tiptoe to whisper something. 'I'm really sorry, Dara,' I say carefully.

'Oh, please.' She whirls around to face me. 'No, you're not. You're *happy*. You always told me it wouldn't last.'

'I never said that,' I say, feeling a quick flare of anger. 'I *never* said that.'

'But you thought it.' After crying, Dara's eyes go from green to practically yellow. 'You always thought it was a bad idea. You didn't *have* to say so.'

I keep my mouth shut because she's right, and there's no point trying to deny it.

Dara draws her knees to her chest and puts her head between them. 'I hate him,' she says, in a muffled voice. 'I feel like such an idiot.' Then, even quieter: 'Why doesn't he think I'm good enough?'

'Come on, Dara.' I'm losing patience with her performance; I've heard the whole monologue before. 'You know that's not true.'

'It is true,' she says, her voice small now. There's a beat of silence. Then she says, even quieter, 'Why doesn't anyone love me?'

That's the essence of Dara: she'll annoy the shit out of you and then break your heart a second later. I reach out to touch her and then think better of it. 'D-bar, you know that's not true,' I say. 'I love you. Mom loves you. Dad loves you.'

'That doesn't count,' she says. 'You guys have to love me.

It's practically illegal not to. You probably just love me so you won't go to jail.'

I can't help it; I laugh. Dara lifts her head up just long enough to glare at me before retreating again, like an injured turtle. 'Come on, Dara,' I say. I unsling my bag and set it down. No point in rushing now. There's no way I'll make it to home-room at all, much less on time. 'You have more friends than anyone I know.'

'Not *real* friends,' she says. 'I just know people.'

I don't know whether I want to hug or strangle her. 'That's ridiculous,' I say. 'I can prove it.' I grab her phone from the bedside table, where it's sitting next to a pile of crumpled tissues stained with lipstick and mascara. She's never bothered to change her password: 0729. July 29. Her birthday, the only password she ever uses, the only password she can ever remember. I pull up her photos and start scrolling through them: Dara at house parties, keg parties, dance parties, pool parties. 'If everyone hates you so much, who are all these people?'

I pull up a grainy picture of Dara and Ariana – at least I think it's Ariana, although she's wearing so much make-up and the picture quality is so bad, it's hard to tell – surrounded by guys who must be in their early twenties at least. One of them has his arm around Dara; he's wearing a cheesy leather jacket and would be hot except for his hair, which is thinning, and gelled into spikes. I wonder when this was taken, and whether poor, brokenhearted Dara was with Parker at the time.

Dara shoves the pillows off her face and sits up, making a grab for the phone. 'What the hell?' She rolls her eyes when I hold the phone out of reach. 'Are you serious?'

'Jesus.' I stand up and make a show of shaking my head

over the picture. 'Ariana looks like a slutty bumblebee in that shirt. Friends don't let friends pair yellow and black.'

'Give it back.'

I take a step backward, dodging her. Dara has no choice but to stand up.

'Ha,' I say, angling away from her as she once again tries to swipe the phone back. 'You're out of bed.'

'This isn't funny,' Dara says. But at least she doesn't look so much like an abandoned doll washed up on a reef of pillows and old sheets. Her eyes are bright with anger. 'This isn't a joke.'

'Who's this guy?' I pull up a second picture of leather-jacket guy. It appears to have been taken in a bar or a basement – somewhere dark and crowded with people. In this one, obviously a selfie, Dara is making a kissy-face at the camera while behind her, Leather Jacket watches. Something in his expression makes me nervous; it's the way Perkins looks when he locates a new mouse hole. 'He looks like he wants to eat your face.'

'That's Andre.' She at last succeeds in grabbing the phone back from me. 'He's nobody.' She hits delete, punching hard with a finger, and then deletes the next picture that comes up, and the next, and the next. 'They're all nobodies. They don't matter.'

She flops onto the bed again, still deleting pictures, jabbing at the phone forcefully as if she can physically splinter the images into non-existence, and mutters something I don't quite make out. But I can tell from her expression that I'm not going to like it.

'What did you say?' I've completely missed homeroom by now and will be late to first period, too. I'll get detention, all for Dara's sake, all because she can't leave anything whole and good and untouched, all because she has to dig and explode and experiment, like a kid making a mess in the kitchen, pretending to be a cook, pretending something *good* will actually come out.

'I said you don't understand,' she says, without looking up. 'You don't understand *anything*.'

'Do you even like Parker?' I say, because now I can't help it, can't keep back the anger. 'Or was it just to see if you could?'

'I don't *like* him,' she says, going very still. 'I *love* him. I've *always* loved him.' I'm tempted to remind her that she said the exact same thing about: Jacob, Mitts, Brent, and Jack.

Instead I say, 'Look. I thought it was a bad idea because of *this*. Because of . . .' I struggle to find the right words. 'You were best friends before.'

'He was *your* best friend,' she fires back, and lies down, curling her legs up to her chest again. 'He's always liked you better.'

'That's ridiculous,' I say automatically, even though, really, I always kind of believed that was true. Was that why I was so shocked when Dara was the one to kiss him? When he kissed her back? Even though it was often the three of us, he was my best friend, my giggle-till-you-snarf-soda, my antidote-to-boredom, my talk-about-nothing person. And Dara was mine, too. For once, I was the apex of the triangle, the high point that kept the whole structure together.

Until Dara once again had to be on top.

Dara looks away and says nothing. I'm sure in her head she's the tragic Juliet, about to pose for her final, premortem photo.

'Look, I'm sorry you're upset.' I pick up my bag from the floor. 'And I'm sorry I apparently don't understand. But I'm late.'

She still doesn't say anything. There's no point asking

whether she plans on going to school. She very obviously doesn't. I wish Mom could be half as hard on Dara as she is in her school, where, apparently, some of the junior boys just refer to her as 'that tough bitch.'

I'm halfway to the door before Dara speaks again.

'Just don't pretend, okay? I can't stand it when you do.'

When I turn around, she's looking at me with the strangest expression – like someone who knows a very juicy, very *secret* secret.

'Pretend what?' I say.

For a second, the sun goes behind a cloud, and Dara's room turns incrementally darker. It's as if someone has held up a palm to Dara's windows, and now, in the shadows, she looks like a stranger. 'Don't pretend you aren't happy,' she says. 'I know you,' she goes on, when I start to contradict her. 'You act like you're so good. But deep down, you're just as screwed up as the rest of us.'

'Goodbye, Dara,' I say, stepping out into the hall. I make sure to slam the door so hard behind me, it rattles on its hinges, listening with satisfaction as something inside – a picture frame? her favorite mug? – crashes to the ground, a responsive echo.

Dara's not the only one who knows how to break things.

AFTER

nick

'IT STILL WORKS, YOU KNOW.'

I haven't realized I've been staring up at the Gateway until Alice comes up behind me. I take a step backward, nearly planting a foot in the paint tray.

She pushes a strand of hair back from her forehead with the inside of her wrist. Her face is flushed, and it makes her eyes look light brown, nearly yellow. 'The Gateway,' she says, jerking her chin toward the huge metal spire. 'It still works. Wilcox gets it inspected every summer. He's determined to run it again. I think he feels bad, you know, like as long as the Gateway stays off-limits it means it really was his fault. The girl's death, I mean. He has to prove the ride is safe.' She shrugs, scratching the tattoo below her left ear with one blue-paint-splattered finger.

When we're not working the rides today, everyone on shift has been tasked with concealing evidence of last night's vandalism. Sometime just before closing, a few idiots with graffiti cans went around decorating various signs around the park with crude illustrations of a certain part of the male anatomy.

Wilcox seemed unfazed this morning. I later heard this happens at least once a summer.

'He petitions the park advisory department every year.' Alice sits down on a small plastic bench shaped like a tree stump. It's rare that Alice sits down. She's always moving, always directing things and calling out orders and laughing. Earlier today I saw her climbing up the scaffolding of the Cobra to get to a kid's backpack that had somehow, inexplicably, become stuck in the gears – swinging, spiderlike, between structural supports, while a small crowd of FanLand employees had gathered, some to cheer her on, some begging her to get down, others scouting for Mr Wilcox and Donna.

I watched Parker watching her, head tilted up to the sky, hands on his hips, eyes sparkling, and felt – what? Not jealousy, exactly. Jealousy is a strong feeling, a feeling that twists your stomach and gnaws your insides to shreds. This was more of a hollowness, like being really hungry for such a long time that you kind of get used to it.

Did he ever look at Dara like that? Does he still?

I don't know. All I know is that he used to be my best friend, and now he doesn't look at me at all. And my other best friend isn't speaking to me. Or I'm not speaking to her.

Last night, seized by an old impulse, I went up to the attic just to check on her and saw she'd added a new sign to her door. Made of pale-green construction paper and decorated with hearts and badly drawn butterflies, it read simply: DON'T EVEN FUCKING THINK ABOUT IT.

'Mature,' I shouted through the closed door, and heard a muffled laugh in response.

'The girl's dad – his name is Kowlaski, I think, or something like that, something with a "ski" – shows up every year and argues that the ride should stay closed,' Alice goes on. 'I guess I understand both sides. The ride is really fun, though. At least, it was. When it's powered up, all these tiny lights come on, so it looks like the Eiffel Tower or something.' She pauses. 'They say she still cries out at night.'

Even though the day is dull and flat and windless, hot as metal, a tiny shiver lifts the hairs on the back of my neck. 'What do you mean?'

Alice smiles. 'It's stupid. It's just something the old-timers say when they're working the graveyard shift. Have you worked the graveyard yet?'

I shake my head. The graveyard shifters – known at FanLand as the gravediggers – are responsible for closing up the park every night, securing the gates against break-ins, hauling trash, emptying the grease traps, and securing the rides and lulling them back into their nightly slumber. I've already heard horror stories from the other employees about shifts stretching until well past midnight.

'Next week,' I say. 'The night before' – *Dara's birthday* – 'the anniversary party.'

'Lucky you,' she says.

'The girl,' I prompt her, because now I'm curious. And it's a relief, weirdly, to talk about the girl, long dead, long broken up into echoes and memories. All morning, the talk has been of Madeline Snow. Her disappearance has sparked a three-county-wide manhunt. Every newspaper is plastered with her image, and the flyers have just multiplied, sprouting like fungus over every available surface.

Mom can't get enough of it. This morning I found her sitting in front of the TV, her hair half-straightened, clutching her coffee without drinking.

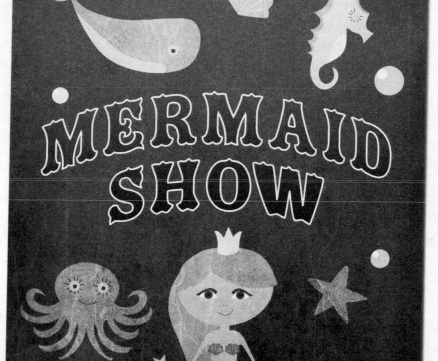

MERMAID SHOW

SHE CAN SWIM WITH SHARKS!

'The first seventy-two hours are the most important,' she kept repeating, information I'm sure she'd regurgitated from a previous news report. 'If they haven't found her yet . . .'

A digitized clock in the upper right quadrant of the TV tracked how long it had been since Madeline had vanished from her car: eighty-four hours and counting.

Alice stands up, shaking out her legs, though she can only have been resting for five minutes. 'It's just a ghost story,' she says. 'Something they say to the newbies to freak them out. Every park has to have a resident ghost. It's, like, a law. I've closed shop here plenty of times, and I've never heard her.'

'Didn't Mr Kowlaski . . .' The question sticks in my throat, huge and gummy. 'Didn't he once tell you that you reminded him of her?'

'Oh, that.' She waves a hand. 'Everyone thinks he's lost his marbles. But he hasn't. He's just lonely. And people do crazy things when they're lonely. You know?' For a moment, her eyes laser-beam onto mine, and I feel a tiny hitch of discomfort in my chest. It's like she knows something – about Dara, about my parents, about how we all fell apart.

Then Maude comes stalking down the path toward us, shoulders hunched, like a linebacker charging toward a touchdown.

'Wilcox sent me,' she says, as soon as she sees us. She's out of breath and annoyed, obviously, to have been sent to deliver messages. 'Crystal didn't show.'

Instantly Alice turns businesslike. 'What do you mean, she didn't show?'

Maude scowls. 'Just what I said. And the show's in fifteen. There are already, like, forty kids waiting.'

'We'll have to cancel,' Alice says.

'No way.' Maude has a BE NICE OR LEAVE pin staked to her T-shirt, just above her right nipple, which is both (a) hypocritical and (b) definitely not part of the FanLand dress code. 'They already paid. You know Donna doesn't do refunds.'

Alice tips her head back and closes her eyes, as she does when she's thinking. She has a thin neck, and an Adam's apple as pronounced as a boy's. Still, there's something undeniably attractive about her. Her dream, she told me once, was to run FanLand after Mr Wilcox. *I want to get old here,* she said. *I want to die right on that Ferris wheel. At the high point. That way it'll be a quick trip to the stars.*

I can't imagine wanting to stay at FanLand, and don't know what she sees in it, either: the endless procession of people, the overflowing trash bags and sticky pulp of mashed-up french fries and ice cream coating the pavilion floors, the toilets clogged with tampons and plastic barrettes and spare change. But lately I can't imagine wanting anything. I used to be so sure: college at UMass, then a two-year break before graduate school for social sciences or maybe psychology.

But that was before Dr Lichme, and lipstick-toothed Cheryl, and the accident. And those dreams, like my memories, seem to be floundering, caught in murky darkness somewhere just out of reach.

'You can do it.' Alice turns to me.

I'm so surprised that it takes me a second to realize she's serious. 'What?'

'You can do it,' she repeats. 'You're Crystal's size. The costume will fit you.'

I stare at her. 'No,' I say. 'No way.'

She's already gripping me by the arm and piloting me back toward the front office. 'It'll take ten minutes,' she says. 'You don't even have to say anything. You just have to swan around on a rock and clap your hands to the music. You'll be great.'

Once a day, a group of FanLand employees does a musical performance for the little kids in the big sunken amphitheater. Tony Rogers stars as the singing pirate, and Heather Minx, who is four foot eleven in a pair of platform wedges, dons a huge, ruffled parrot costume and accompanies him with various well-timed squawks. There's also a mermaid – Crystal, normally, strapped into a shimmery, sequined tail and wearing a fine nylon long-sleeved top with the image of a bandeau shell bikini imprinted on it – to clap and sing along.

I haven't been onstage since I was in second grade. And even that was a disaster. In our second-grade production of *Chicken Little* I completely forgot my cue – and then, in a desperate rush to make it out of the wings before the musical number ended – ran smack into Harold Liu and ended up knocking out one of his teeth.

I try to detach my arm from Alice's grip, but she's surprisingly strong. No wonder she scaled the Cobra this morning in five minutes flat. 'Can't you get Maude to do it?'

'Are you kidding? No way. She'll terrorize the children. Come on, do it for me. It'll be over before you know it.' She practically pushes me into the front office, which is empty. She skirts around the file cabinet and bends down to retrieve the mermaid costume from the corner, where it is folded neatly and sheathed in plastic after every performance. She removes it from its protective covering, shaking the tail out and releasing the faint smell of mildew. The sequins shimmer in the dull light. I fight the wild impulse to turn and run.

'Do I have to?' I say, even though I know what her answer will be.

She doesn't even answer. 'Showtime's in five,' she says, unzipping the tail from waist to fin with one fluid motion. 'So I suggest you strip.'

Seven minutes later I'm standing next to Rogers behind a thick covering of glossy plastic pond fronds, which serves as a makeshift curtain. Heather's already onstage, doing her thing, strutting and flapping her wings and letting the kids pull her tail feathers.

The amphitheater is packed: kids are laughing and clapping, bouncing in their seats, while their parents use the distraction as an excuse to get business done, typing away on smartphones, reapplying sunscreen even as their kids wiggle away from them, puncturing juice boxes with miniature straws. A dog, snow-white and about the size of a large rat, is barking like crazy and making lunging motions whenever Heather gets too close. Its owner, a fat woman wearing a turquoise sweatsuit, can barely keep it in her lap.

The mermaid costume is tight and makes it incredibly difficult to maneuver. I had to waddle down the path, taking miniature, shuffling steps while various park-goers stared.

I feel like I might throw up.

'When the tempo changes, that's our cue,' Rogers says. His breath smells faintly of beer. He bends down and hooks an arm behind my knees. 'Ready?'

'What are you doing?' I try and quick-step backward, but restrained by the costume, I manage only a kind of hop. In one fluid movement, Rogers has swept me up into his arms, carrying me the way a groom would a bride over a threshold.

'Mermaids don't walk,' he practically growls, and then plasters on a huge smile, showing off his gums, as we barrel through the fake foliage and emerge onto the stage, just as the tempo picks up. The kids break out into high-pitched squeals as Rogers bends down and deposits me onto the large, flat rock – actually painted concrete – built for this purpose.

'Wave,' he growls in my ear, before straightening up, still beaming out that smile.

My cheeks already hurt from smiling, and there's a hard knot of fear in my chest. I'm practically naked on top and wearing a goddamn fishtail, in front of a hundred strangers.

I lift my hand and give a quick wave. When several kids wave back, I feel a little better. I try again, with a little experimental flip of my wig – that's the worst part of the costume, I think, a massive, smelly tangle of blond hair with seashells plastered to it – and a girl in the front row leans over to her mom and says loudly over the music, 'Mommy, did you see the pretty mermaid?'

Dara would love this.

Rogers starts into his song, and slowly my nervousness lifts. All I have to do is sit around and ham it up, moving my legs so my fins flop around on the stone, clapping my hands and swaying with the music. I even join in on the choruses: 'Fantasy Land is where dreams come true . . . Fun-shine, Sun-shine, and new friends too . . .'

We've just reached the last verse when it happens. This portion of the song is a summary of FanLand park rules, and Pirate Pete has just warbled past the interdiction on running and has started railing against littering. When he comes to the line, 'Don't be a bum, pick up your gum!' Heather struts her way to the front of the stage, bends over, and displays her flat, feather-bottomed butt to the crowd.

Everyone goes crazy laughing. The dog in the second row

is barking so furiously, and vibrating so hard, it looks like it's about to spontaneously combust.

And suddenly, disentangling itself from its owner's arms, the dog leaps.

Heather screams as the dog chomps down on the big round target of her butt. Fortunately, the costume is thick, and the dog only manages to get a mouth full of feathers and fabric. Heather swings around in a panicked circle, trying to knock the dog loose. All the kids are screeching with laughter, apparently not realizing that this isn't part of the show, as Rogers stands, gape-mouthed, having lost the thread of the music. The fat woman is fighting her way toward the stage, and I stand up to help, forgetting about the mermaid costume and the fact that my legs are suctioned together.

Instead I pitch forward, face-first, landing hard on the ground and cutting my palms on the pavement.

Now the laughter has swelled to an ocean of sound. I can just barely make out cries of *The mermaid, the mermaid!* – individual voices cresting, then subsumed again by the general roar. I roll over onto my back and manage, after two false starts, to wobble to my feet. The fat woman is still trying to detach her dog from Heather's ass. Rogers is doing his best to contain the crowd. I waddle offstage as quickly as the costume will allow, totally ignoring the fact that *mermaids don't walk* and that the song hasn't even finished playing, reaching down to try and yank off the tail as soon as I'm concealed by the palm fronds.

A hand reaches out to steady me. 'Whoa, there. Easy. FanLand limits its employees to one face-plant per day.'

Parker.

'Very funny.' I snatch my arm away.

'Come on. Don't be mad. The kids loved it.' I can tell he's trying hard not to laugh. It's the first time he's smiled at me since I ditched the party. 'Here. Let me help you.'

I stand still while he takes the zipper and eases it down over my legs, tugging gently to get the fabric free of the metal teeth. His fingers graze my ankle, and a feeling passes through me, like a shiver but warm.

Stop. Stop. Stop.

He's Dara's now.

'Thanks.' I cross my arms, hyperconscious of the fact that I'm still wearing the flimsy nylon T-shirt, which makes my boobs look like seashells. He straightens up, slinging the mermaid tail over one arm.

'I didn't know you were gunning for a stage career,' he says, still smiling.

'I'm actually thinking of focusing more on professional self-humiliation,' I say.

'Hmm. Good point. You do have a knack for it. Although I've heard it's a difficult major.' One of his dimples shows, the one on the left, the deeper one. When I was little, like five or six, he once dared me to kiss him there and I did.

'Yeah, well.' I shrug and look away so I won't keep staring at his dimple, which reminds me of other things, times I would be better off forgetting. 'I'm a natural talent.'

'Seems like it.' He takes a step closer, nudging me with an elbow. 'Come on. Let me give you a ride home.'

I almost say no. Things are different now, and there's no point in pretending otherwise.

Gone are the days I used to sit with my bare feet on the dashboard and Parker pretended to get mad about the toe-shaped imprints on the inside of the windshield, while Dara huddled in the backseat, whining about the fact that she never got shotgun. Gone are the days of hunting down weird crap in 7-Elevens and gas stations, of splitting a Big Gulp between the three of us or just driving around with no place to go, windows down, while the ocean thundered somewhere in the distance and the crickets cried out as if the world was ending.

There's no going back. Everyone knows that.

But then Parker slings an arm around my shoulder, and he smells like the same combination of wintergreen and soft cotton, and he says, 'You know what? I'll even let you put your feet up. Even though they smell.'

'They do *not*,' I say, pulling away from him. But I can't help it. I laugh.

'So what do you say?' he says, rubbing his nose and then tucking his hair behind his ear, radio-signal code for when he really wants something. 'For old times' sake?'

And in that second I believe, truly believe, that maybe we can go back.

'Okay,' I say. 'For old times' sake. But—' I hold up a finger. 'You better not say a *word* about that stupid video game you always play. I've had my pain-share for the day, thanks very much.'

Parker pretends to look offended. 'Ancient Civ isn't a game,' he says. 'It's—'

'A lifestyle,' I finish for him. 'I know. You've told me a million times.'

'Do you know,' he says, as we start walking toward the parking lot, 'it took me two years of play just to build my very first arena?'

'I hope that's not a line you use on your first dates.'

'Third, actually. I don't want to seem slutty.'

It's then, walking next to Parker with that stupid costume swinging between us, throwing light in our eyes, that the plan for Dara's birthday begins to take shape.

dara's diary entry

Parker broke up with me today. Again.

Happy fucking Valentine's Day.

The weird thing is, the whole time he was talking, I kept staring at the burn mark on his shoulder and thinking about the time my freshman year we kept a lighter burning until it was hot and then made twin marks in our skin, swearing we would always be best friends. All of us. The three of us. But Nick wouldn't do it, not even after we begged her, not even after she took two shots of straight SoCo and almost puked.

I guess there's a reason people always say she's the smart one.

A mistake, he called it. A mistake. Like getting the wrong answer on a math test. Like turning left instead of right.

You don't even really like me. That's another thing he said. And: We were friends before. Why can't we be friends again?

Really, Parker? You got a 2300 on the SATs. Figure it out.

We talked for almost two hours. Or I should say: he talked. I don't even remember half of what he said. That burn kept distracting me, the little half-moon scar, like a smile. And I kept thinking about the shock of pain when the lighter first touched my skin, so hot it almost felt cold at first. Weird how you can confuse two feelings so different. Cold and hot.

Pain and love.

But I guess that's the whole point, isn't it? Maybe that's why I kept thinking about that time with the lighter. Here's what nobody tells you: 90 percent of the time, when you fall in love, somebody gets burned.

dara

WHEN I GET HOME FROM ANOTHER DAY OF DOING ABSOLUTELY nothing – killing time, riding my bike downtown, flipping through magazines at the CVS and pocketing the occasional lip gloss – I'm surprised to see Ariana standing on the front porch, holding a plastic bag under one arm. She spins around as I bump up onto the lawn with my bike.

'Oh,' she says, as if she wasn't expecting me. 'Hey.'

It's a little after eight o'clock, and Mom must be home by now. Still, Nick's bedroom window is the only one lit. Maybe Mom is in the kitchen, sitting in bare feet with her work shoes kicked under the table, eating soup straight from the can, bathed in the blue light of the TV. The search for Madeline Snow has consumed her – has consumed half the state – even though the news is always the same: there is none.

It's been four days.

I think once again of what Sarah Snow said to me yesterday: *The lying is the hardest part.*

What did she mean?

I rest my bike on the lawn, not bothering with the kickstand, taking my time and letting Ariana sweat it out while I cross to the porch. I can't remember the last time she came over. Even though she's wearing her usual summer outfit, black wedge sneakers and frayed cut-offs so short the pockets stick out, envelope-like, from beneath the hem, plus a vintage T-shirt washed to gray, she looks almost like a stranger. Her hair is gelled into stiff peaks, as if she briefly stuck her head in a tub of Cool Whip.

'What are you doing here?' The question sounds more like an accusation, and Ariana flinches.

'Yeah.' She brings a finger to her lower lip, an echo of an old habit: Ariana sucked her thumb until she was in third grade. 'Seeing you at the party reminded me. I have a bunch of stuff for you.' She presses the plastic bag into my hands, looking embarrassed, as if it contains porn or a severed head. 'Half of it looks like trash, but I don't know. There may be something you wanted in there.'

Inside the bag is a jumble of things: scraps of notepaper, cocktail napkins and paper coasters scrawled over with writing, a sparkly pink thong, a half-used tube of lip gloss, one strappy shoe that appears to be broken, a nearly empty bottle of Berry Crème Body Spray. It takes me a minute to recognize everything in the bag as mine – things I must have left at Ariana's house over the years, things that must have rolled under the front seat of her car.

Suddenly, standing on the porch in front of a dark house with a flimsy plastic grocery bag full of my belongings, I know I'm going to cry. Ariana seems to be waiting for me to say something, but I can't speak. If I speak, I'll break.

'All right.' She hugs herself, shrugs. 'So . . . I'll see you around?'

No, I want to say. *No.* But I let her get halfway across the lawn, halfway back to the maroon Toyota she inherited from her stepbrother, which always smells like her, like clove cigarettes and coconut shampoo. By then my throat feels like it's being squeezed inside a massive fist, and two words pop out before I can regret them: 'What happened?'

Ariana freezes, one hand in her bag, where she has been rummaging for her keys. She doesn't turn around right away.

'What happened?' I say again, this time a little louder. 'How come you didn't call? Why didn't you come by to see if I was okay?'

She does turn around then. I don't know what I was expecting – pity, maybe? – but I'm totally unprepared for how she looks: like her face is a plaster mold on the verge of collapse. Horribly, the fact that she's about to cry makes me feel a teensy, tiny bit better.

'I didn't know what to say. I didn't know what I *could* say. I felt—' She breaks off. And suddenly she is crying, in big hiccuping gulps, without bothering to try and conceal it. I'm shocked into silence. I haven't seen Ariana cry since she was in fifth grade, when we bribed Nick into helping us pierce our ears and Nick was so nervous she slipped and drove the safety pin straight into Ariana's neck. 'I'm so sorry. It was all my fault. I was a terrible friend. Maybe . . . maybe if I'd been better . . .'

All my anger has turned to pity. 'Stop,' I say. 'Stop. You were a great friend. You *are* a great friend. Come on,' I say, when she doesn't stop crying. 'It's all right.' Without knowing it, I've crossed the space between us. When I hug her, I can feel her ribs poking into me. She's so thin she hardly feels real; I think of birds, and hollow bones, and flying away.

'Sorry,' she says again, and pulls back, dragging a hand

across her nose. Her eyes are raw-looking, as if she hasn't slept in days. 'I've just been kind of fucked-up lately.'

'Join the club,' I say, which at least gets a laugh out of her – the ragged, low-throated laugh Ariana claims to have inherited from her grandfather, a cross-country trucker and lifelong two-packs-a-day smoker.

A pair of headlights sweep around the bend, temporarily blinding. It's only then I realize how quiet it is outside. Normally, even as dusk falls, there are kids darting across front yards, shouting, playing Wiffle ball, chasing one another in and out of the woods. Not until Cheryl pokes her head out of the passenger-side window and yells, 'Yoo-hoo!' do I remember I'm supposed to have dinner with my dad tonight.

Ariana seizes my wrist. 'Let's hang out, okay? Let's hang out, just you and me. We can go swimming at the Drink or something.'

I make a face. 'I've had enough of the Drink for a while.' Ariana looks so disappointed I quickly add, 'But yeah, sure. Something like that.' Even as I say it, though, I know we won't. We never used to make plans. Hanging with Ariana was just part of my rhythm, as easy as falling asleep.

It's like the accident punched a hole straight through my life. Now there's only Before and After.

Dad taps the horn. He hasn't turned off the brights yet, and it feels like we're standing on a movie set. Ariana pivots toward the car, raising a hand to her eyes, but she doesn't wave. My parents used to love Ariana, but ever since she shaved half her head freshman year and started scamming on tattoo artists to give her piercings for free, they've soured on her. *It's a shame,* my mom likes to say. *She was such a pretty girl.*

Now it's my turn to apologize. 'Sorry,' I say. 'Dad has custody for dinner, apparently.'

Ariana rolls her eyes. I'm glad she's stopped crying. She looks more like her old self. 'I get it, believe me.' Ariana's parents got divorced when she was five, and since then she's had a stepdad and more 'uncles' than I can count. 'Don't forget what I said about hanging out, okay? Call me anytime. I mean it.'

She's trying so hard, I force a smile. 'Sure.'

She turns and crosses back to her car, grimacing a little as she passes in front of the glare of my dad's headlights. I have the desperate urge to run after her, to slide into the front seat and tell her to gun it, to peel off into the darkness, leaving Dad and Cheryl and the patchwork of sleepy houses and empty lawns behind.

'Ari!' I call out. When she looks up, I lift the plastic bag. 'Thanks.'

'No problem.' She smiles, just a little, even though she still looks sad. 'I always liked it when you called me Ari.'

Then she's gone.

by Margie Nichols

Have the police finally caught a break in the Madeline Snow case?

Sources close to the investigation tell this reporter that the police have named Nicholas Sanderson, 43, an accountant with a home in the upscale beachfront community of Heron Bay, a 'person of interest.'

What does this mean, exactly? According to Frank Hernandez, the commanding officer in charge of the search for Madeline Snow, 'We're investigating a possible connection between Sanderson and the Snow family. That's all. No further comment.'

No further comment? Really? After a little digging, here's what I've learned: Nicholas Sanderson and his wife vacation a good forty-five miles from the Snow residence. They attend different churches, and at no time have Mr or Mrs Snow used Sanderson for his accounting services. Nicholas Sanderson has no children, and no obvious connection to Springfield, where the Snows live.

So what's the connection? Post your thoughts/comments below.

> Doesn't mean anything. Sanderson could've met Madeline anywhere – hanging out at the beach, shopping at Walmart, whatever. Maybe he reached out to her online. Madeline's sister has a car, doesn't she?
> posted by: bettyb00p at 10:37 a.m.

> Why are you assuming there is a connection? Cops are just grabbing at straws, IMHO.
> posted by: carolinekinney at 11:15 a.m.

That guy is the worst!!! Tried to charge me 3K just to do my taxes. What a scam artist.
posted by: alanovid at 2:36 p.m.

bettyb00p is right. Everything happens online nowadays. Was Madeline on Facebook?
posted by: runner88 at 3:45 p.m.

No. I checked.
posted by: carolinekinney at 3:57 p.m.

Still. These sickos always find a way.
posted by: bettyb00p at 4:02 p.m.

See additional 107 comments

JULY 23

dara

8:30 p.m.

UNTIL I TURNED FOURTEEN, MY PARENTS TOOK NICK AND ME TO
Sergei's every other week. Sergei's is wedged between a dentist's
office and a children's shoe store that I have never known a
single person to shop at. There is no actual Sergei; the owner's
name is Steve, and the closest he ever got to Italy was the time
he lived for two years in an Italian neighborhood in Queens,
New York. The garlic is from a jar and the Parmesan cheese
is the crumbly kind that comes in an airtight container, the
kind you can keep in a pantry for years or through nuclear
catastrophes. The tablecloths are paper, and each place setting
comes with a different-colored crayon.

But the meatballs are fluffy and as big as softballs, and the
pizza comes in thick slices, layered with melted cheese, and
the baked ziti is always bubbly brown and crusty at the
corners, just how I like it. Besides, Sergei's is *ours*. Even after
Mom and Dad started making excuses to avoid each other,
claiming late hours at work or developing colds or other
obligations, Nick and I used to go together. For $12.95 we

could get two Cokes and a large pizza and hit up the salad bar, too.

Il Sodi, the restaurant Cheryl has selected, has crisp white linen tablecloths and fresh flowers arranged in the center of every table. The floors are polished wood and so slick even standing up to go to the bathroom makes me nervous. Waiters swan between tables, cranking out fresh pepper and grating fine flakes of cheese onto pasta portions so small they look accidental. Everyone has the pushed and prodded and tugged look that rich people have, like they're just giant pieces of taffy, ready to be molded. Cheryl lives in Egremont, just next to Main Heights, in the house she inherited after her last husband got flattened by an unexpected heart attack the day before his fiftieth birthday.

I've heard the story before, but for some reason she feels the need to tell it to me again, as if she's expecting my sympathy – the phone call from the hospital, her frantic rush to his bedside, regrets about all the things she wishes she got the chance to say – while Dad sits and fiddles with a sweating glass of whiskey on the rocks. I'm not sure when he started drinking. He never used to have more than a beer or two at barbecues; he always used to say alcohol was how boring people had fun.

'And of course it was just devastating for Avery and Josh.' Josh is Cheryl's eighteen-year-old son. He goes to Duke, a fact she has found ingenious ways to work into almost any conversation. I met him once, at a meet-and-greet dinner for the new 'family' in March, and I swear he spent the whole dinner staring at my tits. Avery is fifteen, about as much fun as a Band-Aid, and just as clingy. 'To be honest, even though we lost Robert five years ago, I don't think we'll *ever* be done grieving. You have to give yourself time.' I shoot my dad a look – does she think this is good dinner-party conversation? – but he's studiously avoiding my eyes and instead using his phone under the table. Despite the fact that this dinner was his idea – he wanted some 'quality time' with me, to 'check in,' which I guess is why he didn't invite Nick – he's hardly said a word to me since I sat down.

Cheryl keeps prattling on. 'I wish you'd *talk* to Avery. Maybe we can have a girls' day. I'll treat you to the spa. Would you like that?'

I'd rather spend the day sticking needles under my nails, but of course at that precise moment Dad's eyes tick to mine, both a warning and a command. I smile and make a non-committal noise.

'I'd *love* that. And Avery would *love* that.' Three things about Cheryl: she loves anything having to do with 'girl time,' 'spa time,' or 'sauvignon blanc.' She leans back while three waiters materialize and deposit identical plates of what look like bean sprouts in front of us. 'Micro greens,' Cheryl clarifies, when she sees my face. She has insisted on doing the ordering. 'With chervil and fresh chives. Go on, dig in.'

Digging in is the wrong expression. I've finished the plate of rabbit kibble in about two bites, and I can't help but think of the all-you-can-eat salad bar at Sergei's: the electric glowing cubes of cheddar cheese, the proud trays of iceberg and individual tubs of store-bought croutons and pickled green beans. Even the beets, which Nick and I both agree taste like an open grave.

I wonder where Nick is eating tonight.

'So how's your summer going?' Cheryl says, once the plates have been cleared. 'I hear you're working at FanLand.'

I shoot Dad another look – Cheryl can't even keep Nick and me straight. For Christ's sake, there's only two of us. It's not like I sit around asking how Avery likes Duke. But once again, he has returned to his phone.

'Everything's fine,' I say. No point in telling Cheryl the truth: that Nick and I have been completely avoiding each other, that I've been bored out of my mind, that Mom floats through the house like a balloon, lashed to the TV.

'Listen to this.' Dad speaks up suddenly. '"The police have named Nicholas Sanderson, forty-three, an accountant with a home in the upscale beachfront community of Heron Bay—"'

'Oh, Kevin.' Cheryl sighs. 'Not here. Not tonight. Will you put your phone away for once?'

'—a "person of interest."' Dad looks up, blinking, like a person emerging from sleep. 'I wonder what *that's* about.'

'I'm sure the *Blotter* will tell us,' Cheryl says, swiping the corner of her eye with one perfectly French-manicured fingernail. 'He's been obsessed,' she says to me.

'Yeah. Mom too.' I don't know why, but I get pleasure out of talking about Mom in front of Cheryl. 'It's, like, the only thing she can talk about.'

Cheryl just shakes her head.

I turn to Dad, struck by an idea. I'm still thinking of what Sarah Snow said: *You look familiar.* 'Did the Snows ever live in Somerville?'

He frowns and returns to his phone. 'Not that I know of.'

So that's a dead end. Cheryl, who can't stand to keep her mouth shut for more than .5 seconds, jumps in. 'It's terrible, just terrible. My friend Louise won't even let the twins out on their own anymore. Just in case there's a' – she lowers her voice – '*pervert* on the loose.'

'I just feel so sorry for her parents,' Dad says. 'To keep on hoping . . . to not *know* . . .'

'You think it's better to know?' I say. Once again, Dad looks at me. His eyes are red, bloodshot, and I wonder whether he's already drunk. He doesn't answer.

'Let's change the subject, shall we?' Cheryl says, as once again waiters appear, this time bearing thimble-size portions of spaghetti on vast white plates. Cheryl claps her hands together, and a massive ruby sparkles on one of her fingers. 'Mmm. This looks delicious, doesn't it? Spaghetti with garlic scapes and fresh ramps. I absolutely *love* ramps. Don't you?'

After dinner, Dad drops Cheryl off first, a sure sign he wants to talk to me – which is funny, both because he was almost entirely silent at dinner, and because I'm 90 percent positive he'll drive straight back to Egremont when he's done dropping me off. I wonder what it's like to sleep in the bed of Cheryl's dead ex-husband, and I have a sadistic urge to ask. He white-knuckles the wheel as he drives, leaning forward slightly, and I wonder whether it's because he's tipsy or so he doesn't have to look at me.

Still, he doesn't speak until he's pulled up in front of the house. As usual, only a few lights are burning: Nick's, and the one in the upstairs bathroom. He jerks the car into park and clears his throat.

'How's your mother holding up?' he asks abruptly, which wasn't what I expected him to say at all.

'Fine,' I say, which is only half a lie. At least she goes to work on time now. Most days.

'That's good. I worry about her. I worry about you, too.' He's still gripping the steering wheel, like if he lets go, he might go flying off into outer space. He clears his throat again. 'We should talk about the twenty-ninth.'

It's so typical that he refers to my birthday by the date, as if it's a dental appointment he has to keep. Dad is an actuary, which means he studies insurance and risk. Sometimes he looks at me like I'm a bad return he's made on an investment.

'What about it?' I say. If he's going to pretend it's no big deal, so will I.

He gives me a funny look. 'Your mother and I—' His voice hitches. 'Well, we were thinking we should all get together. Maybe go to dinner at Sergei's.'

I can't remember the last time Mom and Dad were in the same room. Not since a few days after the accident – and even then, they stayed on opposite sides of the minuscule hospital bedroom. 'The *four* of us?'

'Well, Cheryl has to work,' he says apologetically, as if I would have invited her otherwise. Finally he releases his death grip on the wheel and turns toward me. 'What do you think? Do you think that's a good idea? We wanted to celebrate *somehow*.'

I'm tempted to say *Hell no*, but Dad isn't actually waiting for an answer. He slides his fingers behind his glasses and scrubs his eyes. 'God. Seventeen years old. I remember when – I remember when you were both babies, so small I was terrified to hold you . . . I always thought I would crush you, or break you somehow . . .' Dad's voice is thick. He must be drunker than I thought.

'Sounds great, Dad,' I say quickly. 'I think Sergei's would be perfect.'

Thankfully he regains control. 'You think?'

'Really. It'll be . . . special.' I lean over to give him a peck on the cheek, extracting myself before he can wrap me in a bear hug. 'Drive home safely, okay? There are cops everywhere.' It's weird to have to parent your parents. Add it to the list of the two thousand other things that have gone to hell since the divorce, or maybe since the accident, or both.

'Right.' Dad seizes the steering wheel again, bobbing his head, obviously embarrassed by his outburst. 'Looking for Madeline Snow.'

'Looking for Madeline Snow,' I echo, as I slide out of the car. I watch Dad reverse in the driveway and hold up a hand as he passes me again, waving to his dim silhouette in the window. I watch until his taillights turn to tiny, glowing red points, like lit cigarette tips. Once again, the street is quiet, silent except for the constant throaty humming of the crickets.

I think of Madeline Snow, somewhere lost in the darkness, while half the county searches for her.

And it gives me an idea.

nick

IT TURNS OUT THAT MY FAILED TURN AS THE MERMAID WASN'T SO
failed after all – apparently the kids thought it was so uproari-
ously funny that Mr Wilcox decides to make physical comedy,
and specifically my face-plant, a permanent part of the act.
Since we can't count on a real dog to reliably chomp down on
Heather's tail feathers, Wilcox invests in a big, floppy-eared
dog puppet, and Heather works both identities at the same
time – strutting in her costume while wearing the puppet on
her right hand and miming a contest of wills until the culmin-
ating moment, when the dog gets hold of her butt.

Unfortunately I'm stuck in the role of the mermaid for the
foreseeable future. No one else can fit into the tail, and Crystal
never comes back to work. Rumor is that she got busted for
something really bad – Maude even claims the police are
involved.

'Her parents caught her posing for some porn website,'
Maude says, gesturing with a french fry for emphasis. 'She was
getting paid to send naked pics.'

'No way.' Douglas, who is thin and sharp-beaked, like a bird of prey, shakes his head. 'She doesn't even have *boobs*.'

'So? Some guys like that.'

'I heard she was dating some old guy,' a girl named Ida says. 'Her parents flipped when they found out. Now she's on lockdown.'

'She was always bragging about money,' Alice says thoughtfully. 'And she always had really nice stuff. Remember that watch? The one with all the little diamonds?'

'It was a website,' Maude insists. 'My cousin's girlfriend's brother's a cop. There are, like, *hundreds* of girls on there. *High school* girls.'

'Didn't Donovan get busted for the same thing?' says Douglas.

'For *posing*?' Ida squeaks.

'For having *access*.' Douglas rolls his eyes. 'A perv's dream.'

'Exactly.' At last Maude pops the fry in her mouth. Then she drags her finger through a thick glob of ketchup on her plate. That's how she eats fries, in stages: potato, then ketchup.

'I don't believe it,' Alice says.

Maude looks at her pityingly. 'You don't have to,' she says. 'It'll all come out soon enough. You'll see.'

The worst part about being the mermaid is the costume itself, which requires special cleaning and so can't be washed more than once a week. After three days, the tail reeks, and whenever I'm suited up, I make it a point to stay as far away from Parker as possible.

But after a few performances, I find I don't mind being onstage so much. Rogers even shows me how to cushion my fall safely – he was a *thespian* in college, he tells me, with no hint of irony and embarrassment – and after one show, a little cluster of kids even crowds me behind the potted palms and asks for my autograph. I sign: *Stay cool! Love, Melinda the Mermaid.* No idea where Melinda comes from, but it feels right. And suiting up as Melinda keeps me from having to skim the Piss Pool, or scrub puke out of the Whirling Dervish.

Slowly I'm getting the hang of FanLand. I no longer get lost on my way around the park. I know the shortcuts – cutting behind the Haunted Ship brings me straight to the wave pool. Walking through the darkness of the Tunnel lops a full five minutes from the walk between the Lagoon and the dry lands. I know the secrets, too: that Rogers drinks on the job, that Shirley never locks up her pavilion properly because she can't be bothered with the faulty lock on the back door, and that some of the older employees swipe the occasional beer from the cooler as a result, that Harlan and Eva have been screwing around for three summers running and use the pump house as their own personal sex den.

Every day we do more and more prep for the anniversary party: blowing up mountains of balloons and tying them in thick clusters to every available surface; scrubbing and re-varnishing the game stalls; stringing up banners advertising special promotions and events; performing vigilant, military-style maneuvers to keep bands of marauding raccoons (the source of Mr Wilcox's greatest anxiety) from decimating the frozen corn dogs and sugar cones we've stored in all the pavilions.

Mr Wilcox grows increasingly excited, as if he's popping larger and larger rations of caffeine pills. Finally, the day before the party, he's practically vibrating with enthusiasm. He doesn't even speak in full sentences anymore, just walks around repeating random sentence fragments like: 'Twenty thousand people! Seventy-five years! Oldest independent park in the state! Cotton candy free for the under-sevens!'

But his enthusiasm is infectious. The whole park is buzzing with it; a sound perceived but not exactly heard, a sense of anticipation like the moment just before all the crickets start singing at night. Even Maude's permanent scowl has flattened out into something close to a normal expression.

Four of us are assigned to the graveyard shift the night before the party: Gary, a sour-faced man who runs one of the stalls and who has worked at FanLand through three changes of admin – a fact he repeats loudly whenever Mr Wilcox is around; Caroline, a grad student who has spent four summers working at the park and who's struggling through a thesis paper about the role of spectacle in American carnival entertainment; me; and Parker.

Things have become easy between us again; we eat lunch together most days, and time our breaks together, too. In only six weeks, Parker has become a never-ending source of FanLand trivia, much of it related to the park's design and engineering.

'Do you study this stuff at night when you go home?' I ask him one day, after he's been going on and on about the difference between potential and kinetic energy and its application to roller coasters.

'Of course not. Don't be ridiculous,' he says. 'I'm far too busy playing Ancient Civ. Besides, everyone knows the best time to study is first thing in the morning.'

When it's super-hot, we take our shoes off and dunk our feet in the wave pool or take turns with a hose, passing the stream of cold water over our hair and emerging from the back of the pump house sopping wet and happy. He introduces me to the 'Parker lunch classic': pizza covered with the squeezy cheese we use for the nachos.

'You're disgusting,' I say, watching him fold a slice expertly into his mouth.

'I'm a culinary explorer,' he says, grinning so I can see the mashed-up food in his mouth. 'We're very misunderstood.'

The graveyard shift is the hardest and most labor-intensive. As soon as the park gate is shut behind the last family, the other employees rush to shed their T-shirts and duck out through a side exit – a long stream of them, miraculously morphed from identical red skins like a molting snake – before they can be roped into helping the nightly park shutdown.

This includes emptying all 104 trash cans and loading up fresh bags; double-checking every bathroom stall to make sure no terrified children have been left behind by frazzled parents; sweeping up the debris in the pavilions; checking to make sure all entrances and exits are locked and secured; skimming every pool for floating debris and ramping up the chlorine levels overnight, to combat the daily influx of sunscreen-coated children and their inevitable pee; locking up the food carts against the intrusion of raccoons, and making sure no trash has been left behind to tempt them.

Gary delivers our instructions to us with the intensity of a general giving marching orders to an invading army. I'm stuck on Zone B trash duty, which will bring me from the Ship Breaker's Pavilion all the way down past the Gateway.

'Good luck,' Parker whispers, leaning in so close I can feel his breath on my neck, as Gary distributes plastic gloves and industrial garbage bags the size and weight of plastic tarps. 'Remember to breathe through your mouth.'

He isn't kidding: the park trash bins contain a disgusting jumble of half-rotting food, baby diapers, and worse. It's hard work, and after an hour my arms ache from the effort of hauling full bags to the parking lot, where Gary will load them into the Dumpsters. The park looks strange, lit up falsely in the bright electric glow of the floodlights. The paths are striped with deep tongues of shadow, and the rides shimmer in the moonlight, seeming almost insubstantial, like fairy structures that might disappear at any moment. Every so often a voice carries to me across the distance – Caroline or Parker, shouting to each other – but other than the occasional whisper of wind through the trees, it's quiet.

I'm moving underneath the shadow of the Gateway when I hear it: a quiet humming, a sing-song whisper.

I freeze. The Gateway rises above me, steel and shadow, a tower made of silver cobweb. I remember what Alice told me. *They say she still cries out at night.*

Nothing. Nothing but the crickets hidden in the underbrush, the faint hiss of wind. It's almost eleven and I'm tired. That's all.

But as soon as I start moving again, the sound returns, like the faintest cry or a whisper of a song. I whirl around. Behind me is a solid wall of growth, an intricate geometric pattern of woods that divides the Gateway from the Ship Breaker's Pavilion. My stomach is a hard, high knot and my palms are sweating. Even before I hear it again, all the hair on my arms stands up, as if something invisible has just brushed against me. This time the noise is changed, anguished, like a distant sob heard from behind three locked doors.

'Hello?' I choke out. Instantly the sound stops. Is it my imagination, or does something move in the shadows, a bare ghost-impression in the deeper dark? 'Hello?' I call out again, a little louder.

'Nick?' Parker materializes out of the darkness, suddenly

and harshly illuminated as he steps into the circular glow of a lamp. 'You almost done? I've got a virtual half-constructed Roman-style temple waiting for me at home . . .'

I'm so relieved, I nearly throw myself into his arms, just to feel that he's solid and real and alive.

'Did you hear that?' I blurt.

Parker, I see, has already changed out of his work T-shirt. His old backpack, made of corduroy so faded it's impossible to tell what color it once was, is slung over one shoulder. 'Hear what?'

'I thought I heard—' I break off abruptly. Suddenly I realize how silly I'll sound. I thought I heard a ghost. I thought I heard a little girl crying out for her father as she fell through empty space. 'Nothing.' I peel off the gloves, which have made my fingers smell sour, and brush my hair back from my face with the inside of a wrist. 'Forget it.'

'Are you all right?' Parker does the thing he always does when he doesn't believe me: tucks his chin down, stares at me with eyebrows half-raised. I have a sudden flashback of Parker, aged five, looking at me just that way when I told him I could jump across Old Stone Creek, no problem. I broke my ankle; I misjudged the bank height, crashed straight into the water, slipped, and Parker had to carry me home on his back.

'Fine,' I say shortly. 'Just tired.'

And it's true: suddenly I am – aching with an exhaustion so deep I can feel it in my teeth.

'Need help?' Parker gestures to the two bags I've piled next to me: the last remaining load I have to cart out for pickup. He doesn't wait for me to respond before leaning forward and swinging the heaviest bag over his other shoulder. 'I told Gary we'd lock up,' he says. 'Actually, there's something I want to show you real quick.'

'Is it a Dumpster?' I haul the other bag over my shoulder, like Parker's doing, and follow him toward the lot. 'Because I think I've had enough garbage for a lifetime.'

'Don't say that. How could anyone ever get tired of garbage? It's so *authentic*.'

Caroline is just leaving when we reach the lot. Her little Acura, and Parker's Volvo, are the last remaining cars. She rolls down her window to wave as she passes, and Parker loads the trash bags into the Dumpster, throwing them like an old-school sailor tossing canvas bags of fish onto a ship deck. Then he takes my hand – casually, unconsciously, the way he did when we were kids, whenever it was his turn to pick the game we were going to play. *Come on, Nick. This way.* And Dara would trail after us, wailing that we were going too fast, complaining about the mud and the mosquitoes.

It's been years since I've held Parker's hand. I'm suddenly paranoid that my palm is still sweating.

'Are you serious?' I say, as Parker draws me back toward the park gates. There isn't a single inch of FanLand I haven't seen. At this point, there isn't a single inch of FanLand I haven't scrubbed, cleaned, or examined for stray trash. 'I have to be on shift again at nine.'

'Just trust me,' he says. And the truth is I don't want to resist too hard. His hand feels nice – familiar and yet totally new, like hearing a song you only dimly remember.

We loop around the path toward the Lagoon, leaving the Gateway safely in the distance, dim spires rising like a distant city over wide alleys of wooden stalls and concession stands and dark pockets of trees. Now, with Parker next to me, I can't believe how frightened I was earlier. There are no ghosts, here or anywhere; there's no one in the park but us.

Parker leads me to the edge of the wave pool, an artificial beach made out of concrete pebbles. The water, smooth and dark and motionless, looks like one long shadow.

'Okay,' I say. 'Now what?'

'Wait here.' Parker drops my hand, but the impression of his touch – the warmth, the shivery good feeling – takes a second longer to dissipate.

'Parker—'

'I told you to trust me.' He's already backing up, jogging away from me. 'Have I ever lied to you? Don't answer that,' he adds quickly, before I can.

Then he's gone, merging with the darkness. I edge down toward the water, splashing my sneakers experimentally in the shallows, half annoyed at Parker for keeping me out here after shift and half relieved that things are so normal again that Parker *can* annoy me.

Suddenly the motors rumble on, disrupting the stillness. I jump back, yelping, as the water is abruptly illuminated from below in crazy rainbow shades: neon oranges and yellows and purples and blues, shifting Technicolor strata. A wave gathers on the far side of the pool and works its way slowly toward me, causing all the colors to blend and break and re-form. I back up as the wave breaks at my feet, scattering into shades of pink.

'See? Told you it was worth it.' Parker re-emerges, jogging, silhouetted against the crazy light display.

'You win,' I say. I've never seen the wave pool lit up like this; I didn't even know it *could* be. Fingers of light, shimmering and translucent, extend up toward the sky, and I have a sudden, soaring sense of happiness – like I, too, am nothing but light.

Parker and I kick our shoes off and roll up our jeans and sit with our legs half-submerged in the water, watching as the waves gather, crest, break, and retreat, every motion provoking corresponding shifts in the patterns of color. *Dara would love this,* I think, and feel a quick squeeze of guilt.

Parker leans back on his elbows, so his face is partially obscured by shadow. 'Do you remember last Founders' Day Ball? When we broke into the pool and you dared me to climb the rafters?'

'And you tried to pull me in with my dress on,' I say. A burst of pain explodes behind my eyes. Parker's car. The clouded windshield. Dara's face. I squeeze my eyes shut, as if I can make the images disperse.

'Hey.' He sits up again, grazing my knee, just barely, with a hand. 'You okay?'

'Yeah.' I open my eyes again. Another wave breaks over my feet, this one green. I bring my knees to my chest, hugging them. 'It's Dara's birthday tomorrow.'

Parker's face changes. All the light drains from his expression at once. 'Fuck.' He looks away, rubbing his eyes. 'I totally forgot. I can't believe it.'

'Yeah.' I scrape at an artificial pebble with a nail. There's so much I want to say – so much I want to ask him that I've never asked him. It feels as if I have a balloon in my chest; at any second it might burst. 'I feel like I'm just . . . losing her.'

He turns back to me, then, his face twisted with a raw kind of grief. 'Yeah,' he says. 'Yeah, I know.'

That's when the balloon bursts. 'Are you still in love with her?' I blurt out. There's a strange kind of relief in finally asking.

Parker looks at first surprised – then, almost immediately, he shuts down, turns expressionless. 'Why are you asking me that?' he says.

'Forget it,' I say. I stand up. The colors have lost their magic. They're just lights, stupid lights with stupid gels over them, a spectacle made for people too stupid to tell the difference. Like the mermaid costume, made out of cheap sequins and glue. 'I'm tired, okay? I just want to go home.'

Parker stands, too, and puts a hand on my arm when I turn in the direction of the parking lot. 'Wait.'

I shake him off. 'Come on, Parker. Forget I asked.'

'Wait.' This time, Parker's voice stops me. He exhales a long breath. 'Look. I loved Dara, okay? I still do. But—'

'But what?' I wrap my arms around my waist, squeezing back the sudden sensation that I might be sick. Why do I care? Parker can love whoever he wants. He can even love my sister. Why wouldn't he love her? Everyone else does.

'I was never in love with her,' he says, a little more quietly. 'I'm . . . I don't think I've ever been in love.'

There's a long pause. He stares at me as if waiting for me to say something – to forgive or congratulate him, maybe both. Something passes between us, a wordless message I can't begin to decipher. I'm suddenly aware that we're standing very close – so close that even in the dark, I can see stubble on his chin, and see the beauty mark dotting the outside corner of his left eye, like a perfect pen mark.

'Okay,' I say finally.

Parker looks almost disappointed. 'Okay,' he echoes.

I wait by the water while Parker turns off the wave pool again. We retrace our steps to the parking lot in silence. I listen for the voice, for the sing-song call of a ghost in the darkness, maybe crying out for her father, maybe crying out just to be heard. But I hear nothing but our footsteps, and the wind, and the crickets hidden in the shadows, singing for no goddamn reason at all.

text from parker to dara

Hey.

I don't know why I'm texting you.

Actually, I do know why.

I really miss you, Dara.

JULY 28

dara

BEFORE WE WERE BORN, THE MASTER BEDROOM WAS DOWNSTAIRS, and featured an en-suite bathroom with a massive Jacuzzi tub and cheesy gold fixtures. The bedroom was converted first into a den, and then into a combined office/massive closet for all the random shit we accumulated and then outgrew: paper shredders and defunct fax machines, broken iPads and old phone cords, a dollhouse that Nick was obsessed with for .5 seconds before deciding that dolls were 'immature.'

But the tub is still there. The jets stopped working when I was about five and my parents never bothered to replace them, but with the water running from all four faucets, the noise is thunderous and has almost the same effect. The soap dish is shaped like a scalloped seashell. There are divots in the porcelain where you can rest your feet. And for about ten years, my mom has kept the same jar of lemon verbena bath salts perched next to the tub, the label so warped with steam and vapor it has become unreadable.

When we were little, Nick and I used to put on our bathing

suits and take baths together, pretending that we were mermaids and it was our private lagoon. Somehow the fact that we wore bathing suits – and goggles, too, sometimes, so we could go under and blink at each other, communicating through hand gestures and laughing out big bubbles – made it fun. We were so small we could both stretch out easily, side by side, her feet at my head and vice versa, like two sardines packed together.

Tonight, after I've completed the ritual – all four faucets running, a scoop and a half of lemon verbena, wait until the water's so hot it turns my skin pink, then ease in and turn the faucets off one by one – I take a deep breath and go under. Almost instantly my pain evaporates. My broken put-together body turns weightless, my hair fans out behind me, brushing my shoulders and arms, tendril-like. I listen for echoes, but all I hear is the rhythm of my heart, which sounds both loud and strangely distant. Then a secondary rhythm joins the first.

Boom. Boom. Boom.

The sound reaches me even underwater. Someone is knocking – no, *pounding* – at the front door. I sit up, gasping a little.

There's a temporary break in the knocking, and for a moment I think, optimistically, that it was a mistake. Some drunk kid has mistaken our house for a friend's. Or maybe it was a dumb prank.

But then it happens again, slightly quieter but still insistent. It can't be Nick; I'm almost positive Nick is home and asleep, no doubt mentally preparing for our family dinner tomorrow. Besides, Nick knows we keep a spare key under a fake rock next to the planter, like every other family in America.

Annoyed, I haul myself out of the tub, moving carefully on legs that go quickly stiff. Shivering, I towel off, then pull on a pair of thin cotton sleep pants and an old Cougars T-shirt that belonged to my dad in high school. My hair hangs wetly down my back – no time to dry it properly. I grab my phone from the back of the toilet. 12:35.

In the hallway, the latticed windows cut the moonlight into geometric patterns. Someone is moving just beyond the glass, backlit by the porch light. For just a second I hang back, afraid – thinking, irrationally, of Madeline Snow, of hysterical rumors about perverts and predators and girls caught unawares.

Then someone cups a hand to the window to peek inside, and my heart contracts. Parker.

Even before I open the door, it's obvious he's drunk.

'You,' he says. He leans heavily against the house, likely to keep himself on his feet. With one hand, he reaches out as if he's going to touch my face. I jerk away. Still, his hand lingers in the air, hovering like a butterfly. 'I'm so glad it's you.'

I ignore the words – I ignore how good they feel, how badly I've wanted to hear them. 'What are you doing here?'

'I came to see you.' He straightens up, runs a hand through his hair, swaying a little on his feet. 'Shit. I'm sorry. I'm drunk.'

'That's obvious.' I step out onto the porch, easing the door shut behind me, and cross my arms, wishing now that I weren't wearing my dad's old T-shirt, that my hair weren't wet, that I had a *bra* on, for Christ's sake.

'I'm sorry. It's just . . . the whole birthday thing really fucked me up.' Parker looks at me in the way that only he can: chin lowered, watching me with those huge eyes and the lashes thick as brushstrokes, which on anyone else would look girlish. His perfect upper lip, shaped exactly like a heart. 'Remember last year, when we all went to East Norwalk together? And Ariana scored beer from that sleazy guy who worked at the 7-Eleven. What was his name?'

A memory rises up: standing with Parker in the parking lot, doubled over laughing because Mattie Carson was peeing on a Dumpster next to the nail parlor, even though there was a bathroom inside. I don't even remember why Mattie was there. Maybe because he'd offered to bring Super Soakers he'd borrowed from his younger brothers.

Parker doesn't wait for me to answer. 'We tried to break into that creepy lighthouse on Orphan's Beach. And we had a water fight. I creamed you. I totally creamed you. We watched the sunrise. I've never seen a sunrise like that. Remember? It was practically—'

'Red. Yeah. I remember.' It was freezing by then, and my eyes were gritty from the sand. Still, I was happier than I'd been in years – maybe happier than I'd ever been. Parker had lent me his sweatshirt (National Pi Day), and I still have it somewhere. Ariana and Mattie had fallen asleep on a big flat rock, huddled together beneath his fleece, and Nick, Parker, and I sat side by side, a picnic blanket draped around our shoulders like an enormous cape, passing the last beer back and forth, our toes buried in the cold sand, trying to skip stones across the waves. The sky was flat silver, then a dull copper, like an old penny. Then, suddenly, the sun broke free of the ocean, electric red, and none of us could speak or say anything – we just watched and watched, until it was too bright and we couldn't watch anymore.

Suddenly I'm angry at Parker: for reviving the memory of that night; for showing up now, when I'd already convinced myself I was over him; for making everything crack open again. For his perfect lips and his smile and those stormy eyes and the fact that even standing next to him I can feel an invisible force moving between us.

Magnetism, my chem teacher would call it. The seeking of a thing for its pair.

'Is that what you came to say?' I look away, hoping he can't read how badly it aches to be next to him. How badly I want to kiss him. If I don't act angry – if I don't *get* angry – the ache will only deepen. 'To take a stroll down memory lane at nearly one a.m. on a Wednesday?'

He squints, rubbing his forehead. 'No,' he says. 'No, of course not.' I feel a hard squeeze of guilt. I could never stand to see Parker unhappy. But I remind myself that it's his fault: he's the one who showed up out of nowhere, after all this time.

'Look.' Parker's still swaying, and his words are soft around the edges – not slurring, exactly, but like he can't be bothered to make hard sounds. 'Can we go somewhere to talk? Five minutes. Ten, tops.'

He makes a move for the door. But there's no way I'm letting him inside and risking waking up Mom – or worse, Nick. She never said anything about Parker and me, not directly, but I could read on her face how much she disapproved. Worse. I could read the pity, and I knew what she was thinking. One time I'd even heard her friend Isha say it out loud. They were in Nick's room and I was climbing down the trellis and Isha's voice rose up suddenly.

'She isn't prettier than you, Nick,' she'd said. 'It's just that she shoves her tits in everyone's face. People feel bad for her, you know?'

I didn't hear Nick's reply. But at that moment she'd stood up and her eyes slid across the window and I swear, I swear she saw me, frozen, gripping the trellis with both hands. Then she reached out and yanked the curtains shut.

'Come on,' I say, and take hold of Parker's arm, dragging him off the porch. I'm surprised when he fumbles for my hand. I pull away, crossing my arms again. It hurts to touch him.

My car is unlocked. I swing open the passenger door and gesture for him to get in. He freezes.

'Well?' I say.

He's staring at the car as if he's never seen one before. 'In here?'

'You said you wanted to talk.' I walk around to the driver's side, open the door, and get in. After another minute, he climbs in after me. With both doors shut, it's very quiet. The upholstery smells faintly of mildew. I'm still holding my phone, and I half wish it would ring, just to break up the silence.

Parker runs his hands over the dashboard. 'This car,' he says. 'It's been a while since I've been in this car.'

'So?' I prompt him. The car is stuffy, and it's so compact that every time he moves, we bump elbows. I don't want to think about what we used to do in here – and what we didn't do, what we never did. 'You have something you want to say to me?'

'Yeah.' Parker shoves a hand through his hair. It immediately falls back into place. 'Yeah, I do.'

I wait for a long beat of silence. But he says nothing. He doesn't even look at me.

'It's late, Parker. I'm tired. If you just came over to—'

He turns to me suddenly, and the words get caught in my chest: his eyes are two stars pinned to his face, blazing. He's so close I can feel the heat from his body, as if we're already pressed chest to chest, hugging. More. Kissing.

My heart shoots into my throat.

'I came to talk to you because I need to tell you the truth. I need to tell you.'

'What are you talking—?'

He cuts me off. 'No. It's my turn. Listen, okay? I've been lying. I never told you . . . I never explained.'

In the endless stretch of silence before he speaks again, the world outside takes a deep breath.

'I'm in love. I fell in love.' Parker's voice is barely a whisper. I stop breathing altogether. I'm afraid to move, afraid that if I do, everything will disappear. 'Maybe I always *was* in love, and just too stupid to know it.'

You, I think. The only word I can reach, the only thing I can think of: *You.*

Maybe, on some level, he hears me. Maybe in some parallel realm, Parker knows, because just then he says it, too.

'It's you,' he says. And his hands are touching my neck, my face, skimming through my hair. 'My whole life, it's always been you.'

Then he kisses me. And in that second I realize that all the work I've done to forget, to deny, to pretend I never cared about him – all the minutes, hours, days spent taking down our memories, piece by piece – has been totally and completely pointless. The second his lips touch mine – hesitantly, at first, as if he isn't quite sure I'll want it – the second I feel his fingers tighten in my hair, I know there's no use in pretending and there never was.

I am in love with Parker. I have always been in love with Parker.

It's been months since we've kissed, but there's no awkwardness, no strain, like there was with any of the other guys I've been with. It's as easy as breathing: push and pull; give, take, give. He tastes like sugar and something else, something deep and spicy.

At a certain point we break to catch our breath. I'm no longer holding my phone; I have no idea when I dropped it and I couldn't care less.

Parker brushes the hair back from my face, touches my nose with a thumb, sweeps his fingers over my cheeks. I wonder whether he can feel the scar tissue, smooth and alien, and involuntarily I pull back a little.

'You're so beautiful,' he says, and I know he means it, which makes me feel worse. It's been so long, maybe for ever, since anyone has looked at me the way he's looking at me now.

I shake my head. 'I'm all messed up now.' My throat is knotted up and the words come out high, strangled.

'You're not.' He takes my face with both hands, forcing me to look at him. 'You're perfect.'

This time, I kiss him. The knot loosens; once again I feel warm and happy and relaxed, like I'm floating in the world's most perfect ocean. Parker thinks I'm beautiful. Parker has been in love with me all this time.

I'll never be unhappy again.

With one hand he eases aside the collar of my T-shirt, kissing me along my shoulder blade and then up to my neck, moving his lips across my jawline and then to my ear. My whole body is a shiver; at the same time, I'm burning hot. I want everything, all at once, and in that second I know: tonight's the night. Right here, in my stupid mildew-smelling car: I want it all from him.

I grab his T-shirt and pull him closer, and he makes a sound halfway between a groan and a sigh.

'Nick,' he whispers.

All at once, my whole body goes ice-cold. I release him, scrabbling backward, bumping my head against the window. 'What did you say?'

'What?' He reaches for me again, and I swat his hand away. 'What's the matter? What's wrong?'

'You called me by my sister's name.' Suddenly I feel nauseous. That other thing I've been trying to deny – that horrible, deep-down feeling that all along I was never good enough, *could* never be good enough – now surges up, like a monster made to swallow up all my happiness.

He stares at me, then shakes his head, slowly at first, and then with increasing speed, as if he's working up momentum to deny it. 'No way,' he says. But for a second, I see guilt flash across his face, and I know that I'm right, that he did. 'No way. I would never – that's fucked-up – I mean, why would I—?'

'You did. I heard you.' I shove out of the car and slam the door shut so hard the whole car rattles, no longer caring whether I wake anyone up.

He doesn't love me. He never loved me. All along, he's loved *her*.

I was just the consolation prize.

'Wait. Seriously, stop. *Wait.*'

He's out of the car now, trying to intercept me before I can get to the door. He grabs my wrist, and I wrench away, stumbling on the grass, turning over on my ankle so a sharp pain goes all the way up to my knee.

'Let me go.' I've started crying without knowing it. Parker stands there, watching me with an expression of horror and pity and even more guilt. 'Leave me alone, okay? If you love me so much, if you care about me at all, just do me a favor. Leave me the hell alone.'

To Parker's credit, he does. He doesn't follow me to the porch. He doesn't try to stop me again. And once I'm inside, with my face pressed to the cold glass, taking deep, heaving breaths to try and keep the sobs back, I see that he doesn't even wait that long before disappearing again.

BEFORE

nick

'TELL ME AGAIN' – AARON TAKES MY EAR BETWEEN HIS TEETH, pulling lightly – 'what time your mom is coming home?'

He's made me say it three times already. 'Aaron,' I say, laughing. 'Don't.'

'Please,' he says. 'It's so sexy when you say it.'

'She's not,' I say, giving in. 'She's not coming home at all.'

Aaron smiles and moves his mouth from my neck to my jawline. 'I think those might be the hottest words in the English language.'

Something hard and metal is digging into my lower back: the spine, probably, of the pull-out couch. I try to ignore it, try and get into the mood, whatever that means. (I've never understood that phrase; it makes it sound as if moods are something you choose, like putting on a pair of pants. Dara and I once decided that 'sex-mood' would be a leather romper, skintight. But most of the time I just feel like a big pair of sweatpants.)

But when Aaron shifts his weight, leans into me with a knee between my legs, I let out a sharp cry.

'What?' He sits back, instantly apologetic. 'Sorry – did I hurt you?'

'No.' Now I'm embarrassed and scoot backward, instinctively covering my breasts with an arm. 'Sorry. Something was digging into my back. It was nothing.'

Aaron smiles. His hair, true black and silky, has grown out. He brushes it away from his eyes. 'Don't cover up,' he says, reaching out and easing my arm away from my chest. 'You're beautiful.'

'You're biased,' I say. Aaron's the beautiful one. I love how tall he is, and how small he makes me feel; I love the way basketball has defined his shoulders and arms. I love the color of his skin, a cream-gold, like light shining through autumn leaves; I love the shape of his eyes and the way his hair grows silky-straight.

I love so many individual things, points of a compass, dots on a diagram. Yet somehow when it comes to filling in the big picture, to loving *him*, I don't. Or I can't. I'm not sure which, and I don't know that it matters.

Aaron reaches out and grabs my waist, leaning backward and drawing me onto his lap simultaneously, so I'm the one on top. Then he's kissing me again, exploring my tongue carefully with his, running his hands lightly up and down my back, touching me the way he does everything: with cautious optimism, as if I'm an animal who might startle away from his touch. I try to relax, try to stop my brain from firing out stupid images and thoughts, but suddenly all I can focus on is the TV, which is still on, and still replaying old episodes of some competitive grocery shopping show.

I pull away and just for a second, Aaron lets his frustration show.

'Sorry,' I say. 'I'm just not sure I can do this to a soundtrack of *The Price Chopper.*'

Aaron reaches for the remote, which is lying on the floor next to our shirts. 'Do you want to change it?'

'No.' I start to ease off him. 'I mean that's not . . . I'm just not sure I can do this. Right now.'

He catches me by my belt before I can fully push off his lap. He's smiling, but his eyes are even darker than usual, and I can tell he's trying hard not to be annoyed. 'Come on, Nick,' he says. 'We never get to be alone.'

'What do you mean? We're always alone.'

He sits up on his elbows, shaking his hair from his eyes. 'Not really,' he says. 'Not like this.' He half smiles. 'I feel like you're always running away from me.' He puts a hand on my waist and leans back again, pulling me down on top of him.

'What do you want?' I blurt out, before I can stop myself. He hesitates, his lips a fraction away from mine, and pulls away to look at me.

'Everyone thinks we had sex on Founders' Night, you know,' he says.

My heart starts going jackrabbit hard in my chest. 'So?'

'Soooo . . .' He kisses my neck again, progressing slowly up toward my ear. 'If everyone thinks we did it *anyway* . . .'

'You can't be serious.' This time I sit up entirely, moving off his lap.

He exhales, hard. 'Only a quarter serious,' he says, scooting up on the couch so he can sit cross-legged. He rests his elbows on his knees and runs the back of a hand against my thigh. 'You still haven't told me what happened to you on Founders' Night.' He's still smiling that little half smile that doesn't reach his eyes. 'The mysterious disappearing girlfriend.' His hand moves up my thigh; he's teasing me, making a joke, still trying to get me in the mood. 'The magical vanishing girl—'

'I can't do this.' I don't even know I'm going to say the words before I have, but instantly I feel a sense of relief. It's like I've been carrying something hard and heavy behind my ribs and now it's gone, released, removed.

Aaron sighs and withdraws his hand. 'That's all right,' he says. 'We can just watch TV or something.'

'No.' I close my eyes, take a deep breath, think of Aaron's hands and smile and the way he looks on the basketball court, fluid and dark and beautiful. 'I mean, I can't do this. You and me. Anymore.'

Aaron jerks backward as if I've reached out and hit him. 'What?' He starts to shake his head. 'No. No way.'

'Yes.' Now the terrible feeling is back, this time settled in my stomach, a hard knot of guilt and regret. What the hell is wrong with me? 'I'm sorry.'

'Why?' His face is so open in that moment, so raw and vulnerable, a part of me wants to reach out and hug him, kiss him, tell him I was kidding. But I can't. I sit there with my hands in my lap, my fingers numb and alien-feeling.

'I just don't think this is right,' I say. 'I – I'm not the girl for you.'

'Says who?' Aaron starts to reach for me again. 'Nicole—' But he breaks off when I don't move, can't even look at him. For a horrible long moment, as we sit there next to each other, the air between us is charged with something cold and terrible, as if an invisible window is open and a storm is blowing through the room. 'You're serious,' he says finally. It isn't a question. His voice has changed. He sounds like a stranger. 'You're not going to take it back.'

I shake my head. My throat is tight, and I know if I look at him I might break. I'll start to cry, or I'll beg him to forgive me.

Aaron stands up without another word. He snatches up his shirt and yanks it over his head. 'I don't believe this,' he says. 'What about spring break? What about Virginia Beach?'

Some guys from the basketball team plan to take a road trip to Virginia Beach in March. My friend Audrey is going with her boyfriend, Fish; Aaron and I had talked about going together and renting a house with everyone on the beach. We'd imagined clambakes on the beach and long days that tasted like salt. I'd imagined waking up with all the windows open, the cool sting of ocean air, and warm arms around my waist . . .

But not his arms. Not him.

'I'm sorry,' I repeat. I have to get down onto my hands and knees to pick up my shirt. I feel horrible and exposed, as if all the lights have been turned up by a factor of a hundred. Five minutes ago we were kissing, our legs intertwined, the beat-up couch taking on the impression of our bodies. Even though I'm the one who screwed it up, I feel dizzy, disoriented, like I'm watching a movie too fast. I put my shirt on inside out but don't have the energy to fix it. I don't bother with my bra.

'I don't believe it,' Aaron says, speaking half to himself. When he's angry he actually gets quieter. 'I told you I loved you . . . I bought you that stupid stuffed cat for Valentine's Day . . .'

'It's not stupid,' I say automatically, even though it kind of is. I'd thought that was the whole point.

He doesn't seem to hear me. 'What's Fish going to say?' He shoves a hand through his hair. It immediately flops back into his eyes. 'What are my *parents* going to say?'

I don't answer. I just sit there, squeezing my fists so hard my nails dig into the soft flesh of my palms, gripped by a terrible, out-of-control feeling. What the hell is wrong with me?

'Nick . . .' Aaron's voice softens. I look up. He has his hoodie on now, the green one he got doing Habitat for Humanity in New Orleans the summer after sophomore year, the one that always mysteriously smells like the ocean. And in that moment I nearly break. I can see he's thinking the same thing. Scrap the whole thing. Let's pretend this never happened.

Upstairs, a door slams. Then Parker shouts, 'Hey! Anybody home?'

Just like that, the moment vanishes, skittering away into the shadows, like an insect startled by a footstep. Aaron turns away, muttering something.

'What'd you say?' My heart is going again, like it's a fist just itching to punch something.

'Nothing.' He zips up his hoodie. Now he won't look at me. 'Forget it.'

Parker must hear us, or sense us. He's pounding down the stairs before I can yell up to him to stop. When he sees Aaron, he freezes. His eyes tick to me, and to my bra, still lying on the musty carpet. His face goes white – and then, a split second later, completely red.

'Oh, shit. I didn't mean—' He starts to back-pedal. 'Sorry.'

'That's okay.' Aaron looks at me. I know all his moods – but this expression I can't identify. Anger, definitely. But there's something else, something deeper than that, as if he's finally figured out the answer to an impossible math problem. 'I was just leaving.'

He takes the stairs two at a time, forcing Parker to squeeze himself against one wall so Aaron can pass. Parker and Aaron don't like each other and never have. I don't know why. The moment they're together on the stairs feels electric, charged and dangerous; out of nowhere, I'm afraid that Aaron will hit Parker, or vice versa. But then Aaron keeps going and the moment passes.

Parker still doesn't move, not even after the front door slams again, indicating Aaron has left. 'Sorry,' he says. 'I hope I didn't interrupt anything.'

'You didn't.' My cheeks are hot. I wish I could reach out and take my stupid bra – pink, with patterns of daisies on it, like a twelve-year-old's bra – and shove it under the sofa, but that would be even more conspicuous. So instead we both pretend we don't notice.

'Okay.' Parker draws out the word, superlong, as if he knows I'm lying. For a second he says nothing. Then, slowly, he comes down the stairs, edging closer, as if I'm an animal who might be rabid. 'Are you all right? You seem . . .'

'I seem what?' I look up at him then, experiencing a hot flash of anger.

'Nothing.' He stops again, a good ten feet away from me. 'I don't know. Upset. Angry or something.' His next words he pronounces very carefully, as if each one is glass that might shatter in his mouth. 'Is everything okay with Aaron?'

I feel stupid sitting on the couch when he's standing, like I'm at a disadvantage somehow, so I stand up, too, crossing my arms. 'We're fine,' I say. 'I'm fine.' I'd been planning on telling Parker about the breakup – the second I saw his stupid Surf Siders on the stairs, I knew I would tell him, and maybe even tell him why, cry and confess that there's something wrong with me and I don't know how to be happy and I'm an idiot, such an idiot.

But now I can't tell him. I won't. Then I say, 'Dara's not

home.' Parker flinches and turns away, a muscle working in his jaw. Even midwinter, he has the kind of skin that always looks tan. I wish he looked worse. I wish he looked as bad as I feel. 'Well, you're here for her, aren't you?'

'Jesus, Nick.' He turns back to me then. 'We need to . . . I don't know . . . *fix* this. Fix *us*.'

'I don't know what you mean,' I say, squeezing my ribs, hard. I feel like if I don't, I might just come apart.

'You do know what I mean,' he says. 'You are – were – my best friend.' With one hand, he gestures to the space between us, the long stretch of basement, where for years we built pillow forts and competed to see who could withstand tickle wars the longest. 'What happened?'

'What happened is you started dating my sister,' I say. The words come out louder than I intended.

Parker takes a step toward me. 'I didn't mean to hurt you,' he says, his voice quiet, and for a second I want to close the distance between us and bury myself in the soft place between his arm and shoulder blade, and tell him how dumb I've been, and let him cheer me up with bad renditions of Cyndi Lauper songs and weird trivia about the world's largest hamburgers or free-standing structures built entirely from toothpicks. 'I didn't mean to hurt *either* of you. It just . . . happened.' He's practically whispering now. 'I'm trying to stop it.'

I take a step backward. 'You're not trying very hard,' I say. I know I'm being a bitch, but I don't care. He's the one who ruined everything. He's the one who kissed Dara, who *keeps* kissing her, who keeps telling her yes, no matter how many times they break up. 'I'll let Dara know you came by.'

Parker's face changes. And in that moment I know I've hurt him, maybe just as much as he's hurt me. I get a sick rush of triumph that feels almost like nausea, like catching an insect between folds of paper towel and squeezing. Then he just looks angry – hard, almost, like his skin has suddenly tightened into stone.

'Yeah, all right.' He takes two steps backward before turning around. 'Tell her I'm looking for her. Tell her I'm *worried* about her.'

'Sure.' My voice sounds unfamiliar, as if it's being piped in from somewhere a thousand miles away. I broke up with Aaron. And for what? Parker and I aren't even friends anymore. I've screwed up everything. Suddenly I think I might be sick.

'Oh, and Nick?' Parker pauses at the foot of the stairs. His expression is impossible to read – for a second, I think he might try and apologize again. 'Your shirt's on inside out.'

Then he's gone, sprinting up the stairs, leaving me alone.

birthday card from nick to dara

Happy birthday, D.
I have a surprise for you.
10 p.m. tonight. Fantasy Land.
What comes down, must go up.
See you at dinner.

Love,
Nick

P.S. It'll be worth it.

AFTER

nick

ON DARA'S BIRTHDAY, I WAKE UP EVEN BEFORE MY ALARM. Tonight is the night: when Dara and I go back in time. When we become best friends again. When everything gets fixed.

I haul out of bed, pull on my FanLand T-shirt (clean, thankfully) and a pair of jean shorts, and throw my hair into a ponytail. My whole body is sore. In the short time I've been at FanLand, I've already grown stronger, thanks to carting trash and scrubbing out the Whirling Dervish and jogging the claustrophobic network of FanLand pathways. My shoulders ache like they do after the first few weeks of field hockey season, and I have both muscles and dark, splotchy bruises I haven't noticed.

In the hall, I can hear the shower running in Mom's bathroom. This week she's been going to bed at 8:00 p.m. – right after the evening news, and the daily reports about the Madeline Snow case: whether Nicholas Sanderson, the police's only kind-of suspect, is hiding anything; whether it's a good or a bad thing that the police haven't turned up her body; whether she might, possibly, still be alive. Anyone would think Madeline was *her* kid.

I take the stairs to the attic, staying on my tiptoes, as if Dara might startle if she hears me coming. All last night, I thought about what I would to say to her. I even practiced whispering the words to my bedroom mirror.

I'm sorry.

I know you hate me.

Please, let's start over.

Surprisingly Dara's bedroom door is open a crack. I ease the door open with a foot.

In the murky half-light, it looks like a weird alien planet, crowded with mossy surfaces and solid, unidentifiable heaps. Dara's bed is empty. The birthday card I left for her last night is still arranged neatly on her pillow. I can't tell whether she's read it or not.

For years, Dara has been falling asleep in the den – we'll find her the next morning on the couch, enfolded in a blanket, an infomercial spouting off about an all-in-one kitchen knife or a bathroom toilet seat warmer. Once, last year, I came downstairs to the stink of vomit, and found that she'd puked in Mom's Native American clay pot before falling asleep. I cleaned her up, wiping the corners of her mouth with a damp towel, picked off the fake eyelash clinging, furry and caterpillar-like, to her cheek. At one point she just barely woke up and smiled at me through half-lidded eyes.

'Heya, Seashell,' she said, using the nickname she'd made up for me when she was a kid.

That was me: the family janitor. Always cleaning up Dara's messes.

Dr Lichme used to say that maybe I liked it, just a little.

He used to say that maybe helping solve other people's issues kept me from thinking about my own.

That's the problem with therapists: you have to pay them to say the same dumb shit other people will tell you for free.

I thud down the stairs, not bothering to be quiet this time. My left knee is killing me. I must have banged it on something.

When I come downstairs, Mom is just emerging from the bathroom, towel-drying her hair, wearing nothing but work pants and a bra. She freezes when she sees me.

'Were you in Dara's room?' she asks, watching me closely, as if she doesn't trust me not to morph into someone else. She looks awful, pasty-faced, like she hasn't slept.

'Yeah.' When I go into my room to get my shoes, Mom follows me, hovering in the doorway as if waiting for an invitation.

'What were you doing?' she asks carefully. As out of it as she's been, there's no way she hasn't noticed that Dara and I have perfected the art of circling around each other without touching, vacating rooms just before the other person enters, alternating patterns of wake and sleep.

I shove my feet into my sneakers, which have over the summer become deformed, distended into shapelessness by water and sweat.

'It's her birthday,' I say, like Mom doesn't know. 'I just wanted to talk to her.'

'Oh, Nick.' Mom hugs herself. 'I've been so selfish. I never even think about how hard it must be for you to be here. To be home.'

'I'm okay, Mom.' I hate it that my mom gets like this now: one second, fine; the next second, all mess and crumble.

'Good.' She holds the back of her hand against each eye in turn, as if she's pressing back a headache. 'That's good. I love you, Nick. You know that, right? I love you, and I worry about you.'

'I'm fine.' I shoulder my bag and edge past her. 'Everything's fine. I'll see you tonight, okay? Seven thirty. Sergei's.'

Mom nods. 'Do you think – do you think it's a good idea? Tonight, I mean? All of us sitting down together?'

'I think it'll be great,' I say – which, if you're counting, is already the third lie I've told this morning.

Dara's not in the den, although the blankets are all balled up on the sofa and there's an empty can of Diet Coke lying on the ottoman, suggesting that she did spend part of the night downstairs. Dara's like that, mysterious and undirected, always appearing and disappearing at will and never noticing, or maybe just not caring, that other people worry about her.

Maybe she went out last night for an early birthday celebration and wound up sleeping on some random guy's couch. Maybe she woke up early in one of her rare bouts of penitence and will come through the front door in twenty minutes, whistling, make-up-free, bearing a big paper bag full of cinnamon doughnuts from Sugar Bear and a trayful of Styrofoam cups of coffee.

Outside, the thermometer is already at ninety-eight degrees. There's a heatwave due this week, a massive, record-breaking blast of oven-temperature air. Just what we need today. Even before I get to the bus stop, I've chugged through my water bottle, and even though the air conditioning on the bus is on full blast, the sun still seems to beat through the windows and turn the whole interior the murky, musty warm of a dysfunctional refrigerator.

The woman next to me is reading a newspaper, one of those obnoxiously thick ones packed with flyers and coupons and pamphlets advertising sales at a nearby Toyota dealership. The headlines are, no surprise, still given over to the Snow case. On the front page is a grainy picture of Nicholas Sanderson leaving the police station with his wife – both of them walking head down as though against a driving rain.

Nicholas Sanderson just moments after he was cleared of involvement in the Snow disappearance, reads the caption.

'It's a damn shame,' the woman says, shaking her head so that her chin shakes, too. I turn away and look out the window, watching as the coast and its commercial clutter come into view and beyond it, the ocean, white and flat as a disk.

The FanLand sign is partially obscured behind a gigantic mass of balloons, like a multicolored cloud. A short distance away, the owner of Boom-a-Rang, Virginia's Largest Firecracker Emporium, stands outside, smoking a thin brown cigar, looking doleful. In my nine days at FanLand, I have not yet been able to determine the reason for Boom-a-Rang's hours, which seem whimsical to the point of insanity. Who shops for fireworks at eight in the morning?

Inside the park, it's chaos. Doug is herding a group of volunteers – none of them older than thirteen – toward the amphitheater, yelling to be heard over the constant thrum of pre-teen chatter. Even at a distance of twenty feet, I can hear Donna shouting into the phone, probably telling off some food vendor who forgot to deliver a thousand hotdog buns, so I steer clear of the office, figuring I can drop off my bag later. Even Mr Wilcox looks miserable. He passes me on the footpath leading down to the Ferris wheel but barely grunts in response to my hello.

'Don't mind him.' Alice skims my back with a hand as she jogs past me, already sweating freely, a long sheath of napkins tucked under one arm. 'He's a stress case this morning. Parker called in sick, and he's freaking out about staffing.'

'Parker's sick?' I think of the way he looked last night in front of the wave pool, with the colors patterning his face and transforming him into someone unrecognizable, with the light throwing up fingers to the sky.

Alice is already twenty feet in front of me. 'Guess so.' She turns around but continues to half step down the path. 'Wilcox is having a hissy fit, though. And don't even get close to Donna. Someone missed her morning dose of happy.'

'Okay.' The sun is blinding. Every color looks exaggerated, like someone has turned up the contrast on a big remote. I feel weirdly uneasy about Parker, about how we left things last night. Why did I get so upset?

I have another flashback to Dara, to his car, to the night the rain came down in heavy sheets, as if the sky were breaking off in pieces. I blink and shake my head, trying to dislodge the memory.

'You're sure he's okay, though?' I call out to Alice. But she's too far away to hear me.

By 10:00 a.m., it's obvious that even Mr Wilcox has underestimated the crowds. The park has never been so busy, despite temperatures inching past 103 degrees. I refill my water bottle a half-dozen times and still don't have to pee. It's like the liquid is evaporating straight from my skin. As a special treat, and because our little musical number has become something of a sensation, at least for the under-six crowd, we're doing three different shows: ten thirty, noon, and two thirty.

In between shows, I wrestle off the mermaid tail and collapse in the front office, the only interior space with a functioning AC, too sick with heat to care that my underwear is visible to Donna, while Heather removes her parrot costume and paces the room, cursing the weather and fanning out her underarms, wearing nothing but a bra and a pair of Spanx.

It's too hot to eat. It's too hot to smile. And still the people come: rushing, pouring, tumbling through the park gates, a flood of kids and parents and grandparents, teen girls wearing bikini tops and cut-offs, and their boyfriends, shirtless, shorts slung low over bathing suits, pretending to be bored.

By the time two thirty rolls around, I can barely keep a smile on my face. Sweat is dripping between my boobs, behind my knees, in places I didn't even know you *could* sweat. The sun is relentless, like a gigantic magnifying glass, and I feel like an ant sizzling underneath it. The audience is nothing but a blur of color.

Heather mimes her attack by the sock puppet. At that exact moment, the strangest thing happens: all the sound in the world clicks off. I can see the audience laughing, can see a thousand dark cavernous mouths, but it's like someone has severed the feedback to my ears. There's nothing but a dull rushing sound in my ears, as if I'm on a plane several thousand feet in the air.

I want to say something – I know I should say something. But this is my time to stand up, to try and intervene, to save Heather from the dog, and I can't remember how to speak, either, just like I can't remember how to hear. I push myself to my feet.

At least, I think I get to my feet. Suddenly I'm on the ground again, not face forward, as I usually fall, but on my back, and Rogers's face appears above me, red and bloated. He's shouting something – I can see his mouth moving, wide and urgent, while Heather's face appears next to him, minus the bird head, hair plastered damply to her forehead – and then I'm weightless, floating across an expanse of blue sky, or rocking like a baby in my dad's arms.

It takes me a minute to work out that Rogers is carrying me, the way he does before a performance. I'm too tired to protest. *Mermaids don't walk.*

Then his voice, gruff in my ear, popping through the static silence in my brain: 'Take a deep breath now.'

Before I can ask why, his arms release me and I'm falling. There's a shock, electric and freezing, as I hit water. It's a hard reboot: suddenly every feeling powers back on. Chlorine stings my nose and eyes. Underwater, the tail is impossibly heavy, clinging to my skin like a tight casing of seaweed. The pool is absolutely packed with kids and rafts, little legs churning the water to foam and bodies passing above me, momentarily blocking the light. It takes me about a second to realize that Rogers has just thrown me, costume and everything, straight into the wave pool.

I kick off the bottom of the pool. Just before I resurface, I see her: briefly submerged, eyes wide and blond hair extending, halo-like, from her head; briefly visible in between legs scissoring to stay afloat and kids diving beneath the crashing of the waves.

Madeline Snow.

Forgetting I'm underwater, I open my mouth to shout, and just then I break the surface and come out heaving, spitting up water, chlorine burning the back of my throat. The sound has powered back on, along with everything else; the air is filled with shrieking and laughter and the crash of man-made waves against concrete.

I flounder toward the shallows, try and turn around, scanning the crowd for Madeline. There must be sixty kids in the wave pool, maybe more. The sun is dazzling. There are blondes everywhere – ducking, popping up grinning, spouting water from their mouths like fountains, all of them more or less identical-looking. Where did she go?

'You all right?' Rogers is squatting at the edge of the pool, still wearing his pirate hat. 'Feeling better?'

Just then I spot her again, struggling to pull herself onto the deck on arms as skinny as rail spikes. I slosh toward her, tripping on the stupid tail, going face forward down into the water and then dog-paddling the rest of the way. Someone is calling my name. But I have to get to her.

'Madeline.' I get a hand around her arm and she thuds back into the water, letting out a surprised cry. As soon as she turns around, I see it isn't Madeline after all. This girl is maybe eleven or twelve, with a bad overbite and bangs cut blunt across her forehead.

'Sorry,' I say, dropping her arm quickly, even as her mother – a woman wearing denim overall shorts and pigtails, even though she must be in her forties – comes jogging over, her sandals slapping on the wet pavement.

'Addison? Addison!' She drops to her knees on the pool deck and reaches out a hand for her daughter, glaring at me like I'm some pervert. 'Get over here. Now.'

'Sorry,' I say again. The woman only shoots me another dirty look as the girl, Addison, hauls herself out of the pool. Over the constant noise of shouting and laughter, I hear my name again; when I turn, I see Rogers, frowning, skirting the edge of the pool, trying to make his way over to me. I slosh out of the water, suddenly exhausted, feeling like an idiot, and flop onto the deck, my tail dribbling all over the pavement. A little girl wearing a diaper points and laughs delightedly.

'What's going on?' Rogers takes a seat next to me. 'You gonna faint on me again?'

'No. I thought I saw—' I break off, realizing how ridiculous I'll sound. *I thought I saw Madeline Snow underwater.* I work the zipper down to my feet and stand up, holding the tail closed so I don't wind up flashing anyone and getting arrested for indecency. I feel a little better, though, now that my legs aren't suctioned together. 'Did I really faint?'

Rogers straightens up, too. 'Dropped like a pile of rocks,' he says. 'Don't worry, the kids thought it was part of the show. You eat any lunch?'

I shake my head. 'Too hot.'

'Come on,' he says, putting a hand on my shoulder. 'Let's get you out of the sun.'

We pass two clowns and a juggler on our way back to the office – all of them subcontracted from a local entertainment company, though I know Doug is out there somewhere, suited up like a magician, doing card tricks – surrounded by thick knots of delighted children.

Still more people are arriving: so many people, it makes you wonder how all of them could exist, how there can be so many individual lives and stories and needs and disappointments. Looking at the line snaking down from the Plank, while the Whirling Dervish spins around on its track, hurling its passengers in tight ellipses and sending sound waves peaking and crashing, I have the weirdest moment of clarity: all the search parties, all the news stories, all the twenty-four-hour updates and tweet blasts from @FindMadelineSnow are pointless.

Madeline Snow is gone for ever.

I find Alice in the office, taking her own turn in front of the AC. Donna is not there, thankfully, and the phone keeps ringing, barking shrilly four times and then falling silent again when the automated message – *Hello and welcome to Fantasy Land!* – kicks on. Rogers insists that I drink three cups of ice water and eat half a turkey sandwich before clocking out.

'Can't have any accidents on the way home,' he barks, standing over me and glowering as though by the sheer force of eye contact he could make me digest faster.

'You'll come back for the fireworks, right?' Alice says. She has her shoes up on the desk, and the small room smells faintly sour. Alice has explained, with a shrug, that she was working the Cobra when a girl teetered off the ride, grinning, turned to Alice, and puked directly on her shoes.

'I'll be back,' I say. The park has extended hours for the anniversary party: we'll be open until 10:00 p.m., with fireworks beginning at nine. I'm starting to get nervous. Only a few more hours to go. 'I'll be back for sure.'

Tonight Dara and I wake the beast together. Tonight we ride the Gateway up to the stars.

dara's diary entry

Ariana and I went to the Loft to hang out with PJ and Tyson, and then she spent the whole night shoving her tongue down Tyson's throat and trying to convince us to skinny-dip even though it was, like, fifty degrees. There was another guy there who owns a club in East Norwalk called Beamers. He even brought champagne, the real kind. He kept saying I could be a model, until I told him to stop feeding me horseshit. Models are, like, ten feet tall. Still, he was cute. Older, but definitely cute.

He said if I ever needed a job I could waitress for him and make two or three hundred a day, easy. (!!) That sure as shit beats babysitting Ian Sullivan every other day and trying to keep him from putting his cat in the microwave or burning caterpillars with matchsticks. I swear that kid is going to be a serial killer when he grows up.

PJ was in a bad mood because he was supposed to get mushrooms, but I guess his guy ran out. Instead we just drank Andre's champagne and took shots of some nasty shit this girl brought home from France, which tasted like swallowing licorice and rubbing alcohol at the same time.

I know Dr Lick Me would tell me I was just trying to avoid my feelings again, but let me tell you something: it didn't work. All night I kept thinking about Parker. Why the hell is he acting like I have some flesh-eating disease all of a sudden? Hot and cold doesn't even begin to describe it. More like lukewarm and frigid.

So I kept puzzling out little hints and vibes he's been giving me in the past couple of weeks, and all of a sudden I had this moment of total clarity. I've been such a fucking idiot.

Parker's in love with somebody else.

nick

7:15 p.m.

I'M MEETING MOM AND DAD AT SERGEI'S, SINCE THEY'LL BOTH BE coming straight from work. I have no idea how Dara's planning to get there, but she isn't home when I stop in to change. The AC unit is going full blast and all the lights are off; still, the house is old, and just like it has its own rhythms, patterns of creaks and groans and mysterious banging sounds, it has its own internal temperature, which today seems to have settled at around eighty degrees.

I take a cold shower, gasping when the water hits my back, and then throw on the coolest thing I own, a linen dress that Dara has always hated, saying it makes me look like I'm either going to a wedding or about to be sacrificed as a virgin.

Sergei's is a ten-minute walk – fifteen if you go slowly, which I do, trying not to break a sweat. I go around the house and through the backyard, glancing, as always, at the oak tree, half searching for a red flag entwined in its branches, for a secret message from Parker. Nothing but leaves crowd along the heavy branches, shimmering emerald-like in the weakening sun.

I cut into the thicket of trees that divides our property from our neighbors'. It's obvious that Dara has been sneaking out recently. There's a straight path through the growth where branches have been snapped away and the grass trampled.

I emerge onto Old Hickory Lane two houses down from Parker's. On a whim, I decide to stop by and see if he's okay. It isn't like him to flake on work. His car is in the driveway, but the house is quiet and I can't tell if he's home. The curtains in his window – navy-blue stripes, selected by Parker at age six – are shut. I ring the doorbell – the first time I've ever used it, the first time I've ever noticed the Parkers *have* a doorbell – and wait, crossing my arms and uncrossing them, hating that I suddenly feel nervous.

Upstairs, I think I see the curtains twitch in Parker's room. I take a step backward, craning my neck for a better view. The curtains are swinging slightly. Someone's definitely up there.

I cup my hands to my mouth and shout up to him, like I used to do when we were little and needed him to come down for a game of street stickball or to be our third for double Dutch. But this time, the curtains stay still. No face appears at the window. Finally I'm forced to turn around, backtracking down the street, feeling uncomfortable for no reason, as if someone is watching me, observing my progress. I turn around once at the corner; again, I could swear the curtains twitch, as if someone has just yanked them shut.

Frustrated, I turn away. I'm already late, but it's still too hot to do anything but ooze down the street. In less than twenty minutes, I'll be sitting across from Dara.

She'll have to talk to me. She won't have a choice.

My stomach is knotted practically to my throat.

And then, just before I get to Upper Reaches Park, I see her:

She's waiting to board the 22 bus, the one I take to FanLand, standing aside to allow an old woman with a walker to dismount. The halogen lights blazing from the bus shelter bleach her skin practically white and turn her eyes to hollows. She's hugging herself, and from a distance she looks a lot younger.

I stop in the middle of the road. 'Dara!' I shout. 'Dara!'

She looks up, her expression troubled. I wave, but I'm too far away, and standing in a portion of the street swallowed by long shadows, and she must not see me. With a final glance over her shoulder, she slips onto the bus. The doors *whoosh* closed, and then she's gone.

My phone vibrates. Dad's calling, probably to scold me for being late. I press ignore and keep walking to Sergei's, trying to fight a bad feeling. The 22 *does* run through downtown Somerville, but not before it's looped north around the park. If she's planning to show to dinner, it would be far quicker to walk.

But how could she miss her own birthday dinner?

Maybe her knees are acting up, or her back is bugging her today. Still, I unconsciously slow down, afraid that I'll arrive and she won't be there and then I'll know: she isn't coming.

It's a quarter to eight by the time I get to Sergei's, and my stomach turns over: both Mom's and Dad's cars are in the lot, parked next to each other, as if this is just another family dinner. As if I might walk in and get suctioned back in time, see Dad checking his teeth in the polished back of a knife while Mom scolds him, see Dara already flitting around the salad bar, concentrating, like an artist putting the finishing touches on a painting, and making sudden grabs for the croutons or the pickled green beans.

Instead I see Mom sitting alone at the table. Dad is standing in the corner, one hand on his hip, phone plastered to his ear. As I watch, he hangs up, frowning slightly, and dials again.

Dara's not here.

For a second, I feel nauseous. Then the anger comes rushing back.

I weave around the salad bar and push through the usual crowd – kids pegging one another with crayons, parents slugging back mug-size glasses of wine. As I approach the table, Dad turns and gestures helplessly to Mom.

'I can't reach them,' he says. 'I can't reach *either* of them.' But just then he spots me. 'There you are,' he says, presenting his cheek, which feels rough and stinks of aftershave. 'I've been calling.'

'Sorry.' I sit down in the seat across from Mom, next to the empty seat intended for Dara. Better to spit it out. 'Dara's not coming.'

Mom stares at me. 'What?'

I take a deep breath. 'Dara's not coming,' I say. 'We don't need to save her a seat.'

Mom's still looking at me as if I've just sprouted a second head. 'What are you—?'

'Yoo-hoo! Nick! Sharon! Kevin! Incoming. Excuse me.'

I look up and see Aunt Jackie moving toward us, deftly navigating the pattern of tables, clutching an enormous, multi-colored leather bag to her chest, as though to prevent it from rocketing off on its own and taking out water glasses. As always, she's wearing multiple colored strands of big jewelry (*powerful crystals*, she corrected me severely, when I once asked her why she wore so many rocks), so that she looks a little like a human version of a Christmas tree. Her hair is long and loose, swinging halfway to her butt.

'Sorry, sorry, sorry,' she says. When she bends down to kiss me, I catch a quick whiff of something that smells a little bit like damp earth. 'Traffic was terrible. How are you doing?' Aunt Jackie grips Mom's face for a moment before kissing her.

'I'm all right,' Mom says, smiling faintly.

Aunt Jackie studies her face for a minute before releasing her. 'What'd I miss?'

'Nothing.' Dad shakes out his napkin and presents his cheek to Aunt Jackie like he did to me. She plants a big kiss on it, exaggerating the sound, and Dad carefully swipes his skin when she isn't looking. 'Nick was just *informing* us that her sister isn't coming.'

'Don't get angry at me,' I say.

'No one's angry,' Aunt Jackie says brightly, as she sits down next to me. 'No one's angry, right?'

Dad turns back to the waitress and motions that he wants another drink. There's already a whiskey – mostly melted ice, at this point – leaving fat rings on the paper tablecloth.

'I – I don't understand.' Mom's eyes are unfocused, a sure sign she's had a bad day and had to double up on anti-anxiety meds. 'I thought we'd all agreed to have a nice night. To have a *family* night.'

'Maybe what Nick *meant* to say' – Aunt Jackie shoots me a warning look – 'is just that Dara's not here *yet*. It's her birthday,' she adds, when I open my mouth to protest. 'This is her favorite restaurant. She'll be here with us.'

All at once, Mom begins to cry. The transformation is sudden. People always talk about how faces crumble, but Mom's doesn't; her eyes go bright, vivid green right before the tears start flowing, but otherwise she looks the same. She doesn't even try and cover her face, just sits there bawling like a little kid, mouth open, snot bubbling in her nose.

'Mom, please.' I reach for her hand, which is cold. Already people are turning to stare. It's been a long time since Mom has had a fit this bad in public.

'It's all my fault,' she says. 'This was a terrible idea – stupid. I thought going to Sergei's would help . . . I thought it would be like old times. But with just the three of us—'

'What am I, chopped tofu?' Aunt Jackie pipes up, but nobody smiles.

Anger moves like an itch along my spine, into my neck, down into my chest. I should have known she would flake. I should have known she would find a way to ruin this, too. 'This is all Dara's fault,' I say.

'Nick,' Aunt Jackie says quickly, as if I've cursed.

'Don't make this worse,' Dad snaps. He turns to Mom and puts a hand on her back, then immediately withdraws it, as though he's been burned. 'It'll be okay, Sharon.'

'It's not okay,' she says, her voice cresting to a wail. By now, half the restaurant is looking at us.

'You're right,' I say. 'It's not okay.'

'Nicole.' Dad spits out my name. 'Enough.'

'All right,' Aunt Jackie says, her voice low, soothing, as if she's talking to a group of kids. 'Everyone calm down, okay? Let's all calm down.'

'I just wanted to have a nice night. Together.'

'Come on, Sharon.' Dad moves as if to touch her again, but his hand instead finds its way to his whiskey glass, which a waitress has just deposited before scurrying quickly away. A double, judging from the size of it. 'It isn't your fault. It was a nice idea.'

'It's not okay,' I repeat, a little louder. No point in keeping my voice down. Everyone is already staring at us. A busboy coming toward us with ice water catches sight of Mom, turns around, and bolts back toward the kitchen. 'There's no point in pretending. You always *do* this – both of you do.'

At least Mom stops crying. Instead she stares at me, open-mouthed, her eyes all bleary and red. Dad grips his glass so hard, I wouldn't be surprised if the whole thing shatters.

'Nick, honey—' Aunt Jackie starts to say, but Dad cuts her off.

'What are you talking about?' he says. 'Do what?'

'Pretend,' I say. 'Act like nothing's changed. Act like nothing's wrong.' I ball up my napkin and throw it on the table, suddenly disgusted and sorry that I even showed up. 'We aren't a family anymore. You made sure of that when you left, Dad.'

'That's enough,' Dad says. 'Do you hear me?' The angrier Dad gets, the quieter his voice. Now he's speaking in practically a whisper. His face is a mottled red, like someone choking.

Weirdly, Mom has gone totally still, totally calm. 'She's right, Kevin,' she says serenely, her eyes floating up past my head again.

'And you.' I can't help it; I can't stop it. I'm never this angry, but it all boils up at once, something black and awful, like a monster in my chest that just wants to tear, and tear, and tear. 'You're on a different planet half the time. You think we don't notice, but we do. Pills to go to sleep. Pills to wake up. Pills to help you eat, and pills to keep you from eating too much.'

'I said *that's enough*.' Suddenly Dad reaches over the table and grabs my wrist, hard, knocking over a glass of water onto Mom's lap. Aunt Jackie shouts. Mom yelps and leaps backward, sending her chair clattering to the ground. Dad's eyes are enormous and bloodshot; he's holding my wrist so tightly, tears prick my eyes. The restaurant has gone totally silent.

'Let her go, Kevin,' Aunt Jackie says very calmly. *'Kevin.'* She has to put her hand on his and pry his fingers from my wrist. The manager – a guy named Corey; Dara used to flirt with him – is moving toward us slowly, obviously mortified.

Finally Dad lets go. He lets his hand fall in his lap. He blinks. 'God.' The color drains out of his face all at once. 'My God. Nick, I'm so sorry. I should never have – I don't know what I was thinking.'

My wrist is burning, and I know I'm going to cry. This was supposed to be the night Dara and I fixed everything. Dad reaches for me again, this time to touch my shoulder, but I stand up, so my chair grates loudly on the linoleum. Corey pauses halfway across the restaurant, as if he's afraid he might be physically accosted if he comes any closer.

'We aren't a family anymore,' I repeat in a whisper, because if I try to speak any louder the pressure in my throat will collapse and the tears will come. *'That's* why Dara isn't here.'

I don't stay to see my parents' reaction. There's a roaring in my ears, like earlier today, just before I fainted. I don't remember crossing the restaurant or bursting out into the night air but, suddenly, there I am: on the far side of the parking lot, jogging through the grass, gulping deep breaths of air and wishing for an explosion, a world-ending, movie-style disaster; wishing for the darkness to come down, like water, over all our heads.

Nicole Warren
American Lit-Adv
February 28
'The Eclipse'

Assignment: In To Kill a Mockingbird, *the natural world is often used as a metaphor for both human nature and many of the book's themes (fear, prejudice, justice, etc.). Please write 800–1,000 words about an experience of the natural world that might be seen as metaphorically significant, employing some of the poetic techniques (alliteration, symbolism, anthropomorphism) we've covered in this unit.*

One time, when my sister, Dara, and I were little, my parents took us down to the beach to watch a solar eclipse. This was before the casino opened up in Shoreline County and before Norwalk got built up, too, and became a long chain of motels and family-style restaurants and, farther down, strip clubs and bars. FanLand was there, and a gun store; nothing else but gravel-dotted sand and coastline and little dunes, like wind-whipped cream, spotted with sun-bleached grasses.

There were hundreds of other families on the beach, making a picnic of it, spreading out blankets on the sand while the disk of the moon moved lazily toward the sun, like a magnet pulling slowly toward its pair. I remember my mother peeling an orange with her thumb, and the bitter smell of pith.

I remember Dad saying, *Look. Look, girls, it's happening.*

I remember, too, the moment of darkness: when the sky turned to textured gray, like chalk, and then to twilight, but faster than any twilight I'd ever seen. Suddenly we were all swallowed up in shadow, as if the world had opened its mouth and we'd fallen down a black throat.

Everyone applauded. There was a small constellation of flashes in the dark, miniature explosions while people took pictures. Dara put her hand in mine, squeezed, and began to cry. And my heart stopped. In that moment I thought we might be lost for ever in the darkness, suspended in a place between night and day, sun and land, earth and the waves that turned earth back into water.

Even after the moon rolled off the sun, and the daylight came again, a bright and unnatural dawn, Dara wouldn't stop crying. My parents thought she was cranky because she'd missed her nap and had wanted ice cream on the way over, and we did get ice cream, eventually, tall cones too big for either one of us to eat that pooled in our laps on the way home.

But I understood why she was crying. Because in that moment I'd felt it, too: a sheer, driving terror that the darkness was permanent, that the moon would stop its rotation, that the balance would never be restored.

You see, even then, I knew. It wasn't a trick. It wasn't a show. Sometimes day and night reverse. Sometimes up goes down and down goes up, and love turns into hate, and the things you counted on get washed out from under your feet, leaving you pedaling in the air.

Sometimes people stop loving you. And that's the kind of darkness that never gets fixed, no matter how many moons rise again, filling the sky with a weak approximation of light.

nick

8:35 p.m.

I FLING OPEN THE FRONT DOOR SO HARD IT CRACKS AGAINST THE wall, but I'm too pissed to care.

'Dara?' I call her name even though I can tell by feel, by intuition, that she hasn't come home.

'Hi, Nick.' Aunt Jackie emerges from the den, holding a glass filled with what looks like neon-green sludge. 'Smoothie?'

She must have headed to our house in her car straight from the restaurant. Maybe Mom and Dad sent her ahead to talk to me.

'No, thanks.' I'm really not in the mood to deal with Aunt Jackie and her self-help 'wisdom,' which always sounds like it came off the inside of a bottle cap. *Let truth radiate toward you. Focus is about presence. Let go or be dragged.* But she's positioned in front of the stairway, blocking access to my room. 'Are you staying here tonight or something?'

'Thinking about it,' she says, taking a long sip of smoothie and leaving a green mustache around her upper lip. Then: 'That isn't the way to get a response, you know. Not if you really want to talk to her.'

'I think I know my sister,' I say, irritated.

Aunt Jackie shrugs. 'Whatever you say.' She stares at me for a long second, as if debating whether to tell me a secret.

'What?' I ask finally.

She bends over, setting down the smoothie on the stairs. When she straightens up again, she reaches for my hands. 'She isn't *mad* at you, you know. She just misses you.'

Her hands are freezing, but I don't pull away. 'She *told* you that?' Aunt Jackie nods. 'You – you talk to her?'

'Almost every day,' Aunt Jackie says, shrugging. 'I spoke with her for a long time this morning.'

I pull away, taking a step backward, nearly tripping on Aunt Jackie's bag, which is slumped, body-like, in the middle of the hall. Dara used to make fun of Aunt Jackie for her patchouli smell and weird vegan concoctions and endless chatter about meditation and reincarnation. And now they're besties? 'She won't talk to me at *all*.'

'Have you asked?' she says, with a pitying look. 'Have you really *tried*?'

I don't answer. I brush past Aunt Jackie, take the stairs two at a time up both flights to Dara's room, which is also dark, also empty. The birthday card is still sitting on her pillow, exactly where it was this morning. Could she have been out since last night? Where could she have gone? To Ariana's, maybe. Or maybe – suddenly the answer is so obvious I can't believe it didn't occur to me before – she's with Parker. They're probably together on some crazy Dara-inspired adventure, trying to make it to North Carolina and back in twenty-four hours, or camped out together in an East Norwalk motel, throwing potato chips to the gulls from their window.

I pull out my phone and dial Dara's number. It rings five-times before going to voicemail. So either she's busy – if she *is* with Parker, I don't want to think about what she's busy with – or ignoring me.

I text her instead.

Meet me in front of the Gateway @ FanLand. 10 p.m.

I hit send.

There. I've asked, just like Aunt Jackie said I should.

Downstairs, Aunt Jackie has retreated to the den. I root around in the kitchen for a key to Dara's car. Finally I find a spare nestled in the back of the junk drawer, behind a bunch of highlighters and half a dozen matchbooks.

'You going somewhere?' Aunt Jackie calls as I head for the door.

'Work,' I call back, and don't wait for her reply.

Dara's car smells earthy and strange, like there's fungus growing beneath the seat cushions. It's been months since I've been behind the wheel of a car, and a tiny shiver of dread passes through me when I turn the key in the ignition. The last time I drove was on the night of the accident, down on that bleak portion of 101 that shoulders up to the stone-rutted coast, with its thick nests of sandwort and gnarled beach plum trees. I haven't gone back there; I haven't wanted to.

That road leads nowhere.

I back out of the driveway, careful to avoid the trash cans, feeling awkward and a little jumpy behind the wheel. But after a few minutes, I relax. Rolling down the windows, turning onto the highway, gathering speed, I feel the tension in my chest break apart slightly. Dara still hasn't responded to my text, but that doesn't mean anything. She's never been able to resist a surprise. Besides, the 22 goes straight to FanLand. She may have blown off dinner just to get to the park a little early.

At FanLand, the parking lot is still packed, though immediately I can tell the crowd has changed: there are fewer minivans and SUVs, more beat-up secondhand Accords, some thumping with bass, some releasing fine plumes of sweet-smelling smoke from the cracked windows, as kids pass back and forth into the lot to drink or get high. As soon as I park, I start scanning for Dara, ducking low to try and see past the fog-patterned windows without trying to look like I'm looking.

'Hey, sweetheart. Nice ass!' a guy shouts from a nearby car, and his friends erupt into laughter. I can hear a girl shriek in the backseat, 'She does not.'

Three boys, maybe a little younger than I am, are standing in front of Boom-a-Rang's, lighting off sparklers right on the pavement and throwing snaps as hard as they can so they crack off in a cloud of gas.

The fireworks have started. As soon as I pass through the FanLand gates, a huge shower of gold lights up the sky, trailing long tentacles like a glittering sea creature pinned up in the sky. The next one is blue, and then red, these brief, tight bursts, small fists of color.

Dara must be here. She must have come.

I push through the crowds still milling down Green Row, lining up to shoot basketballs through hoops or to try their hand on the strength hammer. It's all lights and flash, the *ring-ring-ring* of games starting and ending, kids shrieking with joy or disappointment, the sky lit up green or purple or startling blue as the fireworks attain some height and, miraculously, transform, scattering like ashes across the underbelly of the clouds. I wonder how high they know to go.

I turn toward the Gateway: it, too, is lit up in flashes, its high point gleaming like a burnished nail.

The lawns are crowded with blankets and picnicking families. I'm skirting the merry-go-round when someone hooks an arm around my neck. I spin around, thinking *Dara*, and am disappointed when it's just Alice, laughing, her hair coming loose from her braids. Immediately, I can tell she's a little drunk.

'We did it!' she says, flinging an arm out as though to take in the sky, the rides, everything: and I remember what she said, that she wanted to die at the very top of the Ferris wheel. 'Where'd you go?'

'I had a thing,' I say. She has changed out of her work shirt and is wearing a flowing tank top that shows off two more tattoos, wing tips peeking out beneath her shoulder straps. I've never seen her without her uniform before, and in that moment she looks almost like a stranger.

'Have some,' she says, as if she can tell what I'm thinking; and passes me a flask from her back pocket. 'You look like you need it.'

'What is it?' I uncap the bottle and take an experimental sniff. Alice laughs when I make a face.

'Jame-o. Jameson. Go on,' she says, nudging me with an elbow. 'Take a load off. FanLand turned seventy-five today. And it doesn't taste *that* bad, I promise.'

I take a swig – not because FanLand turned seventy-five, but because she's right, I do need it – and immediately start coughing. It tastes like lighter fluid going down.

'That's disgusting,' I choke out.

'You'll thank me later,' she says, patting me on the back.

She's right: almost immediately, a fizzy warmth travels from my stomach to my chest, settling somewhere just between my collarbone, like a giggle I'm trying to hold back.

'Wanna come watch from the hill?' she says. 'It's the best view. And Rogers even brought' – she lowers her voice – 'like an *ounce* of pot. We're taking turns in the maintenance shed.'

'I'll be there soon,' I say. Suddenly the insanity of what I'm about to do – what Dara and I are about to do – hits me. Then I really *do* feel the urge to laugh. I take another swig of Jameson before passing the flask back to Alice.

'Come now,' she says. 'You'll never find us.'

'Soon,' I say again. 'I promise.'

She shrugs and starts skipping backward down the path. 'Up to you,' she says, and raises the flask high, so it momentarily picks up the colored reflection from the sky: this time, a sudden dazzle of pink embers. 'Happy anniversary party!'

I raise a pretend glass and watch until she has merged into shadow with the rest of the crowd. Then I take a shortcut, pushing into the stretch of woods that keeps the Gateway relatively isolated: a part of the park once designed, like every other overgrown area, to look tropical and exotic. Stepping off the path feels like stepping into another world. Unlike the other wild stretches, this one has been allowed to grow riotous, and I have to swat creeper vines out of my way and duck underneath the fat, broad leaves of palmetto trees, which reach out like hands to slap me when I pass.

Almost instantly the sound is muffled, as though by a thin sheen of water; the gnats and crickets are buzzing from unseen places, and I can feel the feather-thin sweep of moth wings beating against my bare arms. I shove through the growth, stumbling a little in the dark, keeping my eye on the Gateway's shimmering point. Distantly I hear a *pop-pop-pop* and the roar of the crowd: the finale. All of a sudden the sky is a crazy patchwork of colors, colors with no name, blue-green-pink and orange-purple-gold, as the fireworks come hard and fast.

There's a rustle to my left and muffled laughter; I turn and see a boy hitching up his pants and a girl, laughing, pulling him by the hand. I freeze, terrified for no reason that they'll think I was spying; then I'm alone again, and I move on.

The final display of fireworks goes up as I fight through the last of the growth; in its glow, a sudden shower of bright green that lights the underside of the clouds the same color as a murky ocean, I see that someone is standing by the Gateway, looking up at its high point.

My heart flips. Dara. Then the tendrils of green light fizzle out again and she becomes nothing but a dark brushstroke, a spiky silhouette against the landscape of steel.

I've covered half the distance between us before I realize that it isn't Dara – of course it isn't – the posture's all wrong, and the height, and the clothes, too. But by then it's too late to stop, and already I've half shouted so when he turns around – *he* – I draw up, horrified, with nothing to say and no excuse to give.

His face is very thin and covered with stubble that in the half-dark looks just like shadow smeared across his jaw. His eyes are sunken and yet weirdly overlarge, like pool balls dropped only halfway into their pockets. Even though I've never seen him before, I know him instantly.

'Mr Kowlaski,' I say reflexively. Maybe I need to name him. Otherwise seeing him, coming across him here, in this way, would be too awful. Like how Dara and I used to name the monsters in our closet so we wouldn't be so frightened of them, silly names that reduced their power: Timmy was one, and

Sabrina. Because there is something awful about him, something haggard and also haunted. It's as if he's looking not at me but at a photograph showing a terrible image.

Before he can say anything, Maude appears, shoving past me and immediately linking an arm through Mr Kowlaski's, as if they're partners at a square dance about to do-si-do. She must have been sent to intercept him. As soon as he starts to move, I can tell he's drunk. He's stepping extra carefully, like people only do when they're worried about seeming sober.

'Come on, Mr Kowlaski,' Maude says, sounding surprisingly cheerful. Funny how she only seems happy during a crisis. 'The show's over. The park will be closing soon. Did you drive here?' He doesn't answer her. 'How about a cup of coffee before you go?'

As they move past me, I have to turn away, hugging myself. His eyes are like two pits; and now I feel as if I'm the one who's seeing terrible things, seeing all the times I tried to help Dara, to save her, to keep her safe: the times I lied to Mom and Dad for her, scoured her room for Baggies full of white residue or green nubs, confiscated her cigarettes and then, relenting, gave them back when she put her arms around me and her chin on my chest and stared up at me through those silky-dark lashes; the times I found her passed out in the bathroom and brought her instead to bed, while she exhaled the sharp stink of vodka; the notes I forged for her, excusing her from gym or math class, so she wouldn't get in trouble for cutting; all the bargains I made with God, who I'm not sure I even believe in, when I knew that she'd gone out joyriding, drunk and high, with the random collection of freaks and losers who accumulated around her like a heavy snow, guys who bounced at clubs or managed sleazy bars and hung around high school girls because all the girls their age were too smart to talk to them. *If Dara gets home safe, I promise I'll never ask for anything again. So long as nothing bad happens to Dara, I promise to be extra good. And what happened at the Founders' Day Ball will never happen again.*

I swear, God. Please. So long as she's okay.

How stupid I was to think Dara would come, that she'd be pulled to me, magnet-like, the way she was when we were younger. She's probably out somewhere in East Norwalk, drunk and happy or drunk and unhappy or high, celebrating her birthday, letting some guy slip his hand between her legs. Maybe Parker *is* the guy.

By now, the fireworks are over, and the park is beginning to empty. Already I detect the action of the gravediggers – seven of them on shift to clean up after tonight, including Mr Wilcox himself – in the evidence they're leaving, of trash bags piled neatly by the gates and chairs stacked in high towers.

Two security guards are posted by the gates, making sure that the park clears out. The parking lot has emptied. The boys are gone from in front of Boom-a-Rang, though the air still has that lingering gun-smoke smell of firecrackers. When I finally climb back in Dara's car, I'm so tired I feel it through my whole body, a dull ache in all my joints and behind my eyes.

'Happy birthday, Dara,' I say out loud. I fish my phone from my pocket. No surprise, she never texted me back.

I don't know what makes me call her. A simple desire to hear her voice? Not exactly. Because I'm mad? Not exactly that, either – I'm too tired to be angry. Because I want to know whether I'm right, whether she simply forgot about dinner, whether even now she's sitting on Parker's lap, warm and tipsy and loud, and he has one arm around her waist, pressing his lips in between her shoulder blades?

Maybe.

As soon as the ringtone starts up in my ear, a secondary ring, slightly muffled, sounds in the car, so for a moment I can't tell which is which. I dig my hand in the space between the driver's seat and the door, close my fingers around cool metal, and unearth Dara's phone, which must have somehow gotten wedged there.

It's no surprise that she's been using the car when she isn't supposed to: Dara might not be the best student, but she gets an A+ in any subject that involves breaking rules. But it's weird, and worrying, that she doesn't have her phone. Mom used to joke that Dara should just have the thing surgically attached to her hand, and Dara always said that if scientists could figure out a way to do it, she'd be the first to sign up.

My finger hovers over the text message icon. I'm suddenly uneasy. One time, when I was in fifth grade, I was in the middle of a social studies test – I was filling in the countries of Europe, I remember, on a blank printout of a map – and had just reached Poland when I had the sudden, sharpest pain in my chest, like someone had put a hand around my heart and squeezed. And I knew, I felt, that something had happened to Dara. I didn't realize I'd stood up, knocking my chair backward, until everyone was staring and my teacher, Mr Edwards, told me to sit down.

I *did* sit down, because I had no way of explaining that something had happened. I switched the location of Germany and Poland and didn't even remember to label Belgium, but it didn't matter anyway; halfway through the test, the vice principal came to the door, her face pinched tight like the toe of a nylon stocking, and gestured for me to come with her.

During recess, Dara had attempted to climb the fence that separated the blacktop from the industrial complex on the other side: a factory that manufactured AC components. She'd made it all the way to the top before a teacher, spotting her, had called for her to stop; Dara, losing her footing, had fallen a dozen feet and landed with the blunt, rusted edge of a galvanized pipe, discarded for no apparent reason in the underbrush, lodged partway into her sternum. She was silent on the way to the hospital. She didn't even cry, just kept fingering the pipe and the spot of blood on her T-shirt as if it fascinated her, and the doctor managed to extract the metal successfully and sew her up so smoothly the scar was barely visible, and for weeks afterward she bragged about all the tetanus shots she had received.

Now, sitting in the car, the feeling returns to me like it did that day: the same horrible, squeezing pressure in my chest. And I know, I just *know*, that Dara's in trouble.

All along, I've been assuming she just blew us off tonight. But what if she didn't? What if something bad happened? What if she got drunk and passed out somewhere and woke up and has no way of getting home? What if one of her loser friends tried to scam on her and she ran off without her phone?

What if, what if, what if. The drumbeat of the past four years of my life.

I pull up Facebook. The photo on Dara's profile is an old one, from Halloween when I was fifteen, and Dara, Ariana, Parker, and I crashed a senior party, banking on the fact that everyone would be too drunk to notice. In it, Dara and I are hugging, cheek to cheek, red and sweaty and happy. I wish that photographs were physical spaces, like tunnels; that you could crawl inside them and go back.

There are dozens and dozens of birthday messages posted to her wall: *We love you always! Happy birthday! Save a shot for me wherever you're partying tonight!* She hasn't responded to any of them – unsurprising, since she's without her phone.

What now? I can't call her. I switch back to my phone and pull up Parker's number, thinking that, after all, he might be with her or at least know where she went. But his phone rings only twice before going to voicemail. The pressure is building, flattening out my lungs, as if the air is slowly leaching out of the car.

Even though I know she would kill me for looking through her messages, I pull up her texts, swiping quickly past the one I sent earlier and several in a row from Parker, not sure what I'm looking for, but sensing that I'm getting close to *something*. I find dozens of texts from numbers and names I don't recognize: pictures of Dara, eyes huge and pupils big and black as holes, at various parties I never knew about or was invited to. An unfocused shot – maybe a mistake? – of a guy's bare shoulder. I study it for a minute, wondering whether it's Parker, and then, deciding it isn't, move on.

The next text, and the pictures attached to it, make my heart stop.

This one is almost professional-grade, as if it had been styled and lighted. Dara is sitting on a red sofa in a room almost barren of furniture. There's an AC unit in one corner, and a window, although it's so coated in grime, I can't see beyond it. Dara is dressed in nothing but her underwear; her arms are stiff by her sides, so that her breasts, and the small dark spots of her nipples, are center frame. Her eyes are focused on something to the left of the camera and her head is tilted, like it often is when she's listening. I imagine, immediately, a person standing behind the camera – maybe more than one person – calling instructions to her.

Put your arms down, sweetheart. Show us what you got.

The next picture is a close-up: only her torso is visible. She's tilting her head back, eyes half-closed, sweat dampening her neck and clavicle.

Both pictures were sent from a phone number I don't recognize, an East Norwalk phone number, on March 26.

The day before the accident. I have the feeling of finally hitting ground after a long fall. The breath goes out of me and yet, weirdly, I feel a sense of relief, of finally touching solid earth, of knowing.

This is it: somehow, in these pictures, the mystery of the accident is contained, and the explanation for Dara's subsequent behavior, for the silences and disappearances.

Don't ask me how I know. I just do. If you don't understand that, I guess you've never had a sister.

dara's diary entry

Everyone's always accusing me of loving to be the center of attention. But you know what? Sometimes I wish I could just disappear.

I remember one time when I was little and Nick got mad because I broke her favorite music box, a gift from Mamu. I told her it was an accident, but it really wasn't. I'll admit it, I was jealous. Mamu hadn't given me anything. No big surprise there, right? Nick was always the favorite.

Afterward I felt bad, though. Really bad. I remember I ran away and hid in Parker's tree house with a plan to live up there for ever. Of course I got hungry after an hour or so and came down. I'll never forget how good it felt to see Mom and Dad walking the streets together with a flashlight, calling my name.

I guess that's the really nice thing about disappearing: the part where people look for you and beg you to come home.

nick

10:15 p.m.

A FIST HITS THE WINDOW AND I JUMP, LETTING OUT A YELP. A flashlight skates across the glass. The security guard gestures for me to roll down the window.

'You okay?' he says. I recognize him as one of the men who was standing by the gates, making sure everyone left in an orderly fashion. He probably has instructions to clear the lot, too. My eyes tick to the dashboard. I've been sitting in the car for more than twenty minutes.

'I'm fine,' I say. The guard looks as though he doesn't believe me. He angles a flashlight up to my face, practically blinding me, probably to check my pupils and make sure I'm not drunk or high. I manage to smile. 'Really. I was just leaving.'

'All right, then,' he says, rapping the outside of my car once with his knuckles, for emphasis. 'Just make sure you finish texting before you get on the road.'

I realize I'm still gripping Dara's phone in my hand. 'I

will,' I say, as he turns, satisfied, back toward the gates. I roll up the window again, twist the key in the ignition, punch on the AC. The security guard's words have given me an idea.

I pull up the East Norwalk number attached to the two almost-naked photographs and paste it into a new text. For a minute I sit there, debating, typing and erasing. Finally, I settle on a simple: *Hey. You around?*

It's a crazy gamble, a shot in the dark. I'm not even expecting a response. But almost immediately, Dara's phone dings. I feel a rush of adrenaline all the way to my fingertips.

Who is this?

I ignore that. *Was looking at our pictures again,* I write. And then: *They're pretty hot.* I wipe sweat from my forehead with the inside of my wrist.

For a minute, the phone stays silent. My heart is beating so hard, I can hear it. Then, just as I'm about to give up and put the car in drive, the phone buzzes twice.

Srsly who is this?

I've been unconsciously holding my breath. Now I exhale, a big rush of air, feeling a little like a balloon that has just been punctured.

Rationally, I know that the photographs probably don't mean anything. Dara got drunk, she took her clothes off, she let some creep snap some pictures, and now he doesn't even remember. End of story. I can't explain the feeling, nagging, persistent, that there's some connection here, a way of sewing up the story of the past four months and making sense of it.

It's the same feeling I get when I'm trying to remember the lyrics to a song that keeps looping through my head somewhere just out of reach.

I write DARA, all caps, and leave it at that.

One minute passes, then two. Even though the security guard's face is lost in darkness, I can tell he's watching me.

Ding.

You think this is a fucking joke?

Before I can figure out how to respond, another text comes in.

I don't know what u think ur playing at but u better be careful.

And then another.

This is serious shit whatever u know u better keep ur mouth shut or else!!!

The security guard is moving toward me again. I throw Dara's phone in the cup holder, hard, as if I can shatter it and shatter the messages there, too. I put the car in drive and find myself halfway up the coast before I even realize I've started for home. I'm going way too fast – sixty-five, according to the speedometer – and I slam on the brakes, blood thumping in my ears and air pounding outside my windows, mirroring the distant noise of the surf.

What does it mean?

You think this is a fucking joke?

I think of Dara the way I saw her earlier: boarding a bus, arms crossed, jumping at the sound of her name.

U better keep ur mouth shut or else!!!

What the hell has Dara gotten herself into now?

dara's diary entry

DEAR NICK,

I MADE UP A GAME.
IT'S CALLED: CATCH ME IF YOU CAN.
—D

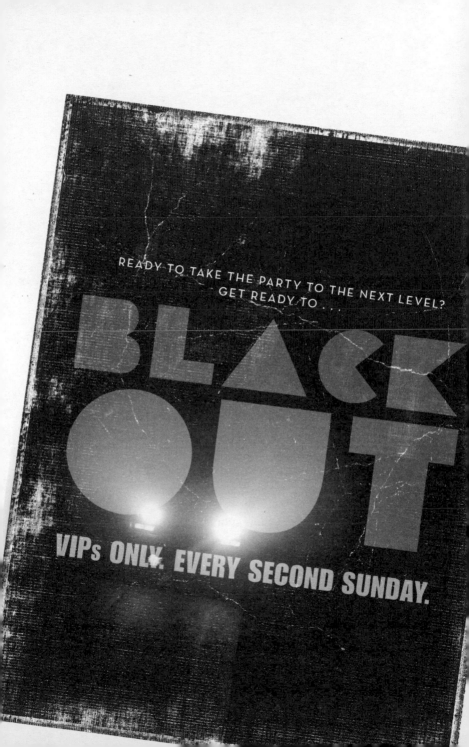

nick

10:35 p.m.

I MIGHT AS WELL HAVE CHUGGED A GALLON OF COFFEE. I FEEL ultra-wired, jumpy, and alert. On the drive home, I keep checking the rearview mirror, half expecting to see a stranger sitting in the backseat, leering at me.

As soon as I enter the house, I see that Aunt Jackie's bag is gone – she must have decided to go home after all. Mom has fallen asleep in the den, her legs entangled in the blankets: a sure sign of sleeping pills. The light from the TV casts the room in blue, sends shifting patterns over the walls and ceilings, and makes the whole scene look submerged. An orange-hued news anchor gazes seriously into the camera above a blazing red graphic that reads SNOW CONSPIRACY? A TWIST IN THE MADELINE SNOW CASE.

Onscreen, the news anchor is saying, 'We'll have more on the new reports from the Snows' neighbor, Susan Hardwell, after the break.' I turn off the TV, grateful for the sudden silence.

How many times have I heard it in the past week? When a person disappears, the first seventy-two hours are the most important.

I saw Dara just before dinner, only a few hours ago, boarding the bus. But she didn't have a bag with her, and she didn't have her phone. So where the hell could she have been going?

In Dara's room I switch on all the lights, feeling a little bit better, less anxious, once the room is revealed in all its mess and plainness. This time, I know exactly what I'm looking for. Despite all of Dara's whining about privacy, she's too lazy to ever hide things successfully, and I find her journal where it always is, at the very back of the smallest drawer in her rickety side table, behind a tangled mess of pens, old phone chargers, condoms, and gum wrappers.

I sit down on her bed, which groans awfully underneath me, as if protesting my trespassing, and open her journal on my lap. My palms are itchy, like they always are when I'm nervous. But I'm compelled by that same indescribable instinct that flattened me all those years ago during that stupid geography test. Dara's in trouble. Dara's been in trouble for a long time. And I'm the only one who can help her.

Dara's handwriting looks like it's trying to leap off the paper: the pages of the journal are packed, covered with scrawled notes, doodles, and random observations.

It happened, starts one, dating from early January. *Parker and I hooked up for real.*

I flip forward a week.

Hook-ups, break-ups, complaints about Mom, Dad, Dr Lichme, and me: it's all there, all the anger and triumph, all channeled into neatly intersecting lines of ink. Some of it I've seen before – I *did* once read her journal, after I found out from my friend Isha that she and Ariana had started in on coke – and I read her note to me afterward, taunting, about what had happened at the Founders' Day Ball. *I'm going to tell Mom and Dad their little angel isn't such an angel after all.*

If only she knew.

From February 15: *Happy Day After Valentine's Day. I'd like to take whoever invented this holiday out to the backyard for a good old-fashioned firing line. Better yet, just string up Cupid and fire arrows in his stupid fat ass.*

From February 28: *Parker's in love with somebody else.* That one makes my heart turn over a little.

And from March 2: *I guess that's the really nice thing about disappearing: the part where people look for you and beg you to come home.* I slow down when I reach March 26: the day the photographs were sent to her from the East Norwalk number, from the guy who warned me – who warned *Dara* – to keep her mouth shut. This entry is relatively short, only a few lines.

There's another party tonight!! Andre was right. It gets easier. Last time I worked for three hours and made over two hundred bucks in tips. The other girls are nice, but one of them warned me about getting too close to Andre. I think she's just jealous because he obviously likes me the best. He told me he's going to be producing a show for TV. Can you imagine what Nick would do if I had my own reality show? She would just die. Then Parker would feel like a real dipshit, wouldn't he?

I know that name, Andre. Dara mentioned an Andre to me months ago. She had pictures of him on her phone.

I flip forward another page. Dara's entry from the morning of the accident is even shorter.

Damn it. I really thought I was getting over him. But today I woke up feeling like shit.

Ariana says I should just go talk to Parker. I don't know.
Maybe I will. Maybe Lick Me was right. I just can't fake my way
out of this one.
    Or maybe I'm finally growing up.

Images come back to me from that night: the rain slick and
steel-colored on Parker's hood, and headlights cutting the world
into blocks of light and shadow. Dara's look of triumph, as if
she'd just crossed a finish line first.

Forward. The entries stop for a while, and I flip past several
blank pages. Dara shattered the bones in her right wrist in the
accident; she couldn't hold a pen or even a fork. The next entry
– the last one, from the looks of it – dates from yesterday, and
is written in all capital letters, like a sign, or something shouted.

DEAR NICK,

I MADE UP A GAME.
IT'S CALLED: CATCH ME IF YOU CAN.
–D

For a second I can do nothing but stare at it, stunned,
reading the message over and over, torn between equal feelings
of relief and anger. Anger wins. I slam the journal shut and
stand up, hurling it across the room, where it thuds against
the window and knocks an empty pencil cup from her desk
on the way down.

'You think this is a fucking game?' I say out loud, and then
feel a sudden chill, as if someone has blown air down my back.
That's almost exactly what Unknown said in response to my
text.

You think this is a fucking joke?

I stand up, kicking my way through piles of her crap, looking for anything out of place, anything that might be a clue about where she's gone and why. Nothing. Just the usual clothing and garbage, the same tornado-style chaos Dara leaves behind everywhere. There are four new cardboard boxes piled in the corner – I guess Mom finally asked her to pick up her shit – but they're empty. I kick one of them and have a short-lived burst of satisfaction when it sails across the room and thuds against the opposite wall.

I'm losing it.

I take a deep breath and, standing in the corner, look again at her room, trying to mentally overlay an image of the room I saw just a few days ago, like fitting slides together and seeing if something doesn't align. And then something clicks. There's a plastic bag at the foot of her bed I'm sure wasn't there earlier in the week.

Inside the bag is a random assortment of stuff: a curling iron, a travel-size bottle of hairspray, a sparkly thong I remove with my pinkie, not sure whether it's clean or dirty. Four business cards, all of them for random businesses like house painters or actuaries. I flip them all onto the bed, one by one, hoping to find some kind of message.

The last card is for a bar, Beamer's. I know the place. It's right off the 101, a half mile south of FanLand, and only a mile or so up the coast from where Dara and I had our accident.

I flip the card over, and right then the whole world sharpens and condenses, funnels down to a name, Andre, and a few numbers scratched in ballpoint. Again, I get that little twinge, like a hidden part of my brain is firing up.I know that number. I texted it less than two hours ago.

U better keep ur mouth shut or else!!!

Weirdly, I don't even feel afraid. I don't feel much of anything at all.

It's not even eleven, and the drive to Beamer's will take me less than twenty minutes.

Plenty of time.

nick

11:35 p.m.

AS SOON AS I PULL INTO THE PARKING LOT AT BEAMER'S, I'M disappointed. I was hoping to see another clue, an immediate sign of Dara's connection to this place. But Beamer's looks like any one of the dozens of bars that clutter East Norwalk, only lonelier: this close to Orphan's Beach, where the currents are vicious and deadly, visitors are fewer and so are businesses. Still, the parking lot is full of cars.

Flyers in the darkened windows advertise Ladies' Nights and drinks with names like Fuzzy Nipple and a VIP party uncreatively named Blackout. There's even a velvet rope in front of the glass doors, which is ridiculous considering there's no one waiting to get in, and the single patron who lingers in the parking lot, smoking a cigarette and talking on his phone, is wearing dirty jeans and a sleeveless Budweiser shirt.

I watch Budweiser stub his cigarette out in a bucket presumably provided for that purpose, exhaling smoke through his nose, dragon-style. I'm about to get out of the car and follow him when the door swings open and I see a bouncer, roughly the shape and size of a humpbacked whale, intercept Budweiser on his way in. Budweiser holds up his hand, probably showing him a stamp, and the bouncer withdraws.

I hadn't counted on needing ID. But of course I do. For a moment, a wave of exhaustion hits me and I think about turning around, angling the car back in the direction of home, leaving Dara to go to hell.

But there's a stubborn part of me that refuses to give in so quickly. Besides, Dara doesn't have a fake, at least as far as I know. She always bragged she didn't need one and could flirt her way into any bar.

If she can do it, I can do it, too.

I flip down the mirror, regretting now the plain scoop-neck tank top and shorts I changed into before leaving the house again, and the fact that I decided to skip anything but a little ChapStick and some mascara. I look pale, and young.

I twist around and reach into the backseat. Like Dara's room, the upholstery is covered in a thick layer of accumulated clothing and trash. It doesn't take me long to find a sequined tank top, some lip gloss, and even a cracked three-pack of dark eyeshadow. I smear on some dark color with a thumb, trying to remember what Dara always said the few times she convinced me to let her do my make-up, and I emerged from the bathroom unrecognizable and always vaguely uncomfortable, like she had slipped me into a whole different skin: Blend from the bottom, go darker in the crease.

I slick on some lip gloss, take my hair down from my ponytail and finger-comb it, and, after checking to make sure that the parking lot is empty of people, swap out tank tops. Dara's sequined tank top hangs so low that a bit of my bra – black, thankfully, and not the printed yellow one I usually wear with a coffee stain directly over my left nipple – peeks out from the top.

I check my reflection one last time and get a momentary shock. Dressed in Dara's clothes, wearing Dara's make-up, I look more like her than I would have thought possible.

I take a deep breath, grab my bag, and step out of the car. At least I changed out of my sneakers to go to dinner, knowing my dad would lecture me if I didn't. My gold gladiator sandals even have a teensy bit of a heel.

The bouncer materializes even before I can get a hand on the door, seemingly rising out of the dark murk beyond the glass panes like an underwater creature surfacing. A rush of sound accompanies him out the door: thudding hip-hop music, women laughing, the chatter of dozens of drunk people.

'ID,' he says, sounding bored. His eyes are at half-mast, low-lidded, like a lizard's.

I force a laugh. It sounds like someone's choking me with a garden hose. 'Really?' I lower my chin, the way Dara always does when she wants something, and blink up at him. But I can feel my left leg twitching. 'I'll be five minutes. Less. I just have to give my friend her wallet.'

'ID,' he repeats, like my words haven't even registered.

'Look,' I say. He's keeping the door open with one foot, and I can just make out a portion of the bar behind him, dimly illuminated by badly unseasonal Christmas lights. Several girls are huddled together over some drinks. Is one of them Dara? It's too dark to tell. 'I'm not here to drink, okay? I'm just looking for my friend. You can watch me. I'll be in and out.'

'No ID, no entry.' He jerks a thumb toward the sign posted on the door, which reads exactly that. Beneath it is another posted sign: NO SHOES, NO SHIRT, BIG PROBLEM.

'You don't understand.' Now I'm getting pissed. And for just a second – white walled inside that hot flash of anger – something clicks, and I get it, and I slip into her skin without meaning to. I toss my hair and reach into my back pocket, extracting the business card I found in Dara's room. 'Andre *invited* me to come.'

It's a huge gamble. I don't know who Andre is or whether he even works here. He might just be some random sleazeball Dara met at the bar. In the photo on Dara's phone, he was wearing a leather jacket and watching Dara with an expression I didn't like. He might have simply grabbed a card to write down his number.

But I'm coasting on instinct now, listening to a low hum of certainty buzzing somewhere deep in my brain. Why write down a number? Why not text it, or program it into Dara's phone directly? There's a message in these numbers, I'm sure of it: a secret code, an invitation, a warning.

The bouncer examines the card for what feels like an eternity, flipping it back to front, front to back, while I hold my breath, trying not to fidget.

When he looks at me again, something has changed – his eyes tick slowly over my face and down to my tits, and I fight the urge to cross my arms. He's no longer bored. He's *evaluating*.

'Inside,' he grunts. I wonder if his vocabulary is limited to the words he needs for the job: *ID, inside, no, entry*. He elbows the door open a little farther, so I just have room to slip by him. A blast of airconditioning greets me, and a heavy cloud of booze-smells. My stomach tightens.

What am I doing?

More importantly: What's *Dara* doing?

It's so loud, I miss what the bouncer says when he next speaks. But he puts a hand on my elbow and points, gesturing me to follow him toward the back.

The bar is crowded, mostly with guys who look at least a decade too old to be as loud and drunk as they are. There are padded red vinyl booths arranged on an elevated platform: one guy is groping his date while she sips a bright-pink drink from the largest cup I've ever seen. A DJ is blasting bad house music from one corner, but there are also four TVs mounted behind the bar and baseball playing on every one, as if Beamer's hasn't decided whether it wants to go for full-on Eurotrash club scene or sports bar. My danger alarm is going off the charts. There's something . . . *off* about the whole place, like it's not a real place but an imitation of a real place, a hastily constructed set piece meant to conceal something else.

I scan the crowd, looking for Dara or even someone who looks like a friend of Dara's. But all the women are older, mid-twenties at least. In her journal, Dara mentioned she was working for Andre. But all the waitresses, too, are older: strapped into micro miniskirts and tight tank tops with the Beamer's logo – two headlights I'm pretty sure are meant to look like nipples – emblazoned across their boobs, looking bored or overwhelmed or just annoyed.

I think of that picture of Dara on the couch, reclining, eyes glazed over, and my stomach knots up.

We move down a narrow hall that leads to the bathrooms. The walls are papered with multicolored flyers – *Wednesday Happy Hour! Fourth of July Bonanza! Ladies' Night Every Sunday!* and more of the strangely monochromatic signs advertising *Blackout* – and photographs. I'm half hoping I'll see a photo of Dara and half praying I won't. But there must be five hundred pictures on the wall, all of them practically identical – tan girls in tank tops aiming kissy-faces at the camera, guys grinning over tequila shots – and we're moving too quickly for me to make out more than a dozen faces, none of them hers.

At the end of the hall is a door marked PRIVATE. The bouncer raps twice and, in response to a muffled command I again don't hear, swings open the door. I'm surprised to see a woman sitting behind a desk, in an office cluttered with boxes full of plastic straws and bar napkins printed with the Beamer's logo.

'Casey,' the bouncer says. 'A girl for Andre.' After shepherding me inside, he immediately abandons us. The door seals out most of the noise from outside. Still, I can feel the pulsating bass rhythm, beating up through my feet.

'Sit down,' the woman – Casey – says, her eyes glued to a computer screen. 'Give me a second. This fucking system . . .' She works her keyboard like she's trying to punch it to death, then abruptly shoves her computer aside. She's probably forty, with brown hair streaked blond and a smudge of something – chocolate? – on her upper lip. She looks like a guidance counselor, except for her eyes, which are a vivid, unnatural shade of blue. 'Okay,' she says. 'What can I do for you? Let me guess.' Her eyes sweep over me, landing on my chest, like the bouncer's did. 'You're looking for a job.'

I decide my best bet is to say nothing. I just nod.

'You eighteen?' she says. I nod again. 'Good, good.' She looks relieved, as if I've passed a test. 'Because it's state law, you know. You have to be twenty-one to waitress, since we don't serve food. But for the private parties, we get to bend the rules.' She's speaking so fast, I'm having trouble keeping up. 'You'll have to fill out an application and a disclaimer, stating you're telling us the truth about your age.'

She slides a piece of paper across the desk to me. Conspicuously, she doesn't ask for my ID, and the 'application' just asks for my name, phone number, and email address, and to sign a statement guaranteeing that I'm of age. When I started work at FanLand, I thought they might ask for a DNA swab.

I hunch over the paper and act like I'm puzzling over it, when really I'm buying time and trying to figure out my next angle. 'I don't have any waitressing experience,' I say apologetically, as if it's just occurring to me. Behind Casey are a series of gray filing cabinets, some of them wedged open because their contents no longer fit. And I know that somewhere buried among all the files and invoices and cheesy Beamer's desktop mouse pads is Dara's application, the confident scrawl of her signature.

I'm now sure. She sat here, in this chair. Maybe she worked here, before the accident. And it's no coincidence that on the night of her birthday, she vanished without taking her cell phone. It all leads back to this place, to this office and to Casey with her bright smile and cold, dazzling eyes. To Andre. To those pictures and his threats.

You think this is a fucking joke?

I need to know.

Casey laughs. 'If you can walk and chew gum at the same time, you'll be fine. Like I said, we don't ask our hostesses to serve. It's against state law.' She leans back in her chair. 'How did you hear about us, by the way?'

She keeps her voice light, but I can sense a sharp undercurrent running beneath the words. For a split second, my mind goes totally blank; I haven't prepared a cover story, and I have no idea what, exactly, I'm supposed to know. I feel like I'm fumbling to grab something slick in cold water: all I get is a rough shape, blunt edges, no details at all.

I blurt, 'I met Andre at a party. He mentioned it.'

'Ah.' She seems to relax fractionally. 'Yeah, Andre's our GM and recruiter. He's in charge of our special events. I should warn you, though' – she leans forward again, crossing her hands on the desk, doing the concerned guidance counselor right before she drops the bomb, *You're failing chemistry, you didn't get into college* – 'we don't have any upcoming parties. I can't say, in all honesty, when we'll be up and running again.'

'Oh.' I do my best to look disappointed, even though I'm still not sure exactly what she means by *parties*. 'Why not?'

She smiles thinly. But her expression stays guarded. 'We're ironing out some kinks,' she says. 'Staffing problems.' She emphasizes the last word slightly, and I can't help but think of the message Andre sent me, or sent Dara: *u better keep ur mouth shut or else!!!*

Is Dara one of his problems?

For a second, I imagine that Casey knows exactly who I am and what I've come for. Then, mercifully, she looks away, returning her attention to the computer. 'I won't bore you with the details,' she says. 'If you want to go ahead and write down your phone number, we'll give you a call when we need you.' She jerks her head toward the one-page application, which I have yet to fill out, and just like that, I know I've been dismissed.

But I can't go yet – not when I've learned nothing.

'Is Andre here?' I say desperately, before I've made the decision to ask. 'Can I talk to him?'

She has gone back to typing. Now she stiffens, her fingers hovering over the keys. 'You can talk to him.' This time when she looks at me, she squints, as if seeing me from a far distance. I look away, blushing, hoping she won't see the resemblance to Dara; now I regret making myself up like her. 'But he'll tell you the same thing I did.'

'Please,' I say, and then, so she won't suspect how desperate I am, quickly add, 'it's just – I really need the money.'

She scrutinizes me for a second longer. Then, to my surprise, she laughs. 'Don't we all?' she says, winking. 'Okay, then. You know where to find him? Down the stairs across from the ladies'. But don't say I didn't warn you. And don't forget to drop off your application with me before you leave.'

'I won't,' I say, standing up so quickly the chair screeches against the floor. 'I mean, thanks.'

Back in the hall, I pause for a moment, disoriented in the sudden darkness. Up ahead, the disco light is whirling, sending showers of purple light around a mostly empty dance floor. The music is so loud it makes my head hurt. Why would anyone come here? Why did *Dara* come here?

I close my eyes and think back to the days before the accident. Weirdly the only thing that comes is an image of Parker's car, and that fogged-up windshield, the rain fizzing on the glass. *We didn't mean to* . . .

I open my eyes again. Two girls spill out of the bathroom, holding hands and giggling. As soon as they start down the hall, I slip after them, noticing for the first time a dark alcove immediately across from the LADIES sign, and stairs leading down to the basement.

The stairs corkscrew around a small, bare landing and abruptly turn from wood to concrete. Another few steps, and I'm deposited in a long, unfinished hallway with cinder-block walls and a paint-splattered concrete floor. The whole basement feels forgotten and disused. In a horror film, this would be where the blond girl goes to die in the opening scene.

I shiver in the sudden chill. It's cold down here and smells like all basements, like moisture barely contained. Naked bulbs encased in mesh hang from the ceiling, and the music is nothing but a dull thudding, like a monster's distant heartbeat. Boxes are heaped at the far end of the hallway, and through one half-open door I see what must be the staff changing room: grim gray lockers, several pairs of sneakers lined up under a bench, and a cell phone buzzing forlornly, performing a quarter-turn rotation on the wood when it does. I get the sudden, prickly feeling of being watched, and I spin around, half expecting someone to jump out at me.

No one. Still, my heart rate won't return to normal.

I'm about to return upstairs, thinking I must have misunderstood Casey's directions, when voices down the hall crest sharply, suddenly, over the music. Even though I don't hear a single word, I immediately know: an argument.

I continue down the hall, moving carefully, holding my breath. With every step the itch in my skin gets worse, as if invisible people are leaning forward to breathe on me. I remember, then, the time Parker dared Dara and me to walk across the graveyard off Cressida Circle at night when we were kids.

'But go quietly,' he said, dropping his voice, 'or they'll reach out and—' He seized me suddenly by the waist and I screamed. Afterward he couldn't stop laughing; still, I never did walk across the graveyard, too afraid that if I did, a hand would reach out and grab me, pulling me down into the rotten earth.

I pass another door, this one gaping open to reveal a dingy bathroom with caulk oozing like thick caterpillars between cracks in the wall. By now the voices are louder. There's a final door, this one closed, a few feet farther on. This must be Andre's office.

The voices abruptly go silent and I freeze, holding my breath, wondering if I've been detected, debating whether I should knock or turn around and run.

Then a girl says, quietly but very clearly, 'The police grilled me for, like, four hours. And I didn't have anything to tell them. I *couldn't* tell them anything.'

A male voice – *Andre* – replies, 'So what the hell are you worried about?'

'She's my best friend. She was drunk. She doesn't even remember getting home. And her *sister's* missing. Of course I'm fucking worried.'

My heart stops beating for the space of a breath, a name: *Madeline Snow. They're talking about Madeline Snow.*

'Lower your voice. And don't feed me some horseshit. You're trying to cover your ass. But you knew what you were getting into when you signed up.'

'You said everything would be private. You said no one would know.'

'I told you to lower your voice.'

But it's too late. Her voice is rising in pitch like steam being forced through a kettle. 'So what did happen that night, huh? Because if you know something, you have to talk. You have to tell me.'

There's a moment of silence. My heart is drumming hard in my throat, like a fist trying to punch its way out.

'Fine.' Her voice is shaking now, skipping registers. 'Fine. Then don't tell me. I guess you can just wait until the police knock down your door.'

The door handle rattles and I jump backward, pressing myself against the wall, as if it will keep me invisible. Then there's a scraping noise, the sound of a chair jumping backward, and the door handle falls still.

Andre says, 'I don't know what the hell happened to that little girl.' The way he says *little girl* makes me feel sick, like I've accidentally eaten something rotten. 'But if I did know – if I *do* know – you really think it's a smart idea to come around here playing Nancy Drew? You think I don't know how to make problems disappear?'

There's a short pause. 'Are you threatening me? Because I'm not afraid of you.' This last part is obviously a lie. Even through the door, I can hear that the girl's voice is shaking.

'Then you're dumber than I thought,' Andre says. 'Now get the fuck out of my office.'

Before I can retreat or react, the door swings open so hard it cracks against the wall, and a girl comes rushing out. Her head is down, but still I recognize her immediately from the paper: the pale skin, the straight fringe of black bangs, and the red lipstick, like she's auditioning for a part in a movie about a vampire from the 1920s. It's Sarah Snow's best friend, the girl who supposedly accompanied her to get ice cream the night Madeline disappeared. She pushes past me roughly and doesn't even stop to apologize, and before I can call out to her, she's gone, darting animal-like up the stairs.

I want to go after her, but Andre has already seen me.

'What do you want?' His eyes are bloodshot. He looks tired, impatient. It's him: the guy from the photo, leather-jacket guy. *He's nobody,* Dara said, months ago. *They're all nobodies. They don't matter.*

But she was wrong about this one.

I try to see him as Dara might have. He's older, maybe early twenties, and his hair is already thinning, although he gels it stiff to conceal the fact. He's good-looking in an obvious way, like someone who spends a lot of time flossing. His lips are too thin.

'Casey sent me down here,' I blurt. 'I mean, I was looking for the bathroom.'

'What?' Andre squints at me. He takes up most of the doorway. He's big – at least six-four – with hands like meat cleavers.

My heart is still going, hard. *He knows what happened to Madeline Snow.* It's not a suspicion. It's a certainty. *He knows what happened to Madeline Snow and he knows where Dara is and he takes care of problems.* It suddenly occurs to me that no one would hear me if I screamed. The music upstairs is too loud.

'You looking for a job?' Andre says, when I don't respond, and I realize that I'm still holding the stupid application.

'Yes. No. I mean, I was.' I shove the paper into my bag. 'But Casey said you guys aren't doing parties right now.'

Andre's watching me sideways, like a snake watching a mouse move closer and closer. 'We're not,' he says. His eyes go over my whole body, slowly, like a long, careful touch. He smiles then: a megawatt, movie-star smile, a smile to make people say *yes*. 'But how about you come in and sit down? Never know when we're going to start up again.'

'That's okay,' I say quickly. 'I don't – I mean, I was kind of looking for a position right now.'

Andre's still smiling, but something shifts behind his eyes. It's like the *friendly* switch has just cut off. Now his smile is cold, scrutinizing, suspicious. 'Hey,' he says, pointing a finger at me, and the certainty yawns open in my stomach: He recognizes me, he knows I'm Dara's sister, he knows I came to find her. All this time, he's been screwing with me. 'Hey. You look familiar. Don't I know you?'

I don't answer. I can't. He *knows*. Without meaning to move, I take off down the hall, walking as quickly as I can without breaking into a run, taking the stairs two at a time. I burst onto the dance floor, pinballing off a guy dressed in a dark purple suit who reeks of cologne.

'Why the hurry?' he calls after me, laughing.

I dodge a small knot of girls swaying drunkenly in heels, squealing along with the song lyrics. Luckily, the bouncer has temporarily abandoned his post — maybe it's too late for new arrivals. I push out into the thick night air, heavy with moisture and salt, taking deep and grateful breaths, like someone emerging from underwater.

The lot is still packed with cars, a tight Tetris formation, bumper-to-bumper — too many cars for the number of people inside. For one disorienting second I can't remember where I parked. I fish my keys from my bag, clicking the car open, feeling reassured when I hear the familiar beep and see head-lights blink expectantly at me. I jog toward the car, weaving between cars.

Suddenly I'm blinded by the sweep of headlights. A small, dark VW cuts by me, spitting gravel, and as it passes under-neath the light I see Sarah Snow's friend hunched behind the wheel. Her name, heard or read a dozen times in the past ten days, returns to me suddenly. *Kennedy*.

I thud a hand down on her trunk before she can fully bypass me. 'Wait!'

She slams on the brakes. I circle around to the driver's side, keeping one hand on her car the whole time, as if it will prevent her from driving away. 'Wait.' I haven't even planned what I'm going to say. But she has answers; I know she does. 'Please.' I place my hand flat on the window. She jerks backward an inch, like she's expecting me to reach through the glass and hit her. But after a second, she buzzes down the window.

'What?' She's holding on to the wheel with both hands, as if she's afraid it might jump out of her hands. 'What do you want?'

'I know you lied about the night Madeline disappeared.' The words are out of my mouth before I know I've even been thinking them. Kennedy inhales sharply. 'You and Sarah came here.'

It's a statement, not a question, but Kennedy nods, a movement so small I almost miss it.

'How did you know?' she says in a whisper. Her expression turns fearful. 'Who are you?'

'My sister.' My voice cracks. I swallow down the taste of sawdust. I have a thousand questions, but can't make a single one come into focus. 'My sister works here. Or at least, she used to work here. I think – I think she's in trouble. I think something bad may have happened to her.' I'm watching Kennedy's face for signs of recognition or guilt. But she's still staring up at me with huge, hollowed eyes, as if *I'm* the one to be afraid of. 'Something like what happened to Madeline.'

Immediately I know it was the wrong thing to say. Now she doesn't look afraid. She looks angry.

'I don't know anything,' she says firmly, as if it's a line she's been practicing repeatedly. She starts to buzz up the window. 'Just leave me alone.'

'Wait.' Out of desperation, I stick my hand in the narrowing gap between the car door and the window. Kennedy lets out a hiss of irritation, but at least she rolls the window down again. 'I need your help.'

'I told you. I don't *know* anything.' She's losing it again, like she did downstairs in Andre's office. Her voice hitches higher, wobbling over the words. 'I left early that night. I thought Sarah had gone home. She was drunk. That's what I thought, when I came into the parking lot and saw the car door hanging open

– that Sarah had been too wasted to remember to close it. That she'd taken Maddie home in a cab.'

I imagine the car, the open door, the empty backseat. Light spilling from Beamer's just like it is tonight, the muffled thud of music, the distant crash of waves. Up the street, the peaked roof of an Applebee's, a few low-rent condominiums clinging to the shore, a diner and a surf shop. Across the street: a greasy clam shack, a former T-shirt shop, now in foreclosure. Everything is so normal, so relentlessly the *same* – it's almost impossible to believe in all the bad things, the tragedies, the dark fairy-tale twists.

One second she was there; the next she was gone.

Without realizing it, I've been holding on to the car as if it will help me keep on my feet. To my surprise, Kennedy reaches out and grips my hand. Her fingers are icy.

'I didn't know.' Even though she's whispering, this is it: the high note, the crescendo. 'It wasn't my fault. *It wasn't my fault.*'

Her eyes are huge and dark, mirrors of the sky. For a second we stand there, only inches apart, staring at each other, and I know that in some way, we understand each other.

'It wasn't your fault,' I say, because I know that this is what she wants – or needs – me to tell her.

She withdraws her hand, sighing a little, like someone who's been walking all day and finally gets to sit.

'Hey!'

I whip around and freeze. Andre has just pushed out of the front doors. Backlit, he seems to be made wholly of shadow. 'Hey, you!'

'Shit.' Kennedy twists around in her seat. 'Go,' she says to me, her voice low, urgent. Then the window zips up and she guns it, her tires skidding a little on the gravel. I have to jump backward to keep from getting crushed; I bang my shin on a license plate, feel a dull nip of pain in my leg.

'Hey, you. Stop!'

Panic makes me slow. I skid across the lot, regretting my sandals now. My body feels unwieldy, bloated and foreign, like in those nightmares where you try to run and find you haven't gone anywhere.

Andre is fast. I can hear his footsteps pounding on the gravel as he ricochets between parked cars.

I reach the car at last and hurl myself inside. My fingers are shaking so badly it takes me three tries to get the keys in the ignition. But I do, finally, and wrench the gear into reverse.

'Stop.' Andre slams up against my window, palms flat, face contorted with rage, and I scream. I punch down on the gas, whipping away from him even as he drums a fist against my hood. 'Stop, damn it!'

I throw the gear into drive, cutting the wheel to the left, my palms slick with sweat even though my whole body is freezing. Little whimpers are working their way out of my throat, spasms of sound. He makes a final lunge at me, as if to throw himself in front of the car, but I'm already pulling away, bumping onto Route 101 and flooring it, watching the speedometer slowly tick upward.

Come on come on come on.

I half expect him to appear again on the road. But I check the rearview mirror and see nothing but empty highway; and then the road curves and bears me away from Beamer's, away from Andre, toward home.

nick

12:35 a.m.

I EXIT THE HIGHWAY IN SPRINGFIELD, WHERE DARA AND I USED TO take music lessons before our parents realized we had less than no talent, and zigzag through the streets, still paranoid that Andre might be pursuing me. Finally I park in the lot behind an all-night McDonald's, reassured by the motion of the employees behind the counters, and the sight of a young couple eating burgers in a booth by the window, laughing.

I pull out my phone and do a quick search of the Madeline Snow case.

The most recent results pop up first, a stream of new blog posts, comments, and articles.

What Does the Snow Family Know? The first article I click on was posted to the *Blotter* only a few hours ago, at 10:00 p.m.

New questions plague the Madeline Snow investigation, it reads.

> *Police have recently turned up evidence that Sarah Snow's statement about the night of her sister's disappearance may be*

flawed, or even fabricated. According to the Snows' neighbor,
Susan Hardwell, Sarah Snow didn't return home until nearly
five o'clock that morning. When she did, she was obviously
intoxicated.

  'She drove right up on my lawn,' Hardwell told me, indicating
an area of churned-up grass by the mailbox. 'That girl's been
trouble for years. Not like the little one. Madeline was an angel.'
  So where was Sarah all that time? And why did she lie?

I click out of the article, wipe my palms against my jeans. It
fits with what Kennedy told me about Sarah: she was drinking
the night her sister disappeared, maybe at one of Andre's mysterious
'parties.' I keep scrolling through the results and pull up an article
about Nicholas Sanderson, the man who'd briefly been questioned
about Madeline's disappearance and then quickly exonerated, not
totally sure what I'm looking for, but full of a vague, buzzing
sense that I'm getting closer, circling around an enormous truth,
bumping into it without fully grasping its shape.

I can barely hold my phone still. My hands are still shaking.
I read half an article before realizing I've been processing only
one out of every few words.

  Police never formally arrested Mr Sanderson, nor did
  they give a reason for his questioning or subsequent release.
  Mr Sanderson's wife had no comment . . .
    '. . . but we're confident that we'll soon reach a
  breakthrough in the case,' stated Chief Lieutenant Frank
  Hernandez of the Springfield PD.

Beneath the article are twenty-two comments. *Let's hope so,*
reads the first one, presumably in response to Lieutenant
Hernandez's last statement.

The pigs are worse than useless. Not worth the tax dollars spent on their pensions, wrote someone named Freebird337.

Someone else had commented on this comment: *People like you make me want to get my gun, and if there are no cops to catch me, maybe I will.*

And below that, Anonymous had written: *he likes young girls*

I stare at those four words over and over: *he likes young girls.* No capitalizations, no punctuation, as if whoever sat down to type had to do it as quickly as possible. There's a sick, twisting feeling in my stomach, and I suddenly realize I'm sweating. I punch on the AC, too scared to roll down the windows, imagining that if I do, a dark hand might come out of nowhere, reaching in to choke me with a monster grip.

It's nearly 1:00 a.m., but I pull up my home number anyway. More and more, I'm convinced that Dara stumbled onto something dangerous, something involving Andre and Sarah Snow and Kennedy and maybe even Nicholas Sanderson, whoever the hell he is. Maybe Dara figured out that Andre was responsible for what happened to Madeline.

Maybe he decided to make sure she kept her mouth shut.

I press my phone to my ear, my cheek damp with sweat. After a while, my home answering machine clicks on – Dara's voice, tinny and unexpected, asking the caller to *speak now or forever hold your peace.* I quickly hang up and try again. Nothing. My mom's probably passed out cold.

I try my dad's cell instead, but the call goes straight to voicemail, a sure sign that Cheryl has spent the night. I click off the call, cursing, shoving a sudden mental image of Cheryl, nipped and tucked and freckled, walking around my dad's house naked.

Focus.

What next? I have to talk to *someone.*

A cop car has just pulled into the McDonald's, and two guys in uniform lumber out, laughing about something, One of them has a hand looped into his belt next to his gun, like he's trying to draw attention to it. Suddenly my next move is obvious. I check my phone again to verify the name: Chief Lieutenant Frank Hernandez, the officer in charge of the Madeline Snow case.

My phone is protesting its low battery, flashing a weak warning light in my direction when I make the last turn indicated by my GPS app and arrive abruptly at the police station, a hulking stone building that looks like a child's idea of an old prison. The precinct is set back on a small parking lot, which someone has attempted to make less bleak by inserting various strips of grass and narrow, dirt-filled garden plots. I park on the street instead.

Springfield is four times the size of Somerville, and even at 1:00 a.m. on a Thursday, the police station is buzzing: the doors hiss open and shut, admitting or releasing cops, some of them hauling in doubled-over drunks or kids high on something or sullen-eyed, tattooed men who look as appropriate to the landscape as those pathetic flower beds.

Inside, high fluorescent lights illuminate a large office space, where a dozen desks are fitted at angles to one another and thickly roped cables snake from computer to computer. There are stacks of paper *everywhere*, in-boxes and outboxes overflowing, as if a blizzard of form work had recently passed through and then settled. It's surprisingly loud. Phones trill every few seconds, and there's a TV going somewhere. I'm struck by the same feeling I had earlier, standing in the Beamer's parking lot and trying to imagine Madeline Snow vanishing in full view of the Applebee's: impossible that dark things bump up against the everyday, that they exist side by side.

'Can I help you?' A woman is sitting behind the front desk, her black hair slicked into so severe a bun it looks like a giant spider clinging desperately to her head.

I take a step forward and lean over the desk, feeling embarrassed without knowing why. 'I – I need to speak to Lieutenant Frank Hernandez.' I keep my voice low. Behind me, a man is sleeping sitting up, his head bobbing to an inaudible rhythm, one wrist handcuffed to a chair leg. A group of cops walk by, rapid-patter talking about a baseball game. 'It's about Madeline Snow.'

The woman's eyebrows – plucked to near invisibility – shoot up a fraction of an inch. I'm worried she'll question me further or refuse or – the possibility occurs to me only now – tell me that he's gone home for the night.

But she does none of those things. She picks up the phone, an ancient black beast that looks like it was salvaged from a junkyard sometime in the last century, punches in a code, and speaks quietly into the receiver. Then she stands up, sliding sideways a little to accommodate her belly, revealing for the first time that she is pregnant.

'Come on,' she says. 'Follow me.'

She leads me down a hallway made narrow by file cabinets, many of them with drawers partially open, crammed with so many files and papers (ever more paper) they look like slack-jawed monsters displaying rows of crooked teeth. The wallpaper is the weird yellow of smoked cigarette stubs. We pass a series of smaller rooms and move into an area of glassed-in offices, most of them empty. The whole layout of the place gives the impression of a bunch of cubic fishbowls.

She stops in front of a door marked CHIEF LIEUTENANT HERNANDEZ. Hernandez – I recognize him from photographs online – is gesturing to something on his computer screen. Another policeman, his hair so pale red it looks like a new flame, leans heavily on the desk, and Hernandez angles the monitor slightly to give him a better view.

I go hot, then cold, as if I've been burned.

The woman knocks and pops open the door without waiting for a response. Instantly Hernandez adjusts the computer monitor, concealing it from view. But it's too late. I've already seen rows of pictures, all those girls dressed in bikini tops or no tops at all, lying or sitting or passed out on a vivid red couch – all those pictures taken of the same room where Dara was photographed.

'Someone to see you,' the receptionist says, jerking a thumb in my direction. 'She says it's about Madeline Snow.' She pronounces the words almost guiltily, as if she's saying a bad word in church. 'What'd you say your name was, sweetheart?'

I open my mouth, but my voice is tangled somewhere behind my tonsils. 'Nick,' I finally say. 'Nicole.'

Hernandez nods at the redheaded policeman and he straightens up immediately, responding to the unspoken signal.

'Give me a minute,' Hernandez says. In person, he looks tired and *rumpled*, almost, like a blanket that's been washed too many times. 'Come in,' he says to me. 'Have a seat. You can just go ahead and stack those anywhere.' The chair pulled up across from his desk is piled with manila files.

The redheaded cop gives me a curious look as he slips by me, and I catch a brief whiff of cigarette smoke and, weirdly, bubblegum. The receptionist withdraws, closing the door, leaving me alone with Hernandez.

I still haven't moved. Hernandez looks up at me. His eyes are bloodshot. 'All right then,' he says lightly, as if we're old friends, sharing a joke. 'Don't sit if you don't want to.' He leans back in his chair. 'You have something to tell me about the Snow disappearance, you said?'

He's being nice enough, but the way he asks the question makes it clear that he doesn't think I'll have anything *important* to tell him. This is a question he's asked a dozen times, maybe a hundred, when some random woman looking for attention comes in to accuse her ex-husband of abducting Madeline, or a random truck driver en route to Florida claims to have seen a blond girl acting strange at a rest stop.

'I think I know what happened to Madeline,' I say quickly, before I can second-guess myself. 'And those pictures you were looking at? I know where they were taken.'

But as soon as I say the words, it occurs to me that at Beamer's I didn't see a room like the one pictured in Dara's photographs. Could I have missed a door somewhere, or a secondary staircase?

Hernandez's right hand tightens momentarily on the armrest. But he's a good cop. He doesn't otherwise flinch. 'You do, do you?' Even his voice betrays no signs, one way or the other, about whether or not he believes me. Abruptly, to my surprise, he stands up. He's a lot taller than I expected – at least six-three. Suddenly the room constricts, as if the walls are shrink-wrap grabbing for my skin. 'How about some water?' he says. 'You want some water?'

I'm desperate to talk. With every second it seems as if the memory of what happened at Beamer's might simply disappear, evaporating like liquid. But my throat is dust-dry, and as soon as Hernandez suggests water, I realize I'm desperately thirsty. 'Yeah,' I say. 'Sure.'

'Make yourself at home,' he says, indicating the chair again.

This time I recognize not just an invitation, but an order. He moves the pile of file folders himself, dumping them unceremoniously onto the windowsill, already mounded with papers, creating a landslide effect. 'I'll be right back.'

He disappears into the hall and I sit down, my bare thighs sticky on the fake leather seat. I wonder if it was a mistake to have come, and whether Hernandez will believe anything I say. I wonder if he'll send out a search party for Dara.

I wonder if she's all right.

He reappears a minute later, carrying a small bottle of water, room temperature. Still, I drink eagerly. He takes a seat again, leaning forward on the desk with his arms crossed. Outside the glassed-in office walls, the redheaded cop goes by, consulting a file, his mouth pursed as if he's whistling.

'Hate this fucking place,' Hernandez says, when he catches me staring. I'm surprised to hear him say *fucking*, and wonder if he did it to make me like him more. It works, a little. 'It's like living in a fishbowl. All right, then. What do you know about Madeline?'

In his absence, I've had time to think about what I want to say. I take a deep breath.

'I think . . . I think her older sister was working at a place called Beamer's on the shore,' I say. 'I think my sister worked there, too.'

Hernandez looks disappointed. 'Beamer's?' he says. 'The bar off Route 101?' I nod. 'They were waitressing there?'

'Not waitressing,' I say, remembering how the woman, Casey, had laughed when I told her I had no experience. *If you can walk and chew gum at the same time, you'll be fine.* 'Something else.'

'What?' He's watching me intently now, like a cat about to pounce on a chew toy.

'I'm not sure,' I admit. 'But—' I take a deep breath. 'But it might have to do with those photographs. I don't know.' I'm getting confused now, losing the thread. Somehow it comes down to Beamer's and that red sofa. But there was no red sofa in Beamer's, at least no red sofa that looked like the one in the photographs. 'Madeline didn't just disappear into thin air, did she? Maybe she saw something she wasn't supposed to see. And now my sister . . . She's gone, too. She left me a note—'

He straightens up, hyperalert. 'What kind of note?'

I shake my head. 'It was a kind of challenge. She wanted me to come find her.' Seeing his confusion, I add, 'She's like that. *Dramatic*. But why would she run away on her own birthday? Something bad happened to her. I can feel it.' My voice cracks and I take another long sip of water, swallowing back the spasm in my throat.

Hernandez turns businesslike. He grabs a notepad and a pen, which he uncaps with his teeth. 'When was the last time you saw your sister?' he asks.

I debate whether to tell Hernandez that I saw Dara earlier in the evening, boarding a bus, but decide against it. He'll no doubt tell me I'm being paranoid, that she's probably out with friends, that I have to wait twenty-four hours before filing a report. Instead I say, 'I don't know. Yesterday morning?'

'Spell her name for me.'

'Dara. Dara Warren.'

His hand freezes, like it has temporarily hit an invisible glitch. But then he smoothly writes the remainder of her name. When he looks up again, I notice for the first time that his eyes are a dark, stormy gray. 'You're from . . . ?'

'Somerville,' I say, and he nods, as if he suspected it all along.

'Somerville,' he repeats. He makes a few more notes on his notepad, angling the paper so I can't see what he's writing. 'That's right. I remember. You were in a bad accident this spring, weren't you?'

I take a deep breath. Why does everyone always mention the accident? It's like it has become my single most important feature, a defining trait, like a lazy eye or a stutter. 'Yeah,' I say. 'With Dara.'

'Two of my men took the call. That was Route 101, too, wasn't it? Down by Orphan's Beach.' He doesn't wait for me to answer. Instead he writes another few words and tears off the sheet of paper, folding it neatly. 'Bad spot of road, especially in the rain.'

I tighten my hands on the armrests. 'Shouldn't you be looking for my sister?' I say, knowing I sound rude and not caring. Besides, even if I wanted to answer his questions, I couldn't.

Luckily he lets it go. He places both fists on the desk to stand up, sliding his bulk away from the desk. 'Give me a minute,' he says. 'Wait here, all right? You want another water? A soda?'

I'm getting impatient. 'I'm fine,' I say.

He gives me a pat on the shoulder as he moves past me to the door, as if we're suddenly buddy-buddy. Or maybe he just feels bad for me. He disappears into the hallway, shutting the door behind him. Through the glass, I watch him intercept the same redheaded cop in the hall. Hernandez passes him the note, and the two of them exchange a few words too quiet for me to hear. Neither of them looks at me – I get the impression this is deliberate. After a minute, both of them move off down the hall out of sight.

It's hot in the office. There's a window AC spitting lukewarm air into the room, fluttering papers on Hernandez's desk. With every passing minute, my impatience grows, that itchy, crawling sense that something is terribly wrong, that Dara's in trouble, that we need to *stop* it. Still, Hernandez hasn't come back. I stand up, shoving the chair back from the desk, too antsy to remain sitting.

Hernandez's notepad – the one he scribbled on while I was speaking – is sitting out on his desk, the top sheet faintly imprinted with words from the pressure of his pen. Seized by the impulse to see what he wrote, I reach over and grab it, casting a quick glance over my shoulder to make sure that Hernandez isn't coming.

Some of the writing is illegible. But very clearly I see the words: *call parents* and, beneath that, *emergency*.

Anger flares inside of me. He didn't listen. He's wasting time. My parents can't do anything to help – they don't *know* anything.

I replace the notepad and move to the door, stepping out into the hall. From the front office comes the burble of conversation and ringing telephones. I don't see Hernandez anywhere. But, coming toward me, a huge tote bag slung over one shoulder, is a woman I *do* recognize. It takes me a second to call up her name: Margie something, the reporter who has been covering the Madeline Snow case for the *Shoreline Blotter* and has been all over local TV.

'Wait!' I shout. She obviously hasn't heard me and keeps walking. 'Wait!' I call, a little louder. A cop, bleary-eyed, looks up at me from another glassed-in office, his expression suspicious. I keep going. 'Please. I need to talk to you.'

She pauses with one hand on the door that leads out to the parking lot, scanning the room to see who was speaking, then has to sidestep as a cop enters from outside, propelling a lurching drunk in front of him. The man leers at me and drawls something I can't make out – it sounds like *Merry Christmas* – before the cop directs him down another hallway.

I catch up to Margie, feeling breathless for no reason. In the glass doors, our reflections have the look of cartoon ghosts: big dark hollows for eyes, sheet-white faces.

'Have we met?' Her eyes are quick, assessing, but she pastes a smile on her face.

The receptionist behind the desk, the one who led me to Hernandez, is watching us, frowning. I angle my back to her.

'No,' I say, in a low voice. 'But I can help you. And you can help me, too.'

Her face betrays no emotion – no surprise, no excitement. 'Help me how?'

She studies me for a minute as if debating whether or not I can be trusted. Then she jerks her head to the right, indicating I should follow her outside, away from the watchful gaze of the receptionist. It's a relief to be out of the stale air of the police station, and its smell of burnt coffee and alcohol breath and desperation.

'How old are you?' she asks, turning businesslike as soon as we're standing on the curb.

'Does it matter?' I fire back.

She snaps her fingers. 'Nick Warren. Is that right? From Somerville.'

I don't bother asking her how she knows me. 'So are you going to help me or not?'

She doesn't answer directly. 'Why are you so interested?'

'Because of my sister,' I reply. If she can dodge a question, so can I. She *is* a reporter, of sorts – and I don't know that I want a story about Dara blowing up in the *Blotter*, not yet. Not until we know more. Not until we have no other choice.

She makes a grabbing motion with her hands – like *all right, show me what you've got.*

So I tell her about my trip to Beamer's and the conversation I overheard outside Andre's office. I tell her that I'm pretty sure that Sarah Snow was working for Andre, doing something illegal. As I talk, her face changes. She believes me.

'It fits,' she murmurs. 'We know Sarah didn't come home until almost five a.m. on Monday. She lied about it initially. She was scared of getting in trouble.'

'What if Madeline Snow saw something she wasn't supposed to?' I say. 'What if Andre decided to . . . ?' I trail off. I can't bring myself to say *get rid of her.*

'Maybe,' Margie says, but frowns, unconvinced. 'It's a stretch. The cops know all about Beamer's. But they've never pinned anything on Andre – nothing major, anyway. A few fines here and there from the health department. And last year an eighteen-year-old came in with a fake ID and then had to get her stomach pumped. But murdering a nine-year-old child?' She sighs. Suddenly she looks twenty years older. 'What do you want from me?'

I don't hesitate. 'I need to know where the photographs were taken,' I say – not a request, a command.

Her expression turns guarded.

'What photographs?' she says. She isn't much of an actress.

'The photographs on the red sofa,' I say, and then add, 'There's no point in pretending you don't understand.'

'How do you know about the photos?' she asks, still dodging the question.

I hesitate. I'm still not sure how much I can trust Margie. But I need her to tell me where those photos were taken. Dara has a connection to that place. Whatever she's afraid of, whatever she's running from – it's connected to that place, too.

'My sister was in one,' I say finally.

She exhales: a long, low whistle. Then she shakes her head. 'No one knows,' she says. 'The photos came from a password-protected site. Members only, super encrypted. All teen girls, most of them still unidentified. Sarah Snow was one of them.'

And Crystal, I think, the mermaid who had to quit FanLand after her parents found pictures of her posing for some weird porn website, at least according to Maude. Crystal is Dara's age: seventeen this summer. Everything is beginning to make a terrible kind of sense.

'The cops caught a lucky break when they got one of the members to talk.' She pauses, looking at me pointedly, and I think of the accountant who was briefly questioned by police, Nicholas Sanderson, and the comment on the *Blotter* posted by an anonymous user: *he likes young girls.* Suddenly I'm positive that this is the 'member' who talked to the police. 'But even he didn't know anything else. It's a private network. Everyone has an interest in keeping it secret – the creator, the members, even the girls.'

A surge of nausea rolls from my stomach to my throat. My baby sister. Suddenly I remember that for years she had an imaginary friend named Timothy the Talking Rabbit; he went wherever we went but insisted on having a window seat, so Dara always took the middle.

How did everything go so wrong? How did I lose her?

'It's Andre.' I'm overcome by anger and revulsion. I should have stabbed him in the face with a letter opener. I should have clawed out his eyes. 'I'm sure it's him. He must have another location – a private place.'

Margie puts a hand on my shoulder. The touch surprises me. 'If he does, if he's the one who's responsible, the police will catch him,' she says, her voice softening. 'It's their *job*. It's late. Go home, get some sleep. Your parents are probably worried about you.'

I jerk away. 'I can't *sleep*,' I say, feeling the wild urge to hit something, to scream. 'You don't understand. *No one* understands.'

'I do understand,' she says, speaking to me gently, consolingly, as if I'm a stray dog and she's worried I might bite, or bolt. 'Can I tell you a story, Nicole?'

No, I want to say. But she keeps going without waiting for a response.

'When I was eleven, I dared my little sister to swim across Greene River. She was a good swimmer, and we'd done it together dozens of times. But halfway to the other bank she started gasping, choking. She went under.' Margie's eyes slide past mine, as if she's still staring out over the water, watching her kid sister drown. 'The doctors diagnosed her with epilepsy. She'd had a seizure in the water, her first. That's why she went under. But afterward, she started having seizures all the time. She broke a rib when she fell down on the curb on her way to school. She was always covered in bruises. Strangers thought she was abused.' She shakes her head. 'I thought it was my fault – that I'd caused her sickness somehow. That it was because I'd dared her.'

Now she looks at me again. For a split second, I see myself reflected in her eyes – I see myself *in* her.

'I became obsessed with keeping her safe,' she says. 'I would hardly let her out of my sight. It almost killed me. It almost killed her.' She smiles a little. 'She went to college all the way in California. After graduation, she moved to France. Met a guy named Jean-Pierre, married him, took French citizenship.' She shrugs. 'She needed to get away from me, I guess, and I can't say I blame her.'

I don't know if she expects the story to make me feel better, but it doesn't. Now I feel worse. She places both hands on my shoulders, ducking a little so we're eye to eye.

'What I *mean*,' she says, 'is it isn't your fault.'

'Nicole!'

I turn and see Hernandez coming across the street, holding two coffees and a bag from Dunkin' Donuts. His face is resolutely cheerful, a gym-teacher smile. 'They always say cops like doughnuts, don't they? I thought we could share one while we wait.'

Cold floods all the way through my body. He's not going to help me. He's not going to help *Dara*.

No one's going to help.

I run, breath high in my throat, heart hammering against my ribs. I hear my name, shouted again and again, until it becomes meaningless: just the wind, or the sound of the ocean, beating invisibly, ceaselessly, somewhere far off in the distance.

SAVE THE
LIGHTHOUSE!!

Join us in the fight to save our beautiful
lighthouse from demolition on June 14.
THE ORPHAN BEACH COMMUNITY ASSOCIATION

Dear Ms. Mauff,

I originally sent this email several weeks ago to an old address I have on file – I'm guessing you've reverted to your maiden name? When it continued to bounce back, I got your new personal email address from a secretary at MLK.

I'm sorry for all the phone tag. I just saw I missed your call this morning. Can you let me know some times you might be available to talk? I have some significant concerns I'd like to share with you, especially in advance of our family session on the sixteenth.

Best,
Leonard Lichme, PhD

Kevin,

I received a very concerning email from Dr Lichme yesterday and have been unable to get through to his office. Has he contacted you?

Sharon

P.S. No, I have no idea what happened to your golf clubs and think it's inappropriate for you to ask me to look for them.

Dr Lichme,

My ex-wife has just informed me that you recently reached out to her with 'significant concerns.' Is there some trouble with Dara I don't know about? And is there some reason that you didn't reach out to me as well? Despite what Sharon might lead you to believe, I am still very much a member of this family. I believe I initially provided you with office and cell phone numbers for this very purpose. Please let me know when I can reach you and/or if you need me to provide you with my phone number again.

Kevin Warren

Dear Mr Warren,

It's not Dara I'm worried about; it's Nicole. But the fact that you would immediately assume otherwise is part of what I'd like to discuss with you and Sharon, preferably together, in my office. Will you be at the family session on March 16, I hope?

In the meantime, I still have your number and will try and reach you this evening.

Best,
Dr Leonard Lichme, Ph.D.

Sharon,

I finally spoke with Dr Lichme. Have you talked to him yet? To be honest, I wasn't too impressed. He suggested that you and I might benefit from Al-Anon, for example, to help 'resolve our impulses to "fix" Dara.' I told him he's the one who's supposed to be fixing her.

He said he's actually more worried about *Nick*. Because Dara acts out, takes drugs, and hangs out with God-knows-who, she's expressing her feelings and so she's supposedly *healthier* than Nick, who's never given us a day's worry in her life. Isn't that a pretty paradox? He kept trying to convince me that because Nick never shows any signs of being in trouble, she's actually the one who *is* in trouble. And for this we're paying $250 an hour (speaking of, you owe me your portion for the month of February. Please mail a check.).

I suppose he knows what he's talking about, but I'm simply not convinced. Nick is a great big sister, and Dara is lucky to have her.

See you on the sixteenth. I hope we can keep it civil.

Kevin

P.S. I wasn't implying you should look for my golf clubs (!). I simply asked whether you had seen them. Please don't make everything a battle.

nick

1:45 a.m.

AS SOON AS I'M BACK ON THE HIGHWAY, I GRAB MY PHONE AND punch in Parker's number. For a second, I'm worried it won't connect: my phone is flashing every five seconds, showing 2 percent battery. *Come on,* I think, *come on, come on.*

Then it's ringing: four, five, six times before clicking over to voicemail.

'Come on,' I say out loud, and punch the steering wheel with a palm. I hang up and redial. Three rings, four rings, five rings. Just before I click off, Parker picks up.

'Hello?' he croaks. I've woken him. No surprise. It's nearly 2:00 a.m.

'Parker?' My throat is so tight, I can barely say his name. 'I need your help.'

'Nick?' I hear rustling, as though he's sitting up. 'Jesus. What time is it?'

'Listen to me,' I say. 'My phone's about to die. But I think Dara's in trouble.'

There's a short pause. 'You think – *what?*'

'At first I thought she was just messing with me,' I rush on. 'But I think . . . I think she might be involved in something big. Something bad.'

'Where are you?' When Parker speaks again, his voice is totally alert, totally awake, and I know he's gotten out of bed.

I could kiss my phone. I could kiss him. I *do* want to kiss him. This fact is huge and solid and impassible, like an iceberg rising suddenly out of the smooth dark water.

'Route 101. Heading south.' I feel a growing sense of vertigo, as if the road in front of my headlights is in fact a long pit and I'm falling.

You can't let me have anything of my own, can you? You always have to be better than me. Dara's voice comes to me at once, a voice as loud as memory. And then I know: I *am* remembering. She said those words to me. I'm sure she did. But the second I try to grasp for the connection, to follow the slick handholds of memory down beneath the water, my mind is enveloped in the same numbing cold, the same undifferentiated dark.

'You're *driving*?' Parker's voice inches higher, disbelieving. 'You need to pull over. Do me a favor and pull over, okay?'

'I need to find her, Parker.' My voice cracks. My phone beeps at me even more insistently. 'I need to help her.'

'Where are you exactly?' he repeats, and his room unfolds in front of me: the old baseball lamp in the shape of a catcher's mitt casting a warm cone of light on the navy-blue carpet; the rumpled sheets that always smell faintly like pine; the swivel desk chair and the clutter of books and video games and faded T-shirts. I imagine him wriggling into a shirt one-handed, rummaging under the bed for his Surf Siders.

'I'm heading toward Orphan's Beach,' I say, because it's the only thing I can think to do. Andre must have a second location, a private place where he brings girls to be photographed. The answer lies along the beach, close to Beamer's, maybe even inside it. They might have a secondary basement; or maybe I missed a doorway somewhere, or a converted storage shed closer to the water. I need proof.

I have an ever-growing sense that this was all planned, at least initially, by Dara. She intended me to find her phone, and the pictures on it. She was leaving me clues so that I would be able to help her.

It was a cry for help.

'Orphan's Beach?' On Parker's end, a door opens and closes with a firm click. Now I see him moving down the hall, navigating by feel, keeping one hand on the wall (papered with faded patterns of ribbons and dried flowers, a design he despises). 'Where we went last year on Dara's birthday? Where we found the lighthouse?'

'Yeah,' I say. 'There's a bar just down the road called . . .' The words turn to dust in my mouth.

Suddenly I know. Images and words flash through my head – the neon Beamer's sign, cocktail napkins imprinted with a logo of twin headlights, to *beam*, a sweep of light – and just like that I know exactly where Andre takes his girls, where he has his parties, where he photographed Dara and Sarah Snow, where something terrible happened to Madeline.

'A bar called what?' Parker's voice sounds distant now, thinner. He's outside. He's hurrying across the grass, holding his cell phone to his shoulder with his chin, rifling through his jeans for his keys. 'Nick, are you there?'

'Oh my God.' I'm clutching my phone so tightly, my knuckles ache.

Just then my phone cuts out, powering down completely.

'Shit.' Cursing out loud makes me feel better. 'Shit, shit, shit.' Then I remember Dara's phone and feel a surge of hope. Keeping one hand on the wheel, I feel around for it in the cup holder, but come up with nothing but an ancient mass of gum, papered together and stuck to the back of a quarter. I reach over to run a hand along the passenger seat, increasingly desperate. Nothing.

Just then an animal – a raccoon or a possum, it's too dark to tell – shoots out from the underbrush and freezes, eyes glittering, directly in the path of my wheels. I jerk the wheel hard into the next lane without checking for cars, expecting to feel a hard thump. After a second, I regain control, correcting my steering before I can plunge past the guardrail and straight past the darkened beachfront houses and into the water. When I look in the rearview mirror, I see a dark shape bolt across the road. Safe, then.

Still, I can't shake loose that spike of panic, the terror of being out of control, of heading over the brink. I must have left Dara's phone at home when I went inside to look through her room. That means I really am alone. The answers are all there, down on that lonely stretch of beach between Beamer's and the accident site, where the currents make it deadly to swim: the answers to what happened to Madeline Snow, and what happened to change my sister; the answers to what happened on that night four months ago, when we went sailing off the edge of the earth and into the darkness.

And a small, persistent voice in my head keeps speaking up, begging me to turn back, telling me I'm not ready for the truth.

But I ignore it, and keep going.

dara

2:02 a.m.

FROM THE OUTSIDE, THE LIGHTHOUSE LOOKS ABANDONED. IT RISES above the construction scaffolding like a finger pointing to the moon. The narrow windows are boarded up with wood bleached a dull gray, and signs declare the whole place off-limits. WARNING, one of them reads, HARD HAT AREA ONLY. But there has been no construction here, not for a long time; even this sign is streaked with salt and warped from weather, graffitied with somebody's tag.

I should have brought a flashlight.

I don't remember how to get in – only that there is a way in, a secret door, like a passage to another world.

I circle the beach, slipping a little on the rocks. In the distance, beyond the boulders, I can see Beamer's lit up, squatting on the shore like a glistening insect, and every so often I hear a car go by on the highway, see a section of beach and stone get lit up by a fast sweep of headlights, though I'm concealed from view by the thick, gnarled hedges of beach grass and pigface that grow up near the divider.

The tide is up. Black mud bubbles up between the stones, and waves foam not four feet from where I stand, forming pools between the rocks whenever they recede. It's a lonely place, a place no one would think to investigate – and yet, less than a thousand feet down the road the lights and chaos of East Norwalk begin.

I duck underneath the construction scaffolding, running a hand along the curve of the lighthouse, paint splintering under my fingers. The only door is boarded up, like all the windows. Still, I keep circling. I've been here before. There must be a way in. Unless . . .

The thought comes to me suddenly. Unless Andre, knowing the cops are getting closer, has covered his tracks.

But almost the instant I think it, my fingers hit something – an irregularity, a minuscule break in the wood. It's so dark beneath the scaffolding I can barely make out my hands, groping along the surface of the lighthouse, a place that has been patched over and nailed shut, as if long ago a hurricane tore out a chunk of the wall and it was only hastily repaired. I push. The wood gives a quarter of an inch, groaning a little when I lean against it.

There's a door here: carved deliberately out of the wall, then made to look like it has been boarded up. But no matter how much I push, it won't release. Could it be locked from inside? I run my fingers against the nearly invisible seam, crying out when I feel the sharp bite of a nail. I suck my finger into my mouth and taste blood. It's just like I thought. The nails aren't actually nailed *into* anything, but simply hammered through the door and then distorted, bent parallel to the wood. Still, it won't open.

I aim a frustrated kick at the door – I need *in* – and then spring backward as the door rebounds, groaning, unhinging like a vertical mouth. Of course. Not push. Pull.

Something stirs behind me. I whip around as the wind lifts and another wave crashes to the shore, foaming between the slick dark rocks. I scan the beach but see nothing but the looming shapes of ancient boulders, the wild tangle of beach grass, and the faint lights of Beamer's twinkling in the distance, turning a portion of the ocean silver.

I slip inside the lighthouse, bending down for a sand-slicked rock I can use to keep the door open. This way, at least a little light breaks up the darkness. Besides, Nick will need in.

If she manages to find me.

Inside, the air smells like stale beer and cigarette smoke. I take a step forward, groping for a light switch, and something – a bottle? – rolls away. I collide with a standing lamp and barely catch it before it crashes to the floor. The lamp, which is cabled to a generator, barely lights up a coiled staircase leading to the lighthouse's upper levels. The room is bare except for a few empty beer cans and bottles, stubbed-out cigarettes, and, weirdly, a man's flattened shoe. Dozens of footprints criss-cross the room, disturbing the heavy layer of sawdust and plaster. Ants swarm a crushed McDonald's bag in the corner.

I drag the lamp toward the staircase. In the light, it looks like a serpent. Then I start to climb.

The red sofa has been removed from the room at the top of the stairs. Even before I find another lamp, I can tell that a large object has been recently dragged across the room – tracks are visible in the dust – and worked, somehow, down the staircase.

But the lamps remain – four of them, with huge bulbs exposed, like lights on a movie set – and the old coffee table, ringed with stains from drink glasses. The AC is still squatting in the corner, its grille choked with dust, and cinder blocks and plywood are stacked just to the left of the stairs, probably from the planned renovations that never materialized. Balled into one corner is a girl's bra – yellow, faded, with bumblebees patterned across the cups.

I stand for a second in the center of the room, fighting the sudden urge to cry. How did I get here? How did any of us get here?

It's all over now: the lying, the struggling, the sneaking around. I remember when my sister and I used to race on our bikes to get home, the burning in my legs and thighs by the time we rounded the final corner, the desire not just to end but to give up, to stop pedaling, to let momentum carry me those final blocks. That's what I'm feeling now – not the triumph of a win but the relief of no longer trying.

But there's one more thing I have to do.

I move around the room, looking for something to tie Andre to Madeline Snow. I'm not sure what, exactly, I'm hoping to find. The truth will out. That phrase keeps running through my head. No. It's the truth will set you free. *Blood will out.*

Blood.

Near one wall is a dark stain, maroonish-brown. I squat down, feeling slightly nauseous. The stain is about the size of a child's palm, and long absorbed into the plank floors. Impossible to tell how old – or new – it is.

Downstairs, the door bangs shut. I stand up quickly, my heart rocketing into my throat. Someone's here. Nick wouldn't have slammed the door. She would be moving carefully, quietly.

There's only one place to hide: behind the stack of plank wood and cinder blocks piled together at the head of the stairs. Moving as quietly as I can, wincing whenever the floor creaks beneath me, I slip into the narrow, dark space between the construction materials and the wall. It smells like must and mouse droppings. I maneuver awkwardly into a crouch, waiting, straining to hear sounds from below – someone moving, walking, breathing.

Nothing. Not a whisper, creak, or breath. I count to thirty and then back down to zero. Finally I shuffle out of my hiding place. The wind must have dislodged the rock from the door.

As I'm straightening up, I catch a glimmer of something silver, half-wedged beneath one of the pieces of plywood. I work it free with my fingers.

The world shrinks down to a narrow point, to a space no wider than a child's outstretched hand.

It's Madeline Snow's charm bracelet – the one we so carefully combed the beach for, back when I joined up with the search party. Her favorite charm bracelet.

I stand up on shaky legs, gripping her bracelet. I edge out into the open.

'What the fuck?'

Andre's voice takes me completely by surprise. I haven't heard him approach. He's standing at the top of the stairs, gripping the banister with white knuckles, his face distorted, monstrous with rage.

'You,' he spits out, and I can't move, can't react. 'What the hell are you doing here?'

He takes two steps toward me, releasing his hold on the banister. I don't think. I just run. I barrel past him and he stumbles backward, giving me just enough space to reach the stairs.

Down, down, down, the metal steps chattering like teeth under my weight, little bursts of pain exploding in my ankles and knees.

'Hey! Stop! *Stop.*'

I hurtle out onto the beach, a sob working its way out of my throat, turn right, fighting blindly up the shore. Andre bursts out of the lighthouse after me.

'Listen. *Listen.* I just want to talk to you.'

I lose my footing on the rocks and go down, accidentally releasing my hold on the bracelet. For one terrifying second, I can't find it again; I rake blindly through the wet sand and the shallow swirls of water, dragging like fingers back toward the ocean. I can hear Andre's footsteps drumming on the beach behind me, the shallow huff of his breathing.

My fingers close on metal. The bracelet. I scoop it up and push back to my feet, ignoring the hard ache in my legs, cutting up the slope toward the highway. Sandwort nips at my bare skin, but I ignore that, too.

I pull myself up between the rocks, using thick ropes of beach grass for purchase, sand slipping beneath my feet, threatening to send me tumbling backward. The growth is so thick, I can barely make out the highway: just the sudden dazzle of headlights, lighting up a vast network of Virginia creeper and sea oats, as a car sweeps by. I keep pushing, holding one arm up to my face to shield it, feeling like I'm the knight in a fairy tale, trying to fight my way through an enchanted forest that just keeps growing thicker and thicker.

But this isn't a fairy tale.

Andre crashes through the underbrush, cursing. But he's falling back. I risk a glance behind me and see a cluster of switchgrass tossing violently as he attempts to work his way around it. At last the growth releases me and all at once the highway is there, the smooth ribbon of pavement glistening like oil in the moon.

I scramble the last few feet up to the road, doubling over,

crunching over empty cans and plastic bags. I hop the divider and turn left – away from Orphan's Beach, away from Beamer's, toward the empty coastline where the houses are unfinished and the beach splinters increasingly into huge formations of stone. I can lose him out there in the darkness. I can hide until he gives up.

I take off down the road, sticking close to the divider. A car blasts by me in a hot rush of sound and exhaust, windows rattling with bass, blaring the horn. Somewhere in the far distance, police sirens are wailing – someone hurt or dead, another life destroyed.

I twist around. Andre has made it up to the highway now. It's too dark to see his face.

'Jesus Christ,' he shouts. 'Are you out of your—'

But whatever else he says gets whipped away as another car blows by.

More sirens now. I haven't been this far south since the night of the accident, and everything looks unfamiliar: on one side of the highway, spiky stones rising up from the beach; on the other, craggy hills and pine trees.

Did Madeline Snow run this way? Did he catch her and bring her back to the lighthouse?

Did she scream?

I turn around again, but there's nothing behind me but empty road: Andre has either given up or fallen back. I slow down, heaving in breaths, my lungs burning. The pain is everywhere now; I feel like a wooden doll about to splinter apart.

The night around me has turned very still. If it weren't for the sirens, still shrieking – getting closer? – the world would feel like an oil painting of itself, perfectly immobile, clothed in dark.

It must have been right around here that Nick and I crashed. A strange feeling comes over me, like there's a wind blowing straight through my stomach. But there's no wind: the trees are motionless. Still, a chill moves down my spine.

Pull over.

Bright starbursts of memory: images suddenly illumined, like comets in the dark.

No. Not until we finish talking.

We are finished talking. For good.

Dara, please. You don't understand.

I said, *pull over.*

Ten feet ahead of me, the divider twists away from the highway. A portion of metal has been snapped clean away. Faded silk ribbons hang side by side along the portion that's still intact. They sway ever so slightly, like weeds disturbed by an invisible current. A battered wooden cross is staked in the dirt, and the huge rock face just beyond the breach is covered in scraps of paper and bits of fabric, mementos, and messages.

Several new bouquets are grouped around the cross, and even from a few feet away I recognize a stuffed animal that belongs to Ariana. Mr Stevens: her favorite teddy bear. She even buys him a Christmas present every year – always a different accessory, like an umbrella or a hard hat.

Mr Stevens has a new accessory: a ribbon around his neck, with a message inked in marker on the fabric. I have to squat down to read it.

Happy birthday, Dara. I miss you every day.

Time yawns open, slows down, stills. Only the sirens shatter the silence.

Notes, water-warped, now indecipherable – faded silk flowers and key chains – and in the center of it all—

A photograph. *My* photograph. The yearbook photo from sophomore year, the one I always said I hated, the one where my hair is too short.

And beneath it, a shiny metal plaque screwed into the stone.

RIP, DARA JACQUELINE WARREN. YOU'LL LIVE IN OUR HEARTS FOR EVER.

The sirens are screaming now, so loud I can feel the noise all the way in my teeth – so loud I can't think. And then, all at once, noise returns to the world in a rush of wind, a tumult of rain that comes sweeping in from the ocean, blowing me backward. The world is lit up in flashes. Red and white. Red and white.

The sirens have stopped. Everything feels like it's going in slow motion – even the hard slices of rain seem to be frozen in the air, a sheet of water turned diagonal. Three cars have pulled onto the shoulder. People are running toward me, turned by the headlights into faceless shadows.

'Nick!' they're shouting. 'Nick! Nick!'

Run.

The word comes to me on the rain, on the soft tongue of the wind against my face.

So I do.

BEFORE

nick

THE SUMMER I WAS NINE WAS A WET ONE. FOR WEEKS IT SEEMED to rain non-stop. Dara even got pneumonia, and her lungs slurped and rattled whenever she inhaled, as if the moisture had somehow gotten inside her.

On the first sunny day in what seemed like for ever, Parker and I crossed the park to check out Old Stone Creek – normally shallow and flat-bottomed and barely two feet across – now transformed into a roaring, tumbling river, barreling over its banks, turning the whole area to swampland.

Some older kids had gathered to throw empty cans in the creek and watch them twirl, bobbing and resurfacing, in the current. This one guy, Aidan Jennings, was standing on the footbridge, jumping up and down, while the water pummeled the wooden supports and went swirling up across his feet.

And then, in one instant, both Aidan and the bridge were gone. It happened that quickly, and without sound; the rotting wood gave way, and Aidan was swept up in a swirl of splintered wood and churning water, and everyone was running after him, shouting.

Memory is like that, too. We build careful bridges. But they're weaker than we think.

And when they break, all our memories return to drown us.

It was raining, too, on the night of the accident.

I didn't mean for it to happen.

He was waiting for me at home after Ariana's party, jogging up and down a little on the front porch, his breath crystal-lizing in the air, his sweatshirt hood tugged up over his head, casting his face in shadow.

'Nick.' His voice was hoarse, as if he hadn't used it in a while. 'We need to talk.'

'Hey.' I tried not to get too close to him as I moved toward the door, rooting in my bag for my keys with fingers that had gone numb from cold. Dara had insisted I stay to watch the bonfire. But the rain had increased steadily, and the fire never materialized: only a blackened, pulpy mess of diesel oil and logs, crushed paper cups and cigarette butts. 'I missed you at the party.'

'Wait.' He grabbed my wrist before I could push open the door. His fingers were icy, his face raw with some emotion I didn't understand. 'Not there. My house.'

I hadn't noticed until he gestured that his car was pulled over a little ways down the road, half-concealed by a group of straggly pines, as if he'd been deliberately trying to stay hidden. He walked a few feet ahead of me, hands shoved deep in his pockets, shoulders hunched against the rain, almost as if he was angry.

Maybe I should have said *no*. Maybe I should have said *I'm tired*.

But this was Parker, my best friend, or my once-upon-a-time best friend. Besides, I didn't know what was coming next.

The drive to his house took all of fifteen seconds. Still, it felt like an eternity. He drove in silence, his hands tight on the wheel. The windshield was almost completely fogged over; the wipers squelched against the glass, sending sheets of water plummeting down toward the hood.

Only after he was parked did he turn to me. 'We haven't talked about what happened on Founders' Day,' he said.

The heat was on, feathering his hair under his trucker hat. *Come to the nerd side,* it said. *We have pi.* 'What do you mean?' I said carefully, and I remember I felt my heart like a fist, squeezing slowly in and out.

'So' – Parker was drumming his hands on his thighs, a sure sign he was nervous – 'it didn't mean anything to you?'

I said nothing. My hands felt like deadweight in my lap, like enormous, bloated things pulled up by a tide.

At the Founders' Day Ball, Parker and I snuck into the pool and climbed up to the rafters, trying to find a way up to the roof. We did, eventually: we found a trapdoor through the old theater. We ditched the dance and sat together for an hour, sharing a bottle of Crown Royal Parker had siphoned from his dad's stash, laughing about nothing.

Until he took my hand in his.

Until there was nothing funny about the way he was looking at me.

We came so close to kissing that night.

Afterward, when the rumor started going around that I'd ditched the dance to hook up with Aaron in the boiler room, I let everyone think it was true.

Rain diced the light from his front porch into crazy patterns. For a while he said nothing. 'All right, listen. Things have been weird between us for months. Don't argue,' he said, when I opened my mouth to protest. 'They have been. It's my fault. Jesus, I know that. It's all my fault. I should have never – well, anyway. I just wanted to explain. About Dara.'

'You don't have to.'

'I *need* to,' he said, with sudden urgency. 'Look, Nick. I screwed up. And now – I don't know how to fix it.'

Cold crept through my whole body, as if we were still outside, standing at the edge of the ruined bonfire, watching the rain fizzle the flames into smoke. 'I'm sure she'll forgive you,' I said. I didn't care if I sounded mad. I was mad.

All my life, Dara had been taking things and smashing them.

'You don't get it.' He took off his hat, shoved a hand through his hair so that it stood up straight, electric, defying gravity. 'I should never have – God. Dara's like a little sister to me.'

'That's gross, Parker.'

'I mean it. I never . . . it just happened. It was all wrong. It was always wrong. I just didn't know how to make it stop.' He couldn't sit still. He jammed his hat back on. He twisted around to face me and then, as though he couldn't stand to, immediately turned away. 'I don't love her. I mean, I do love her. But not like that.'

For a moment, there was quiet. I couldn't see Parker's face – just his profile, the light sliding off the curve of his cheek. Rain drummed against the windshield like the sound of hundreds of tiny feet, stampeding away toward something better.

'Why are you telling me this?' I said finally.

Parker turned back to me. His face was twisted in a look of pain, as if an invisible force had come down on his chest, knocking the wind out of him. 'I'm sorry, Nick. Please forgive me.' His voice was raw. 'It should have been you.'

Time seemed to glitch. I was certain I'd misunderstood. 'What?'

'I mean, it *is* you. That's what I'm trying to say.' His hand found mine, or my hand found his. His touch was warm and dry and familiar. 'Do you – do you understand now?'

I don't remember whether he kissed me, or I kissed him. Does it matter? All that really counts is that it happened. All that matters is that I wanted it. I had never, in my whole life, wanted anything so badly. Parker was mine again: Parker, the boy I'd always loved. The rain kept falling, but now it sounded gentler, rhythmic, like the pulsation of an invisible heart. Steam patterned the windshield, turning the outside world to blur.

I could have stayed like that for ever.

And then Parker jerked back, just as a loud *thump* sounded behind me.

Dara. Her hand splayed on the passenger-side window, her eyes hollowed out by shadow, her hair plastered to her cheeks – and that strange smile on her face. Gloating. Triumphant. As if all along, she'd known what she would find.

For a second, Dara left her hand there – almost as if she expected me to place my hand there as well, almost like a game.

Mirror me, Nick. Do what I do.

I may have moved. I may have called out to her. She withdrew her hand, leaving a ghost imprint of her fingers on the glass. Then this, too, was gone – and so was she.

She had slipped onto the bus before I could catch up to her, the doors hissing shut when I was still a half block away, shouting. Maybe she heard me, maybe she didn't. Her face was white, her shirt dark with rain; standing under the fluorescent lights, she looked like a photo negative, color in all the wrong places. Then the bus slid away beyond the trees, as if the night had opened its jaw to swallow it.

It took me twenty minutes to catch up to the bus on Route 101 in my car, and another twenty before I saw her get off, walking head down on the shoulder, arms crossed against the rain, past blinking-light businesses advertising Bud Light or triple-X videos.

Where was she going? To Beamer's to see Andre? Down to Orphan's Beach and the lighthouse? Or did she just want to get far away, get lost in the rocky beaches of East Norwalk, where the land ran into the angry sea?

I tailed her for another half mile, flashing my headlights, blowing my horn, before she agreed to get in.

'Drive,' she said.

'Dara, listen. What you saw—'

'I said, drive.' But when I started to angle the wheel around, to turn back toward home, she reached out and jerked the wheel in the other direction. I slammed on the brakes. She didn't flinch. She didn't even blink. She didn't seem angry or upset. She just sat there, dripping water onto the upholstery, staring straight ahead. 'That way,' she said, and pointed south – in the direction of nowhere-land.

But I did what she told me. I just wanted the chance to explain. The road was bad; the tires skidded a little when I accelerated, and I slowed down again. My mouth was dry. I couldn't think of a single excuse to give.

'I'm sorry,' I said finally. 'It wasn't . . . I mean, it's not what it looked like.'

She said nothing. The wipers were doing overtime, and still I could barely see the road, hardly see the headlights cutting the rain into splinters.

'We didn't mean to. We were just talking. We were talking about you, actually. I don't even like him.' A lie – one of the biggest lies I'd ever told her.

'This isn't about Parker,' she said, practically the first words she'd spoken since she got in the car.

'What do you mean?' I wanted to look at her but was afraid to take my eyes off the road. I didn't even know where we were going – I recognized, vaguely, the 7-Eleven where we'd stopped the summer before to get beer on the way to Orphan's Beach.

'This is about you and me.' Dara's voice was low and cold. 'You can't let me have anything of my own, can you? You always have to be better than me. You always have to win.'

'What?' I was so stunned I couldn't even argue.

'Don't play innocent. I get it. That's another part of your big act. Perfect Nick and her fuck-up sister.' She was speaking so fast, I could hardly understand her; it occurred to me she might be on something. 'So fine. You want Parker? You can have him. I don't need him. I don't need you, either. Pull over.'

It took me a second to process her request; by the time I did, she had already started to open the door, even though the car was still moving.

And with a sudden, desperate clarity I knew I couldn't let her out: if I did, I'd lose her.

'Shut the door.' I jammed my foot on the accelerator, and she jerked backward in her seat. Now we were going too fast – she couldn't jump. 'Shut the door.'

'Pull over.'

Faster, faster, even though I could hardly see; even though the rain was heavy as a curtain, loud as applause cresting at the end of a play. 'No. Not until we finish talking.'

'We are finished talking. For good.'

'Dara, please. You don't understand.'

'I said, pull over.' She reached over and jerked the wheel toward the shoulder. The back of the car spun out into the opposite lane. I slammed on the brakes, spun the wheel to the left, tried to correct.

It was too late.

We were spinning across the lanes. *We're going to die,* I thought, and then we hit the guardrail, burst through it in an explosion of glass and metal. Smoke was pouring from the engine, and for one split second we were suspended, airborne, safe, and somehow my hand found Dara's in the dark.

I remember it was very cold.

I remember that she didn't scream, or say anything, or make a sound.

And then I don't remember anything at all.

AFTER

nick

3:15 a.m.

I HAVEN'T BEEN PAYING ATTENTION TO WHERE I'M HEADING OR how far I've run until I see Pirate Pete looming above the treeline, one arm raised in a salutation, eyes gleaming bright white. FanLand. His gaze seems to follow me as I jog across the parking lot, transformed by the storm into an atoll: a series of dry concrete islands surrounded by deep ruts of water, swirling with old trash.

The sirens are going again, so loud they feel like a physical force, like a hand reaching deep inside me to shove aside the curtain, revealing quick flashes of memory, words, images.

Dara's hand on the window, and the impression left by her fingers.

RIP, Dara.

We're done talking.

I need to get away – away from the noise, away from those hard bursts of light.

I need to find Dara, to prove it isn't true.

It isn't true.

It can't be.

My fingers are clumsy, swollen with cold. I fumble at the keypad, mistyping the code twice before the latch buzzes open, just as the first of three cars jerks into the parking lot, sirens cutting the darkness into planes of color. For one second, I'm frozen in the headlights, pinned in place like an insect to glass.

'Nick!' Again those cries, that word, both familiar and alien-sounding, like the cry of a bird calling from the woods.

I slip inside the gates and run, blinking away rain, swallowing down the taste of salt, and cut right, sloshing through puddles that have materialized on the sloping pathways. A minute later the gate clangs again; the voices pursue me, overlapping now, drumming down on the sound of the rain.

'Nick, please. Nick, *wait*.'

There: in the distance, through the trees, a flickering light. A flashlight? My chest is tight with a feeling I can't name, a terror of something to come, like that moment Dara and I hung suspended, gripping hands, while our headlights called up an image of a sharp rock face.

RIP, Dara.

Impossible.

'Dara!' My voice gets swallowed up by the rain. 'Dara! Is that you?'

'Nick!'

Closer now – I need to get away, need to show them, need to find Dara. I push into the trees, taking the shortcut, following that phantom light, which seems to pause and then be extinguished at the foot of the Gateway to Heaven, like a candle flame suddenly snuffed out. Leaves lap like thick tongues against my bare arms and face. Mud sucks at my sandals, splatters the back of my calves. A bad storm. A once-in-a-summer storm.

'Nick. Nick. Nick.' Now the word is just a meaningless chant, like the chatter of the rain through the leaves.

'Dara!' I cry. Once again, my voice is absorbed by the air. I push out of the trees onto the walkway that leads to the foot of the Gateway, where the passenger car is still grounded, concealed by a heavy blue tarp. People are shouting, calling to one another.

I turn around. Behind me, a rapid pattern of lights flashes through the trees, and I think then of a lighthouse beam sweeping through the dark sea, of Morse code, of warning signals. But I can't understand the message.

I turn back to the Gateway. It was here I saw a distant light, I'm sure of it; it was here that Dara came.

'Dara!' I scream as loud as I can, my throat raw from the effort. 'Dara!' My chest feels as if it has been filled with stones: hollow and heavy at the same time, and that truth is still knocking there, threatening to drown me, threatening to take me down with it.

Rest in peace, Dara.

'Nick!'

Then I see it: a twitch, a movement beneath the tarp, and relief breaks in my chest. All along this was a test, to see how far I would go, how long I would play.

All along, she's been here, waiting for me.

I'm running again, breathless with relief, crying now but not because I'm sad – because she's here and I found her and now the game is over and we can go home, together, at last. In one corner, the tarp has been loosened from its anchors – smart Dara, to have found a place to hide out from the rain – and I climb over the rusted metal siding and slide beneath the tarp into the dark between the cracked old seats. Instantly I'm hit by the smell: of bubblegum and old hamburgers, bad breath and dirty hair.

And then I see her. She scurries backward, as if worried that I'll hit her. Her flashlight clatters to the ground, and the metal carriage vibrates in response. I freeze, afraid to move, afraid she'll startle away.

Not Dara. Too small to be Dara. Too *young* to be Dara.

And even before I pick up the flashlight and click it on, illuminating a covering of Twinkie wrappers and crushed soda cans, of empty Milky Way wrappers and hamburger buns, all the things raccoons were supposed to have been stealing the past few days; even before the light laps the toes of her pink-and-purple slippers and slips up toward her Disney princess pajama bottoms and finally lands on that heart-shaped face, wide-eyed and pale, the stringy mess of blond hair, the pale blue eyes – even before the voices are on top of us and the tarp disappears so that the sky can fall down on us directly – even before then, I know.

'Madeline,' I whisper, and she whimpers or sighs or exhales; I can't tell which. 'Madeline Snow.'

Feature: It Happened to Me!
Someone Sold My Topless Pics Online
by: Sarah Snow
as told to Megan Donahue

'All I remember is waking up with no idea about how I'd gotten home . . . and no idea about what had happened to my sister.'

My best friend, Kennedy, and I were hanging out at the mall one Saturday when this guy came up to us, telling us we were both really pretty and asking whether we were models. At first I thought he was just hitting on us. He was maybe twenty-four and pretty cute. He said his name was Andre.

Then he said he owned a bar in East Norwalk called Beamer's and asked whether we wanted to make money just for showing up at parties. [Editor's note: Andrew 'Andre' Markenson was the manager of Beamer's up until his recent arrest; the legitimate owners, Fresh Entertainment LLC, were quick to disclaim any knowledge of and to condemn Mr Markenson's activities.] At first it sounded sketchy, but he told us that there would be other girls there and we wouldn't have to do anything besides pass out shots and act friendly and collect tips. He seemed so nice and just, you know, normal. It was easy to trust him.

The first parties were just like he said. All we had to do was dress cute and walk around handing out drinks and be nice to the guys who showed up, and after a few hours we'd walk out with as much as two hundred bucks. We couldn't believe it.

There were always other girls working, usually four or five on a shift. I didn't know a lot about them, except I think they must have been in high school, too. But Andre had been careful about telling us we had to be eighteen, even though he never asked for proof, so I always figured he kind of knew we were underage but was just going to pretend as long as we pretended, too.

I do remember this girl, Dara Warren. She stuck out to me because she died in a car crash only a few days after one of the parties. Then the weird thing is that her sister, Nicole, is the one who found Maddie [Editor's note: Madeline Snow, whose disappearance on July 19 launched a major, county-wide investigation] after she ran away. Crazy, right?

Anyway, Andre always seemed really nice and would tell us all about his life, how he also produced music videos and was a talent scout for TV shows and stuff, even though now I know those were all lies. He sometimes picked a girl to make food runs with him and would come back with burgers and fries for all the girls. He had a really nice car. And he would always give us compliments, tell us we were pretty enough to be models or actresses. Now I know he was just trying to earn our trust.

In April and May and into June there were no parties. I don't know why. Maybe because of cops or something? At the time, he just told us he was busy with some other projects and hinted he was going to be helping cast for a TV show soon. That was a lie, too.

But at the time I didn't have any reason to disbelieve him.

Then in late June, the Blackouts started up again. [Editor's note: 'Blackout' was the name given to the private bimonthly parties, for which guests had to pay a sizable membership fee to be admitted.] The night everything happened, my grandma got sick and my mom and dad had to drive to Tennessee to see her in the hospital, so I was in charge of babysitting Maddie, even though I'd already said I'd be at work. I needed the money because I was supposed to be getting a new car and also, I know it's stupid to say now, but I kind of missed it. The parties were fun and easy and we felt special, you know? Because we'd been chosen.

Maddie had to be in bed by nine, so finally Kennedy and I decided just to bring her along. The parties were usually over by midnight anyway, and we figured she'd just sleep in the backseat. Usually she sleeps through everything – even, like, hurricanes.

Not that night, though.

Andre was being especially nice to me that night. He gave me a shot of this special sweet liquor that tasted kind of like chocolate. Kennedy got mad because I was driving, and I know it was dumb, but I figured one drink wouldn't hurt. But then things started to get . . . weird.

I can't explain it, but I was dizzy and things kept happening and I wouldn't remember them. It was like I was watching a movie but half the footage was missing. Kennedy left early because she was in a bad mood and some guy said something rude to her. But I didn't know that yet. I just wanted to lie down.

Andre told me he had a private office and there was a couch there, and I could nap for as long as I wanted.

That's the last thing I remember until the next morning. I woke up puking. My car was parked halfway on my neighbor's lawn. My neighbor, Mrs Hardwell, was so pissed. I couldn't believe I'd driven home, and I was freaking out. I *couldn't remember anything. It was like someone had cut out a part of my brain.*

When I realized Maddie was gone, I just wanted to die. I was so scared, and I knew it was all my fault. That's why I lied about where we'd gone. In retrospect, I know I should have gone to my parents and the police right away, but I was so confused and ashamed and I thought I could find a way to fix it.

I know now what happened was that Maddie woke up and followed me to the lighthouse, which is where Andre had his 'office.' It wasn't an office at all, just a place he photographed girls so he could sell their pictures online. The police think I must have been drugged, because I don't remember anything.

I guess Maddie got scared and thought I was dead! She's just a little kid. She thought when she saw me lying there without moving that Andre had killed me. She must have cried out, because he turned around and saw her. She was terrified he would kill her, too, so she ran. She was so scared he would come after her she hid for days, stealing food and water and only coming out for a few minutes at a time, usually at night. Thank God we got her home safely.

At first I didn't think I'd ever forgive myself, but after speaking for a long time to other girls who have been through similar situations

< < Page 1 of 3 > >

Dear Dr Lichme,

I understand that earlier this year you saw Nicole Warren for a short time. She was recently admitted to my care at East Shoreline Memorial, and I wanted to reach out to you now both to discuss my initial impressions of her mental state and because she will no doubt need continuing treatment post-release, whenever that will be.

Nicole is physically in good health, and seems both quiet and cooperative, albeit very confused. She seems to have suffered from some major dissociative disorder, which I am still trying to diagnose exactly (provisionally, and although I know the designations are by this point controversial, I'd say it seems to share elements with both MPD/DID and Depersonalization Disorder, no doubt stemming from the major trauma of the accident and her sister's death; additionally, there seem to be indications of a kind of psychogenic fugue state, although not all of the standard characteristics have presented). At some point post-accident – I believe when she returned to Somerville after several months away and was forced to confront evidence of her sister's absence – she began at intervals to inhabit the mind of her deceased sister, patching together a narrative based on various shared memories and her intimate knowledge of her sister's behavior, personality, physicality, and preferences. As time progressed, her delusions intensified and encompassed visual and auditory hallucinations.

As of now, though she has accepted that her sister is

dead, she has little to no recovered memories of the experiences she had while inhabiting her sister's psyche, though I am hoping that changes with time, counseling, and the right combination of medication.

Please give me a call at any time to discuss.

Thanks,

Michael Hueng
O: 555-6734
East Shoreline Memorial Hospital
66-87 Washington Blvd.
Main Heights

Heya, Nick,

How are you doing? Maybe that's a stupid question. Maybe this is a stupid email to be writing – I'm not even sure whether you're getting email. I tried calling your phone, but it was off.

I'm leaving for orientation in less than a week. Crazy! Hopefully I won't get eaten alive in the subway by any giant rats. Or attacked by nuclear-resistant cockroaches. Or mauled by facial-hair-sporting hipsters.

Anyway. Your mom told my mom you might be gone for a few weeks or more. I hate that I'm not going to have a chance to see you. I hope you're feeling better. Shit. That sounds stupid, too.

God, Nick . . . I can't imagine what you've been through.

I guess I just wanted to say hi, and I'm thinking about you. A lot.

—P

Hey—

Not sure if you got my last email. Tomorrow's the big day.
I'm heading to New York. I'm excited, I guess, but I really wish
I could have seen you or at least spoken to you before I left.
Did your mom tell you to call me? She said she was going to
visit, and I asked her to pass along the message, but I'm not
sure if she did. I kept calling my own phone to make sure it
was working, ha.

Anyway, please write. Or call. Or . . . send a carrier pigeon.
Whatever.

Random, but . . . remember when we were kids and I'd tie
a red flag to the oak tree when I wanted you and Dara to
meet me at the fort? I don't know why, but that popped into
my head the other day. Funny how when you're a kid, weird
things have their own kind of logic. Like, things are so much
more complicated but also simpler. I'm rambling, I know.

I'm going to miss FanLand. I'm going to miss Somerville.
Most of all, I'm going to miss you.

xP

East Shoreline Memorial Hospital
66-87 Washington Blvd.
Main Heights

Patient legal name: Nicole S. Warren
Patient ID: 45-110882
Consulting Psychiatrist: Dr Michael Hueng
Consulting Physician: Dr Claire Winnyck
Intake date: July 30
Current date: August 28

GENERAL NOTES:
Patient has made significant improvement over the past
thirty days. Patient initially presented with features of a
major dissociative disorder indicative of PTSD or RTD
(recurrent trauma disorder). Patient seemed anxious and
unwilling to participate in group activities and solo
sessions.
Dr Hueng suggested 100 mg Zoloft/daily and Ambien to
facilitate sleep. Within a few days patient was markedly
improved, displaying renewed appetite and a willingness
to engage with patients and counselors.
Patient seems to understand why she was admitted and
eager to get better. Patient is no longer suffering from
delusions.

PROPOSED COURSE OF ONGOING TREATMENT:
100 mg Zoloft/once daily for management of depression and anxiety
Ongoing therapy, individual and family, with psychiatrist Dr Leonard Lichme

RECOMMENDATION:
Release

Hey, Parker,

Sorry I wasn't able to write or call. I wasn't really feeling up to it for a while. Doing better now, though. I'm home.

By now you're in New York. I hope you're having an amazing time.

—Nick

P.S. Of course I remember the red flag. Sometimes I still look for it.

AFTER

september 2

Dear Dara,

I'm home now. They finally let me out of the loony bin. It wasn't that bad, actually, except for when Mom and Dad visited and stared at me like they were afraid if they tried to touch me I might shatter into dust. We had to do a family session and say a lot of affirmations, like I hear you and respect what you're saying and I see how angry it must make you when I . . . etc. Aunt Jackie would have loved it.

The doctors were pretty nice, and I got to sleep a lot, and we did arts and crafts projects like we were five years old again. I had no idea how many things you could do with Popsicle sticks.

Anyway. Dr Lichme said that whenever I wanted to talk to you, I should write you a letter. So that's what I'm doing now. Except that every time I sit down to write, I don't even know where to begin. There's so much I want to say. There's so much I want to ask, too, even though I know you won't answer.

So I'll settle for the basics.

I'm sorry, Dara. I'm so, so sorry.

I miss you. Please come back.

Love,
Nick

september 26

'THERE.' AUNT JACKIE THUMPS A PALM AGAINST THE LAST cardboard box – overstuffed, straining against the tape like fat against a too-tight belt, and marked in thick black letters *Goodwill*. She straightens up, brushing a stray bit of hair from her face with the inside of her wrist. 'That looks better, doesn't it?'

Dara's room – Dara's old room – is unrecognizable. It's been years since I've seen the floor, now clean-swept and scented with Pine-Sol, beneath the carpet of litter and clothing obscuring it. The old rug is gone, bundled to the curb along with bags filled with stained and ripped jean shorts, broken sandals, faded underwear, and padded bras. The bedspread – a leopard print Dara bought with her own money after my mom refused to get it for her – has been replaced with a pretty floral pattern Aunt Jackie found in the linen closet. Even Dara's clothes are packed away, most of them for donation; dozens of empty hangers swing, creaking, in her closet, as though pushed by a phantom hand.

Aunt Jackie puts an arm around me and gives me a squeeze. 'Are you okay?'

I nod, too overwhelmed to speak. I'm not sure *what* I am anymore. Aunt Jackie offered to do the remainder of the packing herself, but Dr Lichme thought it would be good for me to help. Besides, I wanted to see whether there was anything I could salvage; Dr Lichme gave me a shoebox and told me I should fill it. For three days we've been wading through the swamp of Dara's old belongings. At first I wanted to save everything – chewed-up pens, contact lenses, broken sunglasses – anything she'd touched or loved or handled. After filling up the shoebox in less than ten minutes, I trashed everything and started over.

In the end, I've kept only two things: her journal, and a small gold horseshoe necklace she liked to wear on special occasions. *For luck,* she always said.

The windows are open, admitting the September breeze: a month that smells like notepaper and pencil shavings, autumn leaves and car oil. A month that smells like progress, like moving on. Dad is moving in with Cheryl this weekend; tomorrow, I have a mandated date with Avery, Cheryl's daughter. Mom is in California, visiting an old college friend, drinking wine in Sonoma and taking spin classes. Parker is off at college in New York, probably staying up late and making new friends and hooking up with pretty girls and forgetting all about me. Madeline Snow has started fourth grade – according to Sarah, she's the darling of the whole school. FanLand is closing up for the season.

I'm the only one who hasn't gone anywhere.

'Now there's just one last thing . . .' Aunt Jackie moves away from me, extracting what looks like a bit of scraggly pubic hair from her purse. After a bit more fumbling, she produces a heavy silver Zippo and lights the whole bundle on fire. 'Sage,' she explains as she revolves in a slow circle. 'Purifying.' I hold my breath to keep from coughing, feeling the twin desires to laugh and cry. I wonder what Dara would have said. *Can't she just smoke some weed and be done with it?* But Aunt Jackie looks so solemn, so intense, I can't bring myself to say anything.

Finally she finishes walking the perimeter of the room and shakes the sage branches out the window, casting tiny embers onto the rose trellis, extinguishing the flames. 'All done,' she says. She smiles, but her eyes are tight at the corners.

'Yeah.' I hug myself, inhale, and try to find Dara's scent beneath the bitter stink of the sage, beneath the smell of September and a room newly scrubbed. But it's gone.

Downstairs, Aunt Jackie makes us mugs of oolong tea. In the two weeks she's been staying with us – 'To help out,' she announced cheerfully, when she showed up on our porch with her long hair in braids, carrying an enormous set of misshapen luggage covered in various sewn patches, like some deranged version of Mary Poppins, 'and to give your mom a break' – she has been slowly working the house from top to bottom, treating it like an animal in need of molting, from the new orientation of the living room ('your feng shui was all wrong') to the sudden explosion of living plants in every corner ('much easier to breathe, right?'), to the refrigerator stocked with soy milk and fresh vegetables.

'So.' She slides into the window seat and draws her knees up to her chest, like Dara used to do. 'Have you given any thought to what we talked about?'

Aunt Jackie suggested we try a séance. She said it might help me to speak directly to Dara, to tell her all the things I want to say, to apologize and ask her forgiveness. She swears by it, says she talks with Dara all the time that way. Aunt Jackie actually believes that Dara is hanging there on the other side of existence like some kind of ghostly scarf, pinned to a wall.

'I don't think so,' I tell her. I don't know what scares me more: the idea that I'll hear her, or that I won't. 'Thanks, though.'

She reaches over and grabs my hand, squeezing. 'She isn't gone, you know,' she says, in a quieter voice. 'She'll never be gone.'

'I know,' I say. It's just a different version of what everyone else will tell you; she'll live on inside you. She'll always be there. Except that she did live on inside me – she grew there, rooted like a flower, so gradually I didn't notice. But now the roots have been torn out, the wild, beautiful flower pruned back, and I'm left with nothing but a hole.

The doorbell chimes. For one crazy second I think it might be Parker, even though that makes no sense. He's miles away, at college, moving on like everyone else. Besides, he would never ring the doorbell.

'I'll get it,' I say, just to have an excuse to do something, so Aunt Jackie will stop staring at me pityingly.

It isn't Parker, of course, but Madeline and Sarah Snow.

The two sisters are dressed identically in plaid knee-length skirts and white button-downs, though Sarah's shirt is unbuttoned to reveal a black tank top, and her hair is loose. Her parents, I know, put her in parochial school for her senior year – something about the evil effects of public school education. But she looks happy, at least.

'Sorry,' is the first thing she says, when Madeline bounds into my arms like an overeager puppy, nearly knocking me over. 'Fund-raising. She wanted you to be first.'

'We're selling cookies for my basketball team,' Madeline says, peeling away from me. It's funny to think of Maddie – who's small for her age, and scrawny as a newt – playing basketball. 'Wanna buy some?'

'Sure,' I say, and can't help but smile. Maddie has that kind of effect on people, with a face like a sunflower, all wide and open. The ten days she spent hiding out, sneaking around, worried Andre was coming after her, miraculously don't seem to have traumatized her too badly. Mr and Mrs Snow aren't taking any chances; Sarah told me they've put both their daughters into therapy, twice a week. 'What kinds you got?'

Maddie rattles off a list – peanut butter, chocolate peanut butter, peanut brittle – while Sarah stands there, fiddling with the hem of her skirt, half smiling, never taking her eyes off her younger sister.

In the past month she and I have become friends, or kind of friends, or at least friendly. We've gone with Maddie back to FanLand, this time so she could show us, with a certain degree of pride, how she had managed to stay hidden for so long. I even went swimming at the Snow house, lying side by side on deckchairs with Sarah while Maddie showed off front flips from the diving board, and the Snow parents circled back and forth to check that we were okay, like planets compelled to orbit their daughters. Not that I blame them. Even now, their mom sits in the car, engine on, watching, as if both girls might vanish if she looks away.

'How've you been?' Sarah asks, once Maddie has assiduously marked down my order and then, obeying some eternal rhythm of her own, dashed back toward the car.

'You know. Same,' I say. 'How about you?'

She nods, looking away, squinting against the light. 'Same.

I'm on house arrest, basically. And everyone at school treats me like I'm a freak.' She shrugs. 'But it could be worse. Maddie could be—' She breaks off abruptly, as if suddenly aware of the implication of her words. *It could be worse. I could be you. My sister could be dead.* 'Sorry,' she says, as red creeps into her cheeks.

'That's okay,' I say, and I mean it. I'm happy Maddie made it home safely. I'm happy skeevy Andre is sitting in jail, waiting to get served. It feels like the only good thing that has happened since the accident.

Since Dara died.

'Let's hang out again soon, okay?' When Sarah smiles, her whole face is transformed and she looks suddenly beautiful. 'We can watch a movie at my house or something. You know, since I'm on lockdown.'

'I'd like that,' I say, and watch her move back toward her mom's car. Maddie is already in the backseat. She presses her lips to the glass and blows out, making her face puff up, distorted. I laugh and wave, feel an unexpected pull of sadness. This, the Snows, the new friendship with Sarah – this is just the first of so many things I'll never get to share with Dara.

'Who was that?' Back in the kitchen, Aunt Jackie is stacking apples, cucumbers, and beets on the counter, a sure sign that she's about to threaten me with one of her famous 'smoothies.'

'Just someone selling cookies for school,' I say. I don't feel like fielding questions about the Snows, not today.

'Oh.' Aunt Jackie straightens up, blowing the long bangs out of her eyes. 'I was hoping it might be that boy.'

'What boy?'

'John Parker.' She returns to rummaging in the fridge. 'I still remember how he used to torture you when you were little . . .'

'Parker. No one calls him John.' Even saying his name brings a familiar pain to my chest. I wonder if, even now, he's forgetting me, forgetting *us* – the girl who died, the girl who went crazy – sifting us down through layers of new memories, new girls, new kisses, like sediment slowly compressed at the bottom of a riverbed. 'He's in New York.'

'No, he isn't.' She's stacking items from the refrigerator on the floor now: carrots, soy milk, tofu, vegan cheese. 'I saw his mom at the grocery store this morning. Nice woman. Very calm energy – cerulean, really. Anyway, she told me he was home. Where is that ginger? I'm sure I bought some . . .'

For a second, I'm too stunned by the news to speak. 'He's home?' I repeat dumbly. 'What do you mean?'

She shoots me a quick, knowing look over her shoulder before returning to her search. 'I don't know. I assumed he came back for the weekend. Maybe he was homesick.'

Homesick. The ache in my chest, the space hollowed out by Dara and deepened, refined, when Parker left, is a kind of homesickness. And I realize: Parker was once home to me. A year ago, he would never have come home without telling me. Then again, a year ago he didn't know I was crazy. I hadn't *gone* crazy yet.

'There they are. Hiding behind the orange juice.' Aunt Jackie straightens up, brandishing a knob of ginger. 'How about a smoothie?'

'Maybe in a little while.' My throat is so tight, I couldn't choke down a sip of water. Parker is less than five minutes from me – two minutes, if I were to cut through the woods instead of going the long way – and yet as far away as he's ever been.

We kissed this summer. He kissed *me*. But my memories from that time are distorted, like stills pulled from an ancient movie. I feel as if it all happened to someone else.

Aunt Jackie squints. 'Are you feeling all right?'

'I'm fine,' I say, forcing a smile. 'Just a little tired. I might go lie down for a while.'

She looks as if she doesn't quite believe me. Luckily, she doesn't press. 'I'll be here,' she says.

Upstairs, I head to Dara's room – or what was once Dara's room, and now will become a guest room, clean and impersonal and inoffensively decorated, with framed pictures of Monet prints hanging on walls painted Eggshell #12. Already, it looks much bigger than it ever did, both because it has been cleared of all of Dara's things and also because Dara herself was so big, so alive and undeniable. Everything shrank around her.

And yet in only a few hours we've managed to erase her almost entirely. All of her things – bought, received, painstakingly selected; her tastes and preferences; all the random stuff accumulated over years – all of it sorted, trashed, or packed up in less than a day. How easily we get erased.

The air smells a little like burned sage. I tug the open window even farther and suck a deep breath of the clean air, the smell of summer turning slowly into fall – growth turning to mulch, the greens and blues faded by sun into amber tones.

As I stand there, listening to the wind sing through the withered leaves of the rose bushes, I notice a splash of vivid color in the lower branches of the oak tree, as though a child's red balloon has become entangled there.

Red. My heart skips up to my throat. Not a balloon – a piece of fabric, knotted around a branch.

A flag.

At first I think I must be mistaken. It's a coincidence, or a visual trick, some piece of trash inadvertently blown into the branches. Still, I find myself running downstairs, ignoring my aunt, who calls out, 'I thought you were taking a nap,' and bursting out the front door. I'm halfway to the oak tree before I realize I didn't even stop to put on shoes; the ground is cold and wet beneath my socks. When I reach the oak tree and see the FanLand T-shirt swaying, pendulum-like, on the breeze, I laugh out loud. The sound surprises me. I realize it's been a long time – maybe weeks – since I laughed.

Aunt Jackie's right. Parker's home.

He opens the front door even before I can knock, and even though it has been only two months since I've seen him, I hang back, suddenly shy. He looks somehow different, even though he's wearing one of his usual nerdy T-shirts (*Make Love Not Horcruxes*) and the soft jeans still traced with ink from where he got bored in calc senior year and started doodling. 'You cheated,' is the first thing he says.

'I'm a little too old to fit through the fence,' I say.

'Understandable. I'm pretty sure the fort has been commandeered by old patio furniture, anyway. The chairs launched a pretty major offensive.'

There's a beat of silence. Parker steps out onto the porch and closes the door behind him, but there are still several feet between us and I can feel every inch. I tuck my hair behind my ears, feeling, for just one second, the pattern of imagined scars beneath my fingers, the way it felt to be *her*.

Guilt, Dr Lichme told me matter-of-factly. *On some level you believe you were permanently damaged by the accident. Guilt is a powerful emotion. It can make you see things that aren't there.*

'So you're home,' I say stupidly, after the silence stretches on a second too long.

'Just for the weekend.' He takes a seat on the old porch

swing, which creaks under his weight. After a moment's hesitation, he pats the cushion next to him. 'It's my stepdad's birthday. Besides, Wilcox called and begged for my help shutting down for the season. He even offered to fly me back himself.'

Tomorrow FanLand will close down for the season. I haven't been back to FanLand except for once, with Sarah and Maddie Snow. I couldn't stand the way that everyone greeted me, with fear or gentle reverence, as if I were an ancient artifact that might disintegrate if mishandled. Even Princess was nice to me.

Mr Wilcox has left several messages for me, asking whether I'd be up for helping tomorrow and attending the end-of-the-season FanLand pizza party. So far, I haven't responded.

Parker uses his feet to move us back and forth on the swing. Every time he shifts, our knees bump together. 'How've you been?' he asks. His voice has turned quiet.

I tuck my hands in my sleeves. He smells the same as always, and I'm half-tempted to bury my head in his neck, and half-tempted to run. 'Okay,' I say. 'Better.'

'Good.' He looks away. The sun has started to sink, pinwheeling golden arms through the trees. 'I've been worried about you.'

'Yeah, well, I'm fine,' I say, too loudly. Worried means there's something wrong. Worried is what parents and shrinks say. Worried is why I didn't want to see Parker before he left for New York, and why I didn't respond to any of the messages he's sent me since he arrived at school. But Parker looks so hurt, I add, 'How's New York?'

He thinks about it for a minute. 'Loud,' he says, and I can't help but laugh a little. 'And there are definitely rats, although so far none of them have attacked me.' He pauses. 'Dara would have loved it.'

The name falls between us like a hand, or a shadow passing across the sun. Just like that, I feel cold. Parker picks at a bit of denim unraveling at his knee.

'Look,' he says carefully. 'I've been wanting to talk to you about what happened this summer.' He clears his throat. 'About what happened between . . .' He ticks a finger back and forth between us.

'Okay.' I wish, now, that I hadn't come. Every second, I expect to hear him say it: *It was a mistake. I just want to be friends.*

I'm worried about you, Nick.

'Do you—?' He hesitates. His voice is so quiet I have no choice but to lean in to hear him. 'I mean, do you remember?'

'Most of it,' I answer cautiously. 'But some of it feels . . . not exactly real.'

There's another moment of silence. Parker turns to look at me, and I'm achingly aware of how close we are – so close I can make out the faint, triangular scar where he once took an elbow to the nose during a game of Ultimate; so close I can see a little bit of stubble across his jaw; so close I can see his eyelashes tangled together.

'What about the kiss?' he says, his voice raw, as if he hasn't spoken in a while. 'Did that feel real?'

Suddenly I'm afraid: terrified of what will come next or what won't. 'Parker,' I start to say. But I don't know how to finish. I want to say I can't. I want to say I want to, so badly.

'I meant what I said this summer,' he rushes on, before I can say anything. Then: 'I think I've always been in love with you, Nick.'

I look down, blinking back tears that overwhelm me, not sure whether I feel joyful or guilty or relieved or all three. 'I'm scared,' I manage to say. 'Sometimes I still feel crazy.'

'We all go a little crazy sometimes,' Parker says, finding my hand, interlacing our fingers. 'Remember when my parents got divorced, and I refused to sleep inside for an entire summer?'

I can't help it; I laugh, even as I'm crying, remembering skinny Parker and his serious face and how we used to hang out together inside his blue tent eating Pop-Tarts straight from the box, and Dara would always shake the leftover crumbs onto her tongue. I swipe the tears away with a forearm, but it doesn't do any good; they keep coming, burning up through my chest and throat.

'I miss her,' I blurt out. 'I miss her so much sometimes.'

'I know,' Parker says softly, still squeezing my hand. 'I miss her, too.'

We stay like that for a long time, side by side, holding hands, until the crickets, obeying the same ancient law that pulls the sun from the sky and throws the moon up after it, that strips autumn down to winter and pushes spring up afterward, obeying the law of closure and new beginnings, send their voices up from the silence, and sing.

september 27

'OH MY GOD.' AVERY, CHERYL'S DAUGHTER AND MY MAYBE-SOON-to-be stepsister, shakes her head. 'I can't believe you got to work here all summer. I had to be at my dad's insurance company. Can you imagine?' She mimes holding a phone to her ear. '"Hello, and thank you for calling Schroeder and Kalis." I must have said that, like, forty times a day. Holy shit. Is that a *wave pool*?'

When I told Avery I was going to spend the day helping shut down FanLand, I assumed she would want to reschedule our mandated girl time. To my surprise, she volunteered to help.

Of course, her version of helping has so far involved stretching out on a lawn chair and occasionally switching positions to maximize sun exposure, while offering up a stream of random questions ('Do you think there are so many one-legged pirates because of sharks? Or is it, like, malnutrition?') and observations that range from absurd ('I really think purple reads more nautical than red') to bizarrely astute ('Have you ever noticed that really happy couples don't feel the need to, like, *hang* on each other all the time?').

Weirdly, though, I'm not totally hating her company. There's something comforting about the never-ending rhythm of her conversation, and the way she treats every subject as equally important or equally trivial; I'm not sure which. (Her response earlier this summer to finding out I was in a psychiatric ward: 'Oh my God! If they ever make a movie version of your life, I totally want to be in it.') She's like the emotional equivalent of a lawnmower, digesting everything into manageable, uniform pieces.

'How're you holding up, Nick?' Parker, who's helping dismantle the awnings at one of the pavilions, cups his hands to his mouth to shout to me across the park. I give him a thumbs-up and he grins wide, waving.

'He is so cute,' Avery says, inching her sunglasses down her nose to stare. 'Are you *sure* he isn't your boyfriend?'

'Positive,' I say, for the hundredth time since Parker dropped us off. But even the idea makes me feel warm and happy, like I've had a sip of really good hot chocolate. 'We're just friends. I mean, we're best friends. Well, we were.' I exhale hard. Avery is staring at me, eyebrows raised. 'I'm not sure what we are now. But . . . it's good.'

We have time. That's what Parker said to me last night before I went home, taking my face in his hands, planting a single kiss, lightly, on my lips. *We have time to figure this out.*

'Uh-huh.' Avery looks at me appraisingly for a second. 'You know what?'

'What?' I say.

'You should let me do your hair.' She says this so firmly, so adamantly, as if it's a solution to the whole world's problems

– exactly the way Dara would have said it – I can't help but laugh. Then, swiftly, I get the deep ache again, the dark well of feeling where Dara should be and always has been. I wonder if I'll ever think of her again without hurting.

'Maybe,' I tell Avery. 'Sure. That would be nice.'

'Awesome.' She unfolds, origami-like, from her lounge chair. 'I'm going to get a soda. You want something?'

'I'm okay,' I tell her. 'I'm almost done here, anyway.' I've been stacking chairs around the wave pool for the past half hour. Slowly, FanLand is collapsing in on itself, or retreating, like an animal going into hibernation. Signs and awnings come down, chairs get carted into storage, the stands are shuttered and the rides padlocked. And it will remain, silent and still and untouched, until May – when once again, the animal will emerge, sloughing off its winter skin, roaring with sound and color.

'Need any help?'

I turn and see Alice moving down the walkway toward me, hauling a bucket of filthy water in which a sponge is bobbing slowly across the surface. She must have been scrubbing down the spinning carousel; she insists on doing it by hand. Her hair is in its trademark braids, and with her ripped T-shirt (*Good things come to those who hustle,* it reads) and visible tattoos, she looks like some gangster version of Pippi Longstocking.

'I got it,' I say, but she sets the bucket down anyway and falls in next to me, slinging the chairs easily into towering Tetris formations.

I've only seen her once since I came back from the hospital, and then only from a distance. For a minute, we work together in silence. My mouth feels suddenly dry. I'm desperate to say something, give her some explanation or even apology, but I can't come up with a single word.

Then she says abruptly, 'Did you hear the good news? Wilcox finally approved new uniforms for next summer,' and I relax, and know that she won't ask me anything, and doesn't think I'm crazy, either. 'You *are* coming back next summer, aren't you?' she says, giving me a hard look.

'I don't know,' I say. 'I hadn't thought about it.' Strange to think there will even be a next summer: that time is moving on, and carrying me along with it. And for the first time in over a month, I get just the barest flicker of excitement, a sense of *momentum* and good things coming that I can't yet see, like trying to catch the tail end of a colored streamer dancing just out of reach.

Alice makes a disapproving noise, as if she can't quite believe that everyone else doesn't have the next forty years mapped, plotted, planned, and adequately scheduled.

'We're going to get the Gateway up and running, too,' she says, heaving the last chair into place with a grunt. 'And you know something? I'm going to be first in line to ride that puppy.'

'Why do you care so much?' I blurt out, before I can stop myself. 'About FanLand and the rides and . . . all of it. I mean, why do you love it?'

Alice turns to stare at me, and blood rushes to my face; I realize how rude I must have sounded. After a moment, she turns, lifting her hand to her eyes to shield them from the sun. 'See that?' she says, pointing to the row of now-shuttered game booths and snack vendors: Green Row, we call it, because of all the money that changes hands there. 'What do you see there?'

'What do you mean?' I say.

'What do you *see* there?' she repeats, growing impatient.

I know this must be a trick question. But I say, 'Green Row.'

'Green Row,' she repeats, as if she's never heard the term. 'You know what people see when they come to Green Row?'

I shake my head. I know she doesn't really expect an answer.

'They see prizes. They see luck. They see opportunities to win.' She pivots in another direction, pointing at the enormous image of Pirate Pete, welcoming visitors to FanLand. 'And there. What's that?' This time, she waits for me to respond.

'Pirate Pete,' I say slowly.

She squawks, as if I've said something funny. 'Wrong. It's a sign. It's wood and plaster and paint. But you don't *see* that, and the people who come here don't see that, either. They see a big old pirate, just like they see prizes and a chance to win something on Green Row, just like they see you in that awful mermaid costume, and for three and a half minutes they let themselves believe that you're actually a frigging mermaid. All of this' – she turns a circle, sweeping her arms wide, as if to embrace the whole park – 'is just mechanics. Science and engineering. Nuts and bolts and gears. And *you* know it, and *I* know it, and all the people who come here every single day know it, too. But for just a little while, they *forget* to know it. They *believe*. That the ghosts on the Haunted Ship are real. That every problem can be solved with a funnel cake and a song. That *that*' – she turns and points to the high metal scaffolding of the Gateway, stretching like an arm toward the clouds – 'might really be a gateway to heaven.' She turns back to me and suddenly I feel breathless, as if she's not looking at me but *into* me, and seeing all the ways I've screwed up, all the mistakes I made, and telling me it's all right, I'm forgiven, I can let go now.

'That's what magic is, Nick,' she says, her voice soft. 'It's just faith. Who knows?' She smiles, turning back to the Gateway.

'Maybe someday we'll all jump the tracks and lift off straight into the sky.'

'Yeah,' I say. I look where she's looking; I try to see what she sees. And for a split second I find her, silhouetted by the sky, arms outstretched like she's making snow angels in the air or simply laughing, turning in place; for a split second, she comes to me as the clouds, the sun, the wind touching my face and telling me that somehow, someday, it will be okay.

And maybe she's right.

THE END

Visit Lauren at

www.laurenoliverbooks.com

Find Lauren's books on Facebook at

www.facebook.com/lovedelirium
www.facebook.com/laurenoliverbooks

Follow Lauren on Twitter

@OliverBooks